OUR SONG

OUR SONG

JORDANNA
FRAIBERG

razOr
bill

An Imprint of Penguin Group (USA) Inc.

razor
bill

Published by the Penguin Group
Penguin Group (USA) Inc., 375 Hudson Street, New York, New York 10014, USA
Penguin Group (Canada), 90 Eglinton Avenue East, Suite 700, Toronto, Ontario M4P 2Y3,
Canada (a division of Pearson Penguin Canada Inc.)
Penguin Books Ltd, 80 Strand, London WC2R 0RL, England
Penguin Ireland, 25 St Stephen's Green, Dublin 2, Ireland (a division of Penguin Books Ltd)
Penguin Group (Australia), 707 Collins St., Melbourne, Victoria 3008, Australia
(a division of Pearson Australia Group Pty Ltd)
Penguin Books India Pvt Ltd, 11 Community Centre, Panchsheel Park,
New Delhi–110 017, India
Penguin Group (NZ), 67 Apollo Drive, Rosedale, Auckland 0632, New Zealand
(a division of Pearson New Zealand Ltd)
Penguin Books, Rosebank Office Park, 181 Jan Smuts Avenue, Parktown North 2193,
South Africa
Penguin China, B7 Jaiming Center, 27 East Third Ring Road North, Chaoyang District,
Beijing 100020, China

Penguin Books Ltd, Registered Offices: 80 Strand, London WC2R 0RL, England

Copyright 2013 Jordanna Fraiberg

ISBN: 978-1-59514-268-9

Published simultaneously in Canada

Library of Congress Cataloging-in-Publication Data is available

Printed in the United States of America

10 9 8 7 6 5 4 3 2 1

For Eva

I celebrate myself, and sing myself,
And what I assume you shall assume,
For every atom belonging to me as good belongs to you.

—Walt Whitman, "Song of Myself"

CHAPTER 1

"ALMOST HOME," my father said, clearing his throat. His gray Buick Lucerne coasted down the freeway toward the exit ramp for Vista Boulevard. He said it like it was a good thing.

They were the first words out of his mouth since we'd left the hospital, essentially doubling the number he had uttered since the night of the accident. At least now that he was driving, it wasn't as obvious that he could barely look at me.

You could tell we were practically home from the way the surrounding landscape suddenly transformed from a brown, blotchy mess into a sprawling green landscape, complete with a WELCOME TO VISTA VALLEY greeting emblazoned in pink and yellow tulips. As the founder and head of the Vista Valley Landscape Society, my mother was responsible for all such important decisions. The sign was composed of purple petunias the last time I drove down this stretch—with Derek—on our way back from a debate match. I had only been gone for two weeks, but it was long enough that the flowers had been replanted to welcome spring.

My breath caught every time I saw a flash of red, imagining

it was Derek's Mini Cooper. It was his prized possession, a gift from his parents for leading the Vista Valley High Pioneers to victory at the San Fernando Valley regional debate championships last year. I kept hoping the bright fire-engine-red two-door would magically round the corner, proving nothing had really changed. I would have given everything to rewind time, would have done anything for some miracle that would erase the last two weeks. But that kind of miracle didn't exist.

Besides, I'd already used up my so-called miracle quota. That's what Dr. Farmand had called it, anyway: a miracle. After the accident, my heart stopped beating for almost three full minutes before being restarted by a paramedic. They called it a "near-death experience," but there was nothing near about it. I died. And was brought back to life.

Dr. Farmand and everyone in the hospital kept telling me how lucky I was to be alive. But it didn't feel like the same life I had left behind . . . the carefree one, with Derek.

As we drove down Vista, every storefront reminded me of him, of some moment from our past: Maggiano's, the site of our first date, Abe's Coffee Shop, where we stopped for muffins on the way to school, the China Palace, where we got takeout for movie night every Friday. And Vista Valley Mart, where we shopped just two weeks ago, right before our two year anniversary. . . .

Something snagged in my throat again. I closed my eyes and tried to inhale deeply but nothing flowed in or out.

When I opened my eyes again, we were turning off Vista and nearing the entrance to the Vista Valley Country Club. The wound on the back of my head started to pulse, like a tiny heartbeat. The club was where Derek and I first met, after one of the weekly Sunday brunches my parents always dragged me to. I already knew him from school, of course. Everyone knew Derek O'Brien, captain of the Vista Valley Pioneers Debate Club, president of the student council, and future president of the United States. But I didn't know that Derek knew who *I* was until he pulled up in his golf cart to talk with me while I waited for my father to finish up on the twelfth hole.

Only a few weeks later, I stopped driving my father around the course on Sundays and began driving Derek instead. I could hardly believe my luck. I'd never kissed anyone before, much less had a boyfriend. I wasn't like the other girls at the club, with their blond hair and their tans, with their cute, tiny bodies poking out of their cute, even tinier bikinis. But for some reason, out of all the girls in Vista Valley, I was the one Derek chose. And for the first time in my life, I felt special.

As the car rounded the twelfth hole, a wave of nausea welled up inside me. It suddenly felt like the tinted glass was closing in on me. I wiped my sweaty palm on my jeans and fumbled around for the switch.

"You all right?" My father pressed a button on the side of his steering wheel and the window silently slid open.

I was so sick of that question. For the last two weeks, that's all anyone could ask me, from my parents, to the endless parade of nurses and doctors, to the special counselor sent to assess my psychological "readiness" before releasing me this afternoon.

"I'm fine," I said. Maybe if I said it enough times, someone would eventually believe me. Maybe I would, too.

I extended my arm out into the warm, still air, the car moving too slowly to create the illusion of wind. Staring up at the cobalt sky, I didn't see a single cloud. The sun, a big yellow disc off to the right, looked two-dimensional, like it had been painted onto the sky. The weather was like this practically every day in Vista Valley. Except for the rare time it rained. Like it had that night.

"Don't go this way," I blurted just as my father was about to make a left onto Hyacinth Circle. It was the most direct route home, but he turned off his indicator and continued straight without saying a word.

He didn't need to ask why. It was obvious what I wanted to avoid.

The Buick Lucerne made a right onto our street, Lily Lane. Even with the window down, it still felt like I was viewing the world through the filter of tinted glass. I stared out at the row of almost identical, freshly painted houses, all in matching hues of pastel and white, their perfectly maintained gardens spreading out before them. In the interest of "community harmony," every public aesthetic decision in Vista Valley was planned by committee. I knew this because my mother served on practically every one of them. There wasn't a paint job, holiday decoration, or address plaque that didn't have her fingerprints all over it.

It felt like I was looking at a tableau frozen in time before the accident. As if a thin layer of gauze had fallen over the entire neighborhood, enshrouding it from the rest of the world like a cocoon. *This must be what a parallel universe is like,* I thought.

Everything looked the same, but I suddenly felt like it wasn't. Like everything had been taken apart, brick by brick, flower bed by flower bed, and put back together in the wrong order. Just like me.

Various neighbors appeared as we pulled into our driveway. Oscar Hodes from across the street came out to polish his car; Mrs. Nelson from three doors down decided to bring her trash bins out two days early (my mother would have something to say about that); and the Walton twins, Jasper and Jane, rode their bikes in circles in front of our house. I knew they were all really there to witness my return. There was no doubt that everyone knew what had happened. News always spiraled into gossip in Vista Valley. Especially news like mine.

My mother stood in the open doorway, framed on either side by matching flower boxes displaying her prized orchids. Tugging at her gardening apron, she reminded me of a seventeenth-century Dutch oil painting we studied in art history freshman year, *Portrait of a Mother in Grief*. The only difference was that my mother wasn't wearing black, but she didn't have to. Squinting her eyes to hold back her tears, she acted like she was the one who died, the one who had lost everything. But if I wasn't crying, she had no right to.

"I've got your bag," my dad said, popping the trunk open.

Just then, Noah, my eight-year-old brother, came barreling through the door, practically knocking over my mother. "Ollie's back!"

"The grass, Noah! It's just been fertilized," my mother cried out, but it was too late. Noah was already clomping across, leaving small footprints on the new earth, before taking a running jump into my arms. The weight and force of his body made me stumble back against the car. But it felt good to be hugged, to be his big sister again. I'd been so focused on everything else, I didn't realize how much I had missed him. My mother never brought him to the hospital, saying something about how the restricted visiting hours for children conflicted with his school schedule. But I knew it was really because she didn't want him to know the truth.

"Careful with your sister," my mother warned. "Remember? She's not feeling well. We discussed this."

"I'm fine, Mom," I insisted as he slid off me.

She quickly glanced back at the neighbors, all paused in their activities to stare at us. "Let's get you inside." She took my bag from my father. "There are so many germs in the hospital. Why don't you go take a hot shower while I get this load of laundry started."

That's when it hit me: I was the germ, the blight on her otherwise perfect home.

I followed her inside.

CHAPTER 2

"DON'T YOU LOOK refreshed!" my mother announced as she barged into my room.

"Mom, I'm not dressed!" I said, quickly slipping a shirt over my head. Since the accident, she'd been running on overdrive, checking on me every five minutes. I was hoping it would be different now that I was out of the hospital, that she'd go back to worrying about the trivial domestic things she normally obsessed over, like her orchids. "Can you please knock?"

"Doesn't a nice shower make you feel so much better?" she said, ignoring me. Maybe a shower was all it took for her, but everything was different now. She went over to the bed and held up a pair of pink pajamas. "Didn't you see these adorable new pajamas I got you?"

They were exactly the kind I usually loved, down to the floral embroidery around the collar and cuffs. But I couldn't imagine wearing something so . . . cheerful. Not yet anyway.

"I didn't notice," I said breezily, tightening the drawstring on the torn black sweats I'd opted for instead. "Where's my computer?" I eyed the empty spot where it used to sit on my desk.

"We thought it would be too much stimulation to have it here in your room," she explained, removing a phantom hair from her face. That was my mother's classic tell. The signal that she was uncomfortable, or covering up the truth.

"Then where is it?" Without Internet access in the hospital, it had been a full two weeks since I'd been online. I was desperate to log on to Facebook, to study Derek's page, even though I knew it probably hadn't changed much since the last time I saw it. Like a true politician-in-training, he never posted anything personal.

"Your computer is in the sunroom."

The sunroom wasn't technically a room but a small nook off the kitchen that overlooked the greenhouse. Given that my mother basically lived in exactly one of those two places, it meant that I would have zero privacy. "How am I supposed to get my homework done there?"

"Don't worry about that now. What's important is that you rest."

I gripped my head as a sudden explosion of sound erupted in my brain, like the volume had been cranked up. But I wasn't just hearing my mother's voice. A cacophony of discordant noises ran through my head. Flapping, clapping, crunching: an avalanche of overlapping, jarring sounds, with the almost imperceptible hint of a melody beneath it all, like a ghost. The music was so faint I couldn't even be sure what it was or if it was really there, as if a radio had been possessed, urgently flipping between stations, each one more chaotic than the last, searching, searching, for calm.

"Are you in pain?" my mother asked, rushing toward me.

"I'm fine," I said, reaching for the armchair to steady myself. With the noises ricocheting in my head, I felt off-kilter, like I'd just stepped off a speeding merry-go-round, like I might faint. But no matter how much it was freaking me out, there was no way I could let on what was happening.

A buzzer went off in the kitchen.

"That's the oven," she said, glancing toward the door. "Maybe a good, home-cooked meal will help."

I pushed the noises back until they reduced to a ringing in my ears and followed her downstairs and into the kitchen. A fresh round of nausea washed over me as my mother removed a steaming dish from the oven. I'd barely been able to eat for the last two weeks. The smell and sight of food— even my mother's cooking, which I used to love—turned my stomach.

"Ah, perfect!" she said, testing her recipe. Everything needed to be perfect in my mother's world. Her cooking, her orchids, her house, her family. And now here I was, throwing it all out of balance.

"We're eating in the dining room tonight," she said as I slumped into my usual spot at the kitchen table.

"Why?" The dining room was usually off-limits, reserved for special occasions or when my mother hosted her fellow committee members for luncheons. Or when my father needed to impress some clients.

"Because you're home." I couldn't remember the last time

we'd eaten in there together as a family. She reached for a crystal bowl from the shelf where she kept all her fancy dinnerware. "I thought it would be nice to celebrate the occasion."

"There's nothing to celebrate." I pulled my hair out from under my shirt and fanned it over my shoulders. It helped to relieve the pressure from my long, wet strands tugging down on the scar at the base of my skull. Another unpleasant reminder.

"Well of course there is." She whipped around, clutching the bowl in her hands. "It's a miracle you're . . . back."

I bristled at that word. *For you maybe*, I wanted to say. Because as much as I wanted to feel grateful, I wasn't really back. Not in the way I wanted to be.

I went over to the fridge, where my school calendar was tacked to the door next to Noah's. It listed all the things that happened in the past two weeks, the things that went on without me. The senior talent show, Derek's debate against Paso Verdes High. Our second anniversary . . .

I ran through the events in my head, imagining I had been there, that nothing had changed, that I had spent the last two weeks by Derek's side, the same as the last two years. Love like ours couldn't just vanish into thin air, no matter what happened. And when he saw me at school again tomorrow, I knew that he would realize it, too.

My mother came up behind me and adjusted my hair so that it fell straight down my back. "It'll grow back soon." I nodded silently. She was referring to the square bald patch they had shaved to make room for the stitches. She followed my gaze to the fridge. "I know this breakup has been especially hard on you, but—"

"We didn't break up," I snapped, pulling away. Those words were never uttered. There was still a chance that things could go back to the way they were before the accident. All my hopes were pinned on that chance.

It was true that I still hadn't heard from him since that night. But Derek wasn't the best with the phone. And I knew how focused he got in the middle of debate season. He always told me not to take it personally. But each day without him felt like an eternity, and it had already been fourteen. Fourteen days that had been more painful than the bruises across my body and the stitched gash on my head.

"Maybe it would be better if you stayed home for a few more days, to readjust before going back to school." She scrutinized my face as if she could read my mind before reaching for the phone. "I'm calling Principal Kingston."

"No," I said firmly, putting my hand out to stop her. The thought of waiting any longer to see Derek sent a sharp spasm through my heart. "I'm fine. I want to go back."

She let out a sigh and put the phone down. "We can take it one day at a time."

When I glanced up, I noticed that the rack above the sink that usually displayed her extensive knife collection was now completely empty. That's when I realized that she didn't trust me. She had already come to her own conclusions about what happened that night, no matter how many times we'd gone over it.

• • •

The dining room not only felt too big for the four of us, with the long, rectangular table that could seat twelve, it also felt foreign, like we were guests in someone else's house. Or maybe it was just that I was the one who felt like a guest.

I didn't say much through dinner. Neither did my dad, who checked his BlackBerry every five minutes, while my mother filled the silence by jabbering on about her orchid club and a brand new varietal she couldn't wait to show "the girls." For the past five years, a dozen neighborhood ladies with nothing better to do met each week to trade tips on orchid care. It always seemed like they were secretly competing, as if the color and size of their flowers represented who they were as people. My mom considered herself the Grand Dame of the group. Not just because she was its founder, but because she was the only one with a bona fide greenhouse. She had it built when Noah started school, and it had quickly become her third child.

"Olive, is there something wrong with your meal?" she asked, doling out seconds for Noah. He seemed so much bigger than he did two weeks ago, as if life was bursting out of him.

I moved my food around the plate to make it seem like I was eating. I'd been trying to avoid this very question. My queasiness had only gotten worse as the odor of garlic filled the room. I could still taste the meat on the roof of my mouth, like it had gotten stuck there and would never go away, no matter how much water I drank to try to wash it down. "No, it's just that I ate something before coming home," I lied.

"That's too bad. I wish I had known. I made this especially for you since it's your favorite."

"It is," I agreed. Or it was. I didn't know if I'd ever be able to enjoy meatloaf again. I knew there was no way my mother would understand, not without reinforcing all the conclusions she'd already come to. Plus, it was clear I'd already offended her. She considered it a personal affront if you didn't have seconds, much less finish your first plate (even though she herself was exempt from this expectation). It's one of the reasons she loved it whenever Derek stayed for dinner. His hearty, insatiable appetite was like one giant ego boost. Sometimes I wondered if that was the real reason she liked him: because of the way he made *her* feel. But I couldn't blame her. That was just Derek. When he decided to shine his light on you, there was no resisting its glow. It wrapped itself around you like a second skin, making you forget everything and everyone else.

I reached my hand back through my hair and felt around for the wound. Most of the stitches had already disintegrated, just like Dr. Farmand told me they would. The area where he'd sewed me up was still devoid of nerve endings. He explained that it could stay that way indefinitely.

Tracing my fingertips across the bumpy ridge, I felt like I was touching someone else's skin. Short bits of hair were slowly starting to poke through. They reminded me of the soft stubble that appeared across Derek's face when he tried to grow a beard last year. He was doing it to try to look older so he could buy beer at the gas station by the freeway on-ramp (which was notorious for not carding). Only with his smooth, pink skin and fair, blond hair, the "beard" had the opposite effect. The thin, uneven patches actually made him look younger, like a boy pretending to be a man. Maybe that was why I liked it so much. It somehow made him seem less intimidating, more on my level. Caressing the new patch of peach fuzz on my head, I closed my eyes and imagined it was Derek's cheek.

"Stop fussing with that, Olive," my mother warned, swiping my hand away as she got up to clear the table. "Noah, why don't you go on up and get ready for bed."

I was about to get up too when my mother put her hand on my shoulder. "Your father and I would like to talk to you."

"Okay," I said, twisting my napkin into knots.

She sat back down, throwing my father a pointed glance. "We're concerned about you," she started in before he could offer anything. Not that he would have, anyway.

"I told you I'm fine." I felt like I should plaster it on my forehead.

"And I thank God for that every day. But that's not what I'm talking about. What *we're* talking about," she added, throwing my father another exasperated look.

I still hadn't thought about God, much less thanked him. Besides, if there really were a God with a capital G, how could any of this have happened in the first place? "There *isn't* anything else to talk about."

"We'd just like to go over what happened that night."

"Again?" My body tensed up as the screeching noises in my head rushed back in, like a living, breathing organism had taken my brain hostage.

"Based on the impact, the police report says you had to be speeding—"

"It wasn't my fault," I protested, cutting her off. Snippets of music, pieces of a song, kept pushing through. Was it the song playing on the radio when the car crashed? With the invasive sounds closing in, it was too difficult to hold on to the melody long enough to identify what it was. I only knew that it weighed me down with a haunting sadness.

"Honey . . ." She looked at my father, her eyes pleading for him to back her.

"Your mother isn't saying it's your fault," he finally said, clearing his throat. His voice was flat and distant, like he wanted to be sitting there about as much as I did.

"But it's what you believe," I said, thinking about the now-empty knife rack.

"It's just . . . help us understand," she said, pulling her chair in closer. "It's so unlike you to drive like that. Hyacinth Circle is tricky enough as it is with all those sharp turns. You know that. But at night, in the rain . . . what were you doing, Olive?"

I'd never been in trouble before. Never broken curfew or failed a test or played hooky from school. I *was* the perfect daughter. Why couldn't she just let this one thing go?

"It's like I already told you," I said, trying to recall the exact words I had used when we first talked about it in the hospital. "I forgot I had an English paper due in the morning, and I had to get to the library before it closed."

Clasping her hands, she placed her elbows on the table and leaned forward. "That's not what Derek said."

"What do you mean?" Panic coursed through me. "You talked to him?"

"The police did, naturally. It was his car. You were coming from his house."

Even though they were only the facts, they sounded like accusations. "What did he say?"

"That you had a disagreement." She stared at me like she was waiting for me to slip up, to do or say something that would prove she was right to keep probing.

"It wasn't . . . we didn't . . ." I blinked hard, trying to force back flashes from that night that threatened to pierce through. "What does that even have to do with anything?"

"He said you were upset and left abruptly in his car," she pressed on.

"It was an accident," I whispered, barely able to get the words out.

"That's enough, Marian," my father said, placing his napkin on his plate.

"Where are you going?" she asked as he scraped his chair back and stood.

"I forgot a file at the office." He paused on his way out to kiss the top of my head. "It's good to have you back."

His voice cracked. A well of tears rose up inside me. I could still feel the warmth of his lips even after I heard the front door shut and his engine come to life.

Bam.

The invasion in my head intensified, an audio assault of deafening noises. I felt like I was going to vomit and fall asleep all at once if I didn't get out of there. My mother didn't say anything else as I got up to leave the table. Hopefully that was the end of it and the discussion was over. But with the ethereal tune snaking its way through my brain, growing louder and more melancholy with every note, I feared this was only the beginning.

CHAPTER 3

I SPENT THE next two hours parked in front of the television in the den. A DVR packed with two weeks' worth of shows would normally have been heaven for a TV addict like me. But not even back-to-back episodes of *Hailey's Clinic*, my all-time favorite medical show, could draw me in. I used to love getting lost in the drama of the main characters' lives. Only now their words dissolved into static noise. On the screen, all I could focus on were the nameless patients in the background. Lying in their blue hospital gowns, hooked up to all sorts of machines, I realized they were the ones who were most like me. Not the glamorous actresses playing the parts of the doctors.

"Need anything?" my mother asked, poking her head in for about the tenth time. I had been waiting for her to go to bed so I could finally use the computer in peace, without the risk of her monitoring my every click of the mouse. But she kept clanging away in the kitchen, like she was deliberately trying to outwait me so I couldn't get online. I didn't understand what she was afraid of. I guess that on top of everything else, she was from the generation that was suspicious of the Internet, convinced it was dangerous.

I quickly closed my eyes, pretending to be asleep. She came in anyway, pried the remote from my hand, and turned off the system. "Let's get you into bed," she said, gently nudging my shoulder.

"What time is it?" I asked, throwing out a fake yawn.

"Almost ten."

I figured she wasn't going to rest until I did what she wanted. I reluctantly stood up and followed her down the hall. "I'll drive you in the morning," she said when we got to my room. "But you have to be ready by seven fifteen because it's my day for Noah's carpool."

Clearly my old routine of driving myself to school in my dad's old Honda was no longer an option. The truth was that I wasn't ready to drive yet anyway. I wasn't so sure I ever would be. But I didn't need my mother making that decision for me.

Too tired to fight with her, I nodded and said good night, closing the door behind me. I let out a deep sigh as I heard my mother retreat down the hall. Leaning back against the door, I took in the sight of my bedroom. It was obvious she had already done a sweep. My folder of old homework assignments had been moved to the other side of the desk, and a few knickknacks had been rearranged on the shelf. I'm not sure what she was expecting to find.

She had also unpacked my bag from the hospital. Even though I hadn't worn anything besides a hospital gown for the last two weeks, she washed all the clothes she had brought me.

They sat in a neat pile on top of my dresser, right next to the Ziploc bag containing the gold chain with the heart pendant Derek gave me for my birthday last year. *So that you will always have my heart,* he had written in the card. It was the closest he had come to saying, "I love you."

The paramedics removed the necklace in the ambulance when they were trying to revive me. It had been sitting in this tiny plastic bag ever since. With all the bandages and IV tubes and sponge baths in the hospital, they wouldn't let me put it back on until I got home. I slowly unsealed the baggie. The chain slid out onto my hand. It was so thin and delicate. My fingers trembled as I unlatched the back and slipped it around my neck. It felt cold against my skin, just like it had the first time Derek put it on me. I hoped the fact that this necklace survived, intact, was a sign that we would too.

My knees suddenly felt weak. There were signs of him everywhere. The pictures of us tacked all over my bulletin board. The bouquet of pink roses he had given me on our first Valentine's Day, now dried and preserved in a clear box on the bookshelf. His blue debate team sweatshirt hanging over the desk chair. He had forgotten it the last time he was here. My stomach twisted into knots thinking the very thing I'd been trying so hard to avoid. What if it really was the last time he'd be in my room? I ran over and pressed the sweatshirt to my nose. If I inhaled deeply, I could still make out the scent of his Old Spice deodorant.

Just then my cell began to ring. I scrambled to find it in my purse, where I was sure I had left it. It wasn't there, no doubt thanks to my mom. I frantically tore through the room, chasing the muffled sound, until I finally found the phone buried under the pile of laundry. I picked up without checking the caller ID. There was no point, since Derek's number was blocked, anyway. He took his privacy to an extreme, like he was already an elected official. A real one that is, outside the walls of Vista Valley High.

"Hello?" I was out of breath.

"You sound strange. Did I wake you?"

I let out a disappointed sigh and collapsed on the bed. It wasn't Derek. It was my best friend Annie. "I couldn't find my phone. My mom unpacked for me. Of course."

"Of course," Annie agreed. She knew what my mom was like. "You thought it was him again," she added. She also knew what I was like.

"I'm just a little out of it," I said, even though we both knew I was lying.

I reached over and absentmindedly ran my fingers over the old, hand-painted wooden box on my nightstand. Annie got it for me on her trip to India for her sweet sixteen. In a nutshell, that was the difference between Annie and the rest of the girls in Vista Valley. While most of them were trying to outdo each other on the elaborate party front, Annie was roaming the streets of Delhi, handing out pens and chocolates to homeless kids.

"I told you to give me a special ringtone so you can avoid this problem. Something peppy to match my awesome personality. I swear I'm just going to do it tomorrow so that you don't have a coronary every time I call." She paused for a beat. "Another one that is."

"Very funny," I snorted. I didn't mind Annie's making jokes like that because I knew how much she cared. She was also the only one besides my parents who had called and visited me in the hospital.

"So, what's it like being home so far?"

"It's great. The entire neighborhood came out and gawked at my return, like I'm some kind of circus freak. My dad's practically gone mute and my mom's on overdrive, running around like a headless chicken on speed. At least Noah's acting normal."

"So what you're basically saying is nothing's really changed."

Annie had a way of cutting through the crap. It was probably because both her parents were shrinks, like she was born with a special gene that helped her see things the way they really were. And she wasn't afraid to say it.

"Anyway, I'm calling because I'm gonna come get you in the morning," she said.

The lump in my chest dislodged. A barrage of tears bubbled up. I thought about all the times that Derek had taken me to school, of his trademark honk when he pulled up outside: three quick beeps in a row. "Everyone always does two," he used to say. "Three is how you'll know it's me."

I sat up and opened the wooden box on the bedside table. Inside were all the fortunes I'd secretly been saving from our Friday Chinese take-out dates. I only kept the ones about love. Both his and mine. Derek didn't know. He already thought I was enough of a hopeless romantic. Wedging the phone between my ear and shoulder, I reached in and pulled out a fortune. My other hand grabbed hold of the pendant as I read the black words printed out on the small piece of white rectangular paper: *Everything will now come your way.*

Now more than ever, I needed it to be true.

"Hello?" Annie tapped her fingers against the phone. "You still there?"

"Of course," I said, releasing the gold heart. I slipped the fortune back in the box and closed it, trying to snap myself out of it. "You sure you don't mind picking me up?"

"Please, you're my best friend."

We had been best friends since we were twelve, when fate paired us together for an assignment in social sciences. Sometimes I wondered if we'd be friends now if we hadn't met when we were so young. All it took was one glance to see how different we were. Annie was what I liked to call a gamine. She was petite, but what she lacked in size she more than made up for in confidence. In her vintage scarves and dresses, she looked like she lived in New York City, not the San Fernando Valley, land of the strip mall. Her short pixie cut perfectly framed her delicate face. She was the only one I knew who could pull off such a different look without becoming a total outcast.

My hair was long and landed halfway down my back, just like all the girls at school. And I was much taller and bigger than Annie too. No matter how many times she told me my curves were sexy, all I felt when I looked in the mirror was round and chubby. It was the reason I wore loose shirts and avoided form-fitting dresses. It was also the reason I never let Derek see me naked.

"It's a good excuse for me to try to be on time for a change," she said. "Now get some sleep. I'll be there at eight."

I slipped under the covers and tried to get comfortable. I hoped that now that I was here, in my own bed, I would finally be able to sleep, but my mind raced with thoughts of Derek. How was he going to react when he first saw me tomorrow? When would it be? By our lockers where we usually met up? On the stairwell between classes? In the cafeteria at lunch? I didn't know if I could wait that long.

I flung off the covers and jumped out of bed. Pausing by the door, I strained to listen for signs of my mother scurrying around like a domesticated mouse, but even mice had to sleep. Thankfully, the house was completely silent. I quietly opened the door and crept toward the sunroom.

Even though this had been our home for the last eight years, there was something unfamiliar about the moonlit shadows in the darkened halls. It almost felt like I was walking down them for the first time. Family pictures covered the walls. My mom had spent hours picking the perfect shots and placing them in chronological order, starting all the way back with my parents' wedding photo. The most recent picture was this year's annual Christmas family portrait, taken in the garden by Vista Valley's preeminent photographer. My mother made us wear matching red and green tops for extra holiday spirit. With our fake smiles and perfectly brushed hair, we looked so stiff and unnatural, like wax figures. I wondered what next year's portrait would look like, and if I could still manage a smile.

It took a few minutes for the computer to come to life. I

stared out the window and into the garden, but it was so dark that nothing was visible. It was already late enough that nobody was awake except for me. I waited until the beach ball on the screen stopped spinning, then went straight to Facebook. I checked Derek's page first, even before my own. As expected, nothing had changed. He barely used social networking except to post stuff to the debate team page. His relationship status still said single, just like it had for the last two years. He said it had nothing to do with me; he just hated having his personal life exposed and didn't want the things he posted online to haunt him forever. I understood, but the idea that I could ever be something that haunted him kind of stung.

But I tried to stay positive. Derek always said that if you wanted to achieve your goals, you had to act *as if*. Meaning, *as if* you'd already gotten what you wanted. It wasn't enough to hope you could win a debate. You had to tell yourself you were already a winner before it even began. You had to believe it the way you believed an indisputable fact. That's why I told myself I *was* going to Georgetown next year, along with Derek.

I clicked over to my own page. It hadn't changed much either since I last logged on. A few kids from my class had posted things like "Hope ur ok" and "we miss u." But that was about it. It wasn't like the onslaught of messages you get on your birthday. Maybe it was better that no one seemed to notice. It made it easier to go back tomorrow, to pretend that nothing happened. To act *as if*.

I heard the sound of a car pulling into the driveway, followed by the front door slowly creaking open. It was my father and he was headed this way. "Come on, come on," I said under my breath, trying to make the computer go back to sleep.

As soon as the screen went dark, I darted into the kitchen. It was too late to make a run for my room. I peered out into the hall. He wasn't carrying his briefcase or the alleged file he had gone to the office to get. He must have decided to finish his work there; otherwise why was he coming home at two in the morning? He unfastened his tie as he got closer. With no other escape, I ran out the back door into the garden.

Standing barefoot in the cool, damp grass, I watched through the window as the kitchen lights went on and my father sat down with a glass of scotch. After a few minutes he got up and stood by the door, stirring the cubes around his glass as he peered outside. It was almost like he knew I was there.

I retreated further back along the footpath so he wouldn't see me, even though I knew I was invisible in the black night. I felt a sharp jab in my side as I passed the greenhouse. The moonlight cast shadows of the headless, flowerless orchids inside, making them loom large against the glass, like killer plants.

The last time I had been in the greenhouse was three months ago, with Derek, the night before Christmas break. He had always wanted to fool around in there, but I always resisted. The idea of lying in the dirt surrounded by glass walls made me feel more exposed than usual. But he said it would be the best present I could ever give him.

My top was off and my pants unzipped when my mother came barging in looking for her gardening log. Leave it to Derek to think on his feet, he instantly flattered my mother on her impressive collection of plants. That was all it took for her to launch into a long-winded lecture on the history of the orchid while I huddled in the corner feeling around for my shirt. Derek had wanted to have sex really badly that time. If my mother hadn't ruined it, maybe we would have. Maybe my first time would have been that night.

I slid down on the grass and leaned back against the willow tree. I stared ahead at the house. It was only a few hundred feet away, but it might as well have been a few hundred miles. It felt like a thick glass wall had been erected in my absence. The one-way kind, where I could see in, but no one could see out.

The kitchen light finally went out and I sank deeper into the cool earth. I looked up at the sliver of moon poking through the layers of feathery branches, at the smattering of stars shining through, casting a soft glow across my body. I pretended they were beaming down on some other town. On some other girl.

Not me.

CHAPTER 4

ANNIE PICKED ME up at eight o'clock on the dot. She was never on time.

"Look at you! So prompt," I said, sliding into the front seat of her 1977 turquoise Volkswagen Beetle. Annie could pull off the whole retro-cool vibe, but if I were the one behind the wheel, the irony would have been completely lost and there'd be nothing retro or cool about it. Like I'd ever get behind the wheel again.

"NO. WAY." She was yelling at the radio, in response to a caller's request. "That song totally sucks! There should be some kind of veto system for people with such horrible taste. Where's my phone?!"

She scrambled around in her purse with one hand while simultaneously pulling away from the curb, the old engine chugging like a caboose. She was addicted to the Bobby and Darin morning show and had their request line on speed dial. The one time she actually got through, we were already in class when her song came on the air. But that didn't stop her from trying. Or from having daily one-way arguments with the deejay.

"Wow, you look great, Ol," she said as the sound of a busy signal filled the air.

"A shower and real clothes kind of help."

"I don't know. I think you rocked hospital gown chic."

"Um, yeah. No thanks. I'll be happy if I never see another hospital gown."

"Did my ears hear that correctly? Does this mean that your die-hard devotion to *Hailey's Clinic* has finally come to an end?"

"Guess so." I shrugged, thinking about last night.

"Now that's cause for celebration."

"You're such a snob." The only shows Annie normally watched were costume period dramas on PBS or artsy foreign films with subtitles.

"That's what Jessica says," Annie laughed.

Jessica was Annie's best friend from her old school in L.A., before she moved to Vista Valley in the fifth grade. They lost touch for a while but reconnected last summer when they worked at the same camp. They were pretty much inseparable after that, or as inseparable as you can be when you live thirty miles apart.

"You know that 'snob' is just another way of saying I have excellent taste." Annie reached over and turned up the volume. "Finally! A song I can get behind. You almost lost me, Bobby and Darin, you almost lost me."

"How is Jessica?" I asked. "Have you guys been able to talk much?"

Jessica moved to Paris with her family just after Christmas. It happened suddenly, when her mom got one of those job offers you can't refuse. Even though she didn't say it, I could tell that Annie missed her. She cared about Jessica a lot, but I never felt jealous. Somehow, our friendships felt different. They didn't compete or overlap. It was kind of like the way I had room for both Derek and Annie in my life. They fulfilled different needs.

"It's hard with the time difference." She made a sudden left onto Pine. Thankfully, she was taking the long route, the one that avoided Hyacinth Circle.

With that thought, the volatile sounds came slamming back into my head, like even the act of avoidance was a reminder. I stared at the clock's blinking red lights. If I focused hard enough, I could squeeze the sounds out until they blended together into a fuzzy hiss.

I leaned my head against the seat and stared out at the view whizzing past. It was all the same, one perfect storybook house after another, block after block. A series of immaculately trimmed flowers and hedges and glistening minivans, scenes of cheerful mothers in sweater sets with their stiff smiles, waving goodbye to the rectangular yellow vehicles carting their children away. I felt a pang in my chest as I thought back to when I was one of those pigtailed kids on the bus, with my own cheerful mother waving me off. Life was so simple back then.

Life was so simple up until two weeks ago.

"You all right?" Annie asked, glancing over.

"Mm-hmm." I dug my fingers into the cracked leather seat. Every passing block brought us that much closer to school. I thought about my Facebook page and how no one seemed to notice I was gone. But maybe it'd be different when I got to school. Maybe it'd be just like walking in to your own surprise party after you thought everyone'd forgotten your birthday. Maybe everyone was just waiting to see me to say how worried they were, how much they missed me, how happy they were that I was back. Maybe that's what Derek was waiting for, too.

"I wish you'd stop thinking about him," Annie said. It was eerie how she could get inside my head like that. "Don't even try to deny it."

"Wow." I made a show of looking at the flashing red numbers on the dashboard clock. It was an hour behind. Annie never got around to changing it for daylight savings, so it was only correct for half the year. "It only took you five whole minutes to bring him up."

"Are you kidding? I've been keeping my mouth shut for the last two weeks, not to mention the last two *years*."

Derek was the one thing we hardly ever talked about. It was definitely a giant omission given he was practically my whole life, but Annie made her feelings about him clear right at the start. As far as she was concerned, he was arrogant, selfish, and a Republican on top of it all. I tried to convince her that it didn't make him a bad person. She just didn't know the real Derek the way I did. The one who helped me with my homework and hid funny notes in my school bag. The one who brought me chicken soup from Nate's Deli when I was sick and cute souvenir teddy bears when he came home from family vacations.

"He doesn't deserve you Ol," she said, waving her arms around for emphasis.

"The road," I said as the car wavered over the double yellow line.

She repositioned her hands on the wheel. "The guy didn't even have the decency to come see you in the hospital!"

Just hearing it out loud was like getting a kick to the stomach. "It's not that simple."

When Annie had asked me about the accident, I told her the same thing I had told my parents: why I was in a hurry that night, why I was in Derek's car. When she also pressed me about why he never called, I told her to stop asking.

She let out a frustrated sigh. "At least tell me you're not going to just let him off the hook."

Only that was exactly what I was planning to do. The sooner things went back to normal, the sooner I could put everything behind me. Behind *us*. "You don't get it."

How could she, when she'd never had a real relationship? How could she understand that when you find true love, there were certain things you became willing to accept, whatever the price? Annie was always so busy with her art and photography it was like she didn't even notice that her love life was missing.

"I just hope that you really do," she said, making a right onto Glen Oaks. The red brick building that housed Vista Valley High surfaced in the distance.

As we entered the school parking lot, traces of the sporadic melody grew more intense in my head, rising above the other clamoring sounds. It sounded as if it was being strummed out on the delicate strings of an acoustic guitar. The beat was slow and quiet, almost sweet-sounding, like a lullaby. But the thing about lullabies is that beneath their dulcet rhythms lurks something darker, like a warning or a harbinger of danger to come.

I strained my neck, scanning the row of cars for a pop of red in the sea of mostly white, silver, and black SUVs. I knew it was impossible; I'd seen the pictures. But still, I secretly hoped that Derek's Mini had magically survived, just like I had.

"Hello, you're in the way," Annie said, slamming on the brakes. Katie Richards and Melanie Garcia, two girls from our grade, stepped out into the car's path. "It's not like I'm some Prius sneaking up on them," she said, revving the engine for emphasis.

Katie had recently started dating one of Derek's friends from the debate team, and the two of us were just starting to become friends. I started to say hi but stopped mid-wave when Katie glanced over her shoulder and turned away. She hurried off, whispering something to Melanie. My stomach tightened into a ball of knots.

"Here, take these." Annie removed her giant pink plastic sunglasses and handed them to me. "It's going to be fine."

"You better be right," I said, slipping them on. The dark shades dimmed the sunshine and all the surrounding bright colors. It reminded me of being in the garden last night, safe under the cover of darkness. I had stayed until dawn, staring at the fractured moon, the smattering of stars across the sky. They shone so brightly, like tiny diamonds, until they gradually faded away as the sun rose.

"I'm always right," she said, pulling into an empty spot.

"Not that you're arrogant or anything," I teased. She sounded just like Derek. They were both so confident and sure of themselves. It was one of the things I loved and envied most about them. Sometimes I wondered if the real reason Annie didn't like Derek was that they were actually alike. More than either of them would ever admit.

I pulled the visor lower and checked myself out in the mirror. "Wow." The pink frames covered half my face. I was almost unrecognizable. "I never thought I'd say this, but I actually like the way these look on me."

"They're yours," Annie said. She opened the glove compartment and pulled out an almost identical pair in black. She was obsessed with accessories, especially sunglasses. She said the right style could determine your whole vibe. Though the reason I liked the glasses had nothing to do with the way they framed my cheekbones or complemented my outfit. I liked them because wearing them helped me feel like someone else.

We rounded the building and joined a steady stream of students heading toward the entrance. It was like stepping onto one of those moving sidewalks in an airport. The flow of people kept pushing me forward. I couldn't step off even if I wanted to. Once inside, I took off the sunglasses, immediately shielding my eyes from the bright fluorescent lights. The sound of the clanking metal lockers and the roar of overlapping conversations were practically deafening. Just being here around so many people was like an assault to my senses. Squinting, I checked the time on the massive clock above the front doors. The first bell was going to ring any minute.

I bolted toward the back stairs. It was the fastest route to our lockers. I didn't want to miss the chance to catch Derek before he disappeared in the Pioneer. That was what the debate team called their practice room, but it really felt more like a private club with a strict members-only policy. In the two years we'd been dating, I hadn't been inside once.

"Hey, slow down," Annie said, shuffling behind me with at least five bags flying off her.

"Maybe you should travel lighter." Between her school-books, her camera equipment, her lunch cooler, and whatever else she deemed necessary to lug around, she was also known as the Bag Lady.

The first bell rang. "I don't want to be late my first day back," I said, taking the steps two at a time.

"We still have seven minutes until the second bell!" she huffed from a few steps behind.

The closer I got, the faster my legs moved, like they were trying to outpace the quickening beat of my heart. I could feel the adrenaline coursing through me. When I got to the third floor landing, I leaned against the wall in the empty stairwell, trying to collect myself. I needed to act as calm and normal as possible when I walked through the doors.

Annie appeared beside me and I turned to face her. "Do I look okay?"

"Beautiful," she said, brushing the hair off my face.

I pulled the heart pendant out from under my shirt and walked through the double doors. As we made our way down the hall, it suddenly grew quieter, like regular conversation had given way to hushed whispers. I could practically feel everyone's eyes boring into my back. It was mostly freshmen at this end of the hall so I shook it off, telling myself it was normal, that the freshmen always knew who the seniors were.

But it was the same when we got to the senior section at the other end of the floor. The only difference was that everyone seemed to look the other way as I passed, like they were deliberately avoiding my gaze. It was exactly what Katie had done in the parking lot.

I scanned the hall, looking for Derek, for some sign of his cropped blond hair bobbing in the crowd. None of this would matter if he were on my side. One sweep of his arm around my shoulder would make everything else go away.

I wasn't like Annie, who was too busy and cool to care what anyone else thought of her. I also wasn't like the mass of popular copycats at school, with their manicured nails and matching outfits. I was more like a formless blob in between—the type of girl who blends into the background until something makes you stop and notice her. And for me, that something was Derek. Being his girlfriend gave me a place. Because of him, I belonged. Because of him, I was a part of something much bigger.

But when we got to our lockers, he was nowhere in sight. I was too late. A panicky feeling overcame me. What if he was avoiding me? I tried to push the thought away, to remind myself of all the other times I couldn't reach Derek in the past. There was always a reason, like when he forgot to charge his cell battery or practice ran late. I was always scared that something was wrong, or worse, that it was over. But I had always been wrong. There was even the time he didn't call for five days after our first real fight, which ended up being a stupid misunderstanding. I kept telling myself that one day we'd be able to look back and chalk this time up to an even bigger misunderstanding.

My hands were shaking so much it took me three tries to punch in my locker combination. When I finally got it open, a goofy Polaroid of me and Derek from New Year's Eve stared back at me. I was so nervous I felt like I was going to throw up.

"Want me to walk you to class?" Annie asked, sidling up next to me.

I reached inside for my books. "Thanks, but I'll be okay."

"Meet you back here for lunch then?"

I nodded yes as the second bell rang and watched Annie retreat the other way down the hall. The hushed voices seemed even louder now that I was alone, like the escalating rumble of an approaching wave.

Fixing my gaze on the floor, I waited until the hall cleared and began making the trek to homeroom.

CHAPTER 5

I SPENT THE rest of the morning in a fog, waiting for each period to end, for another chance to see Derek. We didn't have a single subject together this semester, but I still knew his schedule by heart and had a mental map of where he was at all times. As soon as each bell rang, I was first out the door. I calculated which route to take so I had the best chance of intercepting him, even if it was in the completely wrong direction for my next class. It was worth lingering in the halls, enduring the whispers, if it meant I would see him. But I didn't. It was like he'd somehow slipped through the cracks.

At least my teachers acted halfway normal and didn't broadcast the fact that I had been gone for the last two weeks. It seemed as if they were instructed not to say anything. I didn't get in trouble for having the wrong books or for not following along. I was normally a front row student, diligently taking notes, but I now found it was easier to bide my time in the back, away from the stares.

"Hey," Annie said, approaching my locker. "Ready?"

It was finally lunch. "Just about." I shoved my books in my locker then glanced back across the hall toward Derek's.

"Have you seen him yet?" she asked, following my gaze.

I shook my head no. "Have you?"

"I have the unfortunate displeasure of being in three classes with him, so yes, I spent half the morning with him."

I had begun to wonder if he was even here, if perhaps he was the one who had disappeared. But now that Annie confirmed he was at school, I knew where I could find him. "Do you mind if we eat in the cafeteria?"

Annie hated cafeteria food and always packed her own organic lunch, which she usually ate in the darkroom. She was the yearbook photo editor and always had tons of work she crammed into any spare minute. She also didn't mind eating alone. She called it her "Zen time." My so-called Zen time was when I was with Derek, which is why I ate right next to him in the cafeteria every day.

"Let's go," she said, dangling her compact navy blue cooler in her hand.

I tugged on the heart around my neck as we passed the debate team room. It was in the old teacher's lounge, right next to the cafeteria.

"Ol?" Annie reached over and touched my arm. I didn't realize I had stopped. I shook it off and released the pendant before continuing on toward the cafeteria.

I felt queasy as soon as we walked in. The air, heavy with the smell of fish and garlic, lingered in my nostrils. I scanned the packed room for Derek's table. He and his friends had been eating in the same spot since freshman year, but no one was there yet. I always liked the fact that he had such a close-knit group of friends, which seemed unusual for guys. Maybe it was just because they were all on the debate team, but they always stuck together, and made a pact to stay friends for the rest of their lives. They called themselves the Circle of Trust, or the COT for short. They even joked about the golf retreats they'd go on when they were older, how they'd leave the wives and kids behind, just like their dads. I always liked hearing them talk about the future like that, imagining that by then, I'd be Derek's wife, and we'd have our own kids. It made it feel like we'd be together forever, too.

"Nerd Herd alert, twelve o'clock," Annie said as we got to the back of the food line.

I whipped my head up to the front of the line, where Simon Glass, Dylan Nelson, and Max Samansky had just finished paying. They were carrying their trays off toward their table.

"Keep your voice down," I whispered, glancing around to make sure no one heard her.

"What? If they get to give themselves a lame name, I can too."

"I told you, it's private." Annie hated cliques of any kind, but I had always secretly wanted to belong to one. The COT may not have been mine, but it was the closest I'd come.

"Ooh, yum. Brown mystery meat, brown mystery fish, and brown potatoes. I'm sensing a theme here," Annie said, inching her tray along the glass display.

I kept straining my neck toward the entrance, waiting for him to arrive. Where was he?

"Wow, that broccoli looks like it's been sitting there so long it's also turning brown. I think I might even feel bad for it," she said, nudging my arm.

"Mm-hmm," I murmured, turning around to face her. "You feel bad for who?"

Just then something flashed in her eyes. I turned around. My heart raced. There he was. Like an apparition. With his neat, parted blond hair, in his uniform of khakis and a button-down, he greeted his friends as he sauntered into the line, flashing his perfect smile. He looked exactly the same.

That is, until he lifted his gaze, until his eyes locked on me, until his smile faded and his face went slack. He did an about face, went right to his table, and sat down without his lunch. That's when I noticed that someone else was sitting in my place, right next to Derek. A cheerleader named Betsy Brill, the most popular girl in school. Her long, wavy blond hair cascaded over her shoulders like she'd just come from the salon, and her toned, tanned shoulders poked out of her sleeveless dress as if she were eating in a five star establishment, not the grimy cafeteria.

What the hell was she doing there?

A sharp pain worked its way up my spine. With one eye trained on me, Betsy leaned over and whispered something in Derek's ear. I wanted the floor to open up and swallow me whole.

The intense flapping sounds gushed back in. Like a caged bat struggling to be free, the escalating melody ricocheted against my skull, drowning everything else out. The notes climbed higher and higher, like they might take flight before coming to an abrupt stop, mid-note. It was just how I felt: stuck, unable to move forward, like the end was missing.

Boom.

My tray slipped through my fingers and crashed to the floor, splattering food and lemonade everywhere.

All conversation came to a grinding halt. Everyone turned and stared. I kept waiting for Derek to turn around, too. To stand up in front of the whole school and defend me. Instead, he kept acting like I didn't exist.

I glanced toward the exit. It felt like it was fifty miles away. *Stay steady*, I told myself as I put one foot in front of the other, my flip-flops squeaking across the wet floor. *Don't look back, just keep moving.*

Pretty soon I was running. Across the cafeteria, through the swinging door, down the hall, past the debate room. I didn't slow down until I reached the girls' bathroom and darted into the last stall. Doubled over the toilet, I began to dry heave, but nothing came out.

A group of girls came busting through the door. The clack of their heels and high-pitched chatter bounced against the linoleum tiles, breaking the silence. Peeking through the crack of the stall door, I could see who they were: Betsy Brill's posse. The Queen Bees. Everyone always knew who the popular girls were, no matter what grade they were in. They were like local celebrities. As they crowded around the mirror, I watched them admiring their perfect reflections. That was another thing about the popular girls. Their skin always looked flawless, even under the bright glare of the fluorescent lights.

"Ohmygod," one of them said. They were mid-conversation. It didn't take long to figure out what they were talking about. "I can't believe she can show her face around here . . ."

Or who they were talking about: me. With nowhere to go, I retreated to the wall behind the toilet, closed my eyes, and tried to block them out. But I couldn't. Their words came at me like daggers, even louder than the phantoms in my head.

"I heard she tried to run him down but he got out of the way just in time."

"Can you imagine? That'd be, like, murder."

"Yeah, instead it was just a suicide mission."

"Too bad she didn't succeed."

"But she totally did! Didn't you hear she was dead and came back to life?"

"Ew, she's like a zombie!"

They roared with laughter. I slid down to the floor, my feet poking out from under the stall. They were too caught up to even notice. They had already made up their minds about me, anyway. Apparently everyone had. It didn't matter that none of it was true. That I would never hurt Derek. That I didn't want to die.

I laid my head down on the sticky floor and watched their feet retreat out the door. The melody erupted, each note more despondent than the one before. It was the sound of my pain, taunting me. I was reminded of the instructional video we watched for lifeguard training last summer, about how drowning is never the way it looks in the movies, with all sorts of screaming and splashing. It was the opposite: silent, stealthy, deadly. That's when I realized there was no point resisting. This song was a part of me now, like a heartbeat, as fragmented and incomplete as I was.

CHAPTER 6

"HONEY?" MY MOTHER poked her head through the door, then proceeded to charge right in. In the last week, she'd perfected the art of simultaneously knocking and entering, like she might catch me in the middle of doing something dangerous. "You're not dressed and we needed to leave ten minutes ago!"

I quickly tucked the wooden box under the pillows. I had been reading the fortunes over and over, like the act of repetition would give them a better chance of coming true. "I'm not going."

She marched over to the windows and yanked open the drapes. The sunshine blinded me momentarily. "But it's Easter!"

We weren't religious, but my mom was on the club's Easter brunch decorating committee (of course). My stomach constricted into knots as I thought about last year's brunch, when I sat at Derek's table, with his family. I'd barely seen him all week since the cafeteria incident. The few times we crossed paths in the halls, he looked the other way. "I don't care," I said, pulling the duvet over my head to shield my eyes from the bright glare.

"You might feel better if you put on a nice outfit and get some fresh air."

"No, that's what would make *you* feel better." She was wearing a new coral dress with a matching cardigan and her fancy, triple strand pearls. She saved them for special occasions.

"I'm worried," she said. "You're not yourself."

"I'll be fine."

"I think you should talk to someone."

"You mean you?" I said, kicking the covers.

"No, I mean a professional. Someone who can help."

My body stiffened. Suddenly it seemed like I could hear the voices and laughter of the girls in the bathroom, like they were here, in my room, looming behind my mother, taunting *you're crazy* over and over. "Aren't you the one who said I could take my time?"

"There's a difference between taking your time and hiding." She sat down and ran her fingers through my tangled strands of hair, fanning them out on the pillow. "You can't spend the rest of your life in bed."

"I don't need a shrink," I said, springing out of bed. The sudden movement caused my blood to rush to my head. I steadied myself against the dresser so she wouldn't notice I was dizzy. "I'll be ready in five."

The Buick was idling in the driveway when I finally emerged fifteen minutes later.

"You can't go in jeans." My mother threw her hands up in frustration.

"Leave it, Marian," my father said.

"Fine." She reached into her purse and pulled out a travel-size comb. "Just brush your hair, okay?"

As soon as I was buckled into the backseat next to Noah, my mother glanced at the clock and nudged my father to get moving. She was always anxious about getting to places early. She held back from chastising me for making them wait, but I could practically see her biting her tongue.

She pulled down the visor and began reapplying her already heavily coated coral lipstick. "Are those new sunglasses?" she asked, peering at me through the mirror.

"Sort of." I was wearing Annie's giant, pink plastic pair. It was easier to pretend no one was looking at me when I had them on. It reminded me of Buck, our black Lab, who died when I was eight. He would always cement his eyes shut when he was caught doing something bad, as if blocking out the world meant he too would become invisible. Now I understood why he did it and suddenly longed to be curled up in his warm, slick fur. My father and I had buried him together in the backyard. I cried myself to sleep for weeks after. My dad promised we'd get another puppy, but then we moved and my mom got pregnant and everyone forgot about Buck. Except for me.

"You don't need to wear them in the car with these windows so heavily tinted. It's not good for your eyes."

She hated that my father had the windows done and complained it made it seem like he was some kind of chauffeur for the mob. It was also her typical, indirect way of letting me know she didn't like the glasses.

"Don't worry, Mom."

She turned toward my father and began rattling off all the things she had to check once we got there—the flower arrangements, the tablecloths, the Easter baskets. Her nonstop chatter sounded like the drone of a persistent fly. Every once in a while, she interrupted her stream of consciousness to tell my dad to slow down, pointedly glancing back at me each time.

"You're the one who's in such a rush, Marian." He sounded tired.

And it was no wonder. I had been sneaking out into the garden every day since I'd been home, and every night around two in the morning, my dad would appear, like clockwork. First, the kitchen light would go on and he'd get a glass to measure out his scotch. Then he'd loosen his tie and remove his jacket before moving over to the window. Swirling his drink, he'd just stare out into the darkness. I always dozed off while he was standing there. It was practically the only time I slept. Maybe because I knew he was watching over me, even if he wasn't aware of it.

I stared out the darkened window at the matching whitewashed, mission-style buildings. I used to think they were transplanted from Spain or something. Even the McDonald's had a quaint, old-fashioned feel to it, making it seem like it was actually a fancy, stand-alone restaurant, not some run-of-the-mill fast food chain. But now, as I looked closer, all the buildings seemed so fake, like a movie set, with nothing real behind their facades.

"Oh darn, don't tell me," my mother cried out, peering down at her legs.

"What's wrong?" my father said evenly. He never got rattled by her intensity.

"There's a tear in my stockings below the hemline. I was so distracted I left the spare pair in the vestibule." That was my mother, always planning for a potential emergency.

"Can't you just go bare? They're skin color anyway."

"No I *cannot*, Henry," she snapped, like it was the most absurd suggestion ever.

My cheek muscles tightened, trying to stifle a smirk as my father made a U-turn in the middle of the road. It had been a while since I'd smiled.

"What are you doing?" my mother asked, finally taking her eyes off the rip.

"Going home so you can change."

"We don't have time. Just take me to the drugstore, it's closer."

My dad parked in front of Vista Valley Mart while my mom ran inside. Noah started humming the theme song to *Spiderman*.

"Come on, Ollie, name that tune," he said breathlessly between notes. It was a game I taught him on the long drive to Arizona last year, when we went to visit one of my mom's cousins.

I slumped lower in my seat, trying to quell my nausea. All I could think about was the last time I was here, with Derek, and what we had come to buy. Our second anniversary was coming up and I had convinced myself I was finally ready. Technically, Derek was the one who bought the condoms—and picked them out—while I nervously kept a lookout for our nosy neighbor,

Mrs. Miller, who was shopping in the next aisle. I knew she would report every detail back to my mother if she spotted me. It was the neighborhood code. Derek thought my paranoia was funny and chased me around the store, waving the box in the air before pulling me into a bear hug in a fit of laughter. Back then, all I could think about was whether Mrs. Miller had seen us. Now, I would have given anything to laugh like that with him.

My mother practically jumped out of the moving car when we finally pulled up to the main entrance to the club. "We'll meet you inside, Henry. Olive, can you give me a hand?" She passed me a box of toys from the trunk, prizes for the Easter egg hunt.

My Dad and Noah went to park while I followed her inside. I held my breath and kept my head down as we walked through the lobby. I knew Derek would be here with his family, and there would be no avoiding him. But maybe it would be different here. Maybe it would remind him of how things used to be, of the fact that this was where we met, on a beautiful, sunny Sunday, just like this one.

I made my way to the table where Noah eventually joined me. My dad was checking on his tee-off time, while my mother was flitting this way and that, tending to last minute details.

"Check this out!" Noah sprang from his seat to show me his latest tae kwon do moves. Sometimes I wished I could be more like him: carefree, oblivious to what other people thought. Maybe it was because he was a boy, or because he was eight years old. Either way, I was never like that.

Just then Derek's family came into the dining room. They

were all there, even Greg and Ashley, his brother and sister, who were home from college. Ashley always intimidated me. She was a senior at Vista Valley High back when I was a freshman, and all the guys in the entire school were in love with her. Not only was she smart and beautiful, but she was an amazing swimmer. Her reputation lived on through all the trophies she had won, still on display in the glass cabinets in the school halls. She swam for Stanford now and was probably going to make it to the next Olympics. His brother Greg was just as impressive: a senior at Georgetown, he already had a job lined up at the White House for after he graduated. Derek wanted to be just like him. He never said it, but he didn't have to. Greg was the real reason Derek was so obsessed with going to Georgetown next year.

My heart clenched in my chest thinking about Georgetown, about next year. By then everything would be back to normal, I told myself. By then, he'd see me differently, the way he used to, before that night.

"Ollie, you're not watching!" Noah swung his arms in front of my face, knocking over a glass of water.

"Careful," I hissed as it clanked over the silverware, sending water in every direction. But it was too late. Ashley looked right at me with no hint of recognition before whispering something in her mother's ear. Mrs. O'Brien quickly glanced up, her posture straightening like a cat's, as they shuffled to their table, only four over from ours. Derek was so engrossed in conversation with Greg and his dad that he hadn't noticed me yet. Mrs. O'Brien made sure to keep it that way, guiding Derek to the opposite end of the table, where I had a lovely view of the back of his head.

"There's Derek!" Noah was already on his way to greet him, but I managed to grab hold of his arm. "Ow, you're hurting me."

"Sorry," I said, releasing my grip. "It's just that Derek's busy now. Show me another move. You're really good."

"Why doesn't he come over anymore?" Noah just stood there, staring at me. "Did you guys have a fight or something?"

My heart sank and I struggled to choke back a sob. Noah loved Derek and looked up to him like a big brother. I never thought about how everything that happened, and how acting like it *didn't* happen, affected him too.

"What's going on here?" My mother appeared, immediately mopping up the wet tablecloth with her napkin. "Noah, did you do this?"

"It was my fault," I covered. Taking the blame was the least I could do, if I couldn't tell him the truth about everything else. That was the one thing my mother and I agreed on. We were both trying to protect Noah, even if it was for different reasons.

I stared down at my plate throughout lunch, moving my food around to make it look like I was eating. Luckily my mom was too preoccupied making sure everyone else was having a good time to notice.

Once dessert was served, she leaned into the table toward my father. "Is everything settled with the insurance claim?"

"Not yet." He cleared his throat, like there was something stuck in it.

"It's been over three weeks. What's the hold up?"

My stomach contorted into knots. They were talking about the accident.

"These things take time, Marian. I said I would tell you when I got the report from the appraiser."

Derek was laughing at something Greg said. He still hadn't noticed I was right behind him.

"I sent Carolyn a flower arrangement." She glanced over her shoulder at Derek's mother. "But I never heard a word."

"That's not necessary, Marian. It's all being handled," my father said. "I'm on top of it."

"I should go over and say something." My mother whipped out the compact from her purse and began reapplying her lipstick. "I don't feel right about this."

She didn't feel right about it? I was the one everyone was talking about. *What about me?* I wanted to scream. But I remained silent, slumped in my seat, reminding myself that causing a scene wasn't going to help anyone, least of all me.

"Do whatever you like." My father put his napkin on the table and got up from his seat. "But I have to go. It's tee-off time."

Finding my legs, I pushed my chair back and stood to follow him.

"Where are you going, honey?" my mother asked, as if she'd dipped her voice in a vat of syrup. She only spoke to me that way in public, when she was within earshot of others.

"To get the cart." She couldn't possibly expect me to sit there while she marched up to Mrs. O'Brien, who clearly wanted me to disappear even more than Derek did.

"I was hoping you'd help me with the egg hunt. You used to love it when you were younger. Remember?"

"I want to go with Dad." It wasn't just that I wanted to

escape before she did anything humiliating, but that I genuinely felt like being with him. Being the only ones awake in the middle of the night made it seem like we had some sort of secret bond. Even if I was the only one aware of it.

"Honey, I don't think it's such a great idea for you to drive the cart today."

"But I always do. I've driven it a million times."

"Henry?" she said with a strain in her voice, trying to get my dad to reinforce her position.

But he didn't have to. It was obvious she didn't trust me driving a vehicle of any kind, even one that went five miles an hour on grass.

"Forget it. I'm going home." I took off before she could stop me. I knew she wouldn't raise her voice or run after me. Not here.

I slipped out through the back of the clubhouse and started across the golf course. It was the quickest way home. I didn't care about the risk of getting struck by flying balls. Part of me wanted one to hit me. Maybe it would knock me out of my misery for good this time.

Even though I never played, the location of every fairway, putting green, and hole was cemented into my brain. It wasn't just from carting my dad around, but from all the times Derek and I had sneaked off to fool around here. Practically every square inch of the perfectly manicured course contained a memory from our past. My heart ached as I got to the fairway leading up to the twelfth hole. That was where it all began. When I reached the pole with the little flag marking the cup, I dug my heel into the green. Chunks of mud and grass came flying up and scattered over the surface.

"Hey, what are you doing?" One of the groundskeepers emerged from a nearby bunker and started lumbering toward me. "Young lady, stop!"

But I had already bolted down the other side of the green, the slope of the rough increasing my speed. On foot, he was both too far away and too fat to catch me. But I kept running, cutting diagonally into the shrubs behind the swampy pond that spilled out onto the far end of the parking lot. There was a service entrance a few hundred feet ahead that would land me out on the street.

As I snaked around the lot, I heard the crisp snap of a club making contact with a ball. Instinctively, I ducked and stopped in my tracks. Looking up, I spotted the white ball arcing over a row of parked cars, its dimpled indentations glinting off the sun like a star. It was heading right for the roof of a silver Mercedes, but luckily landed in the hedges just a few feet to its side.

Where had it come from? The ball was too far from the course to be a stray, and the driving range was all the way over on the other side of the clubhouse. A few seconds later, I heard another snap, followed by another ball flying overhead. This time, I traced its path backward: to the silhouette of a guy standing on the roof of an old Jaguar.

Who was he and what was he doing hitting balls out *here*? It was definitely against club regulations, and no one *ever* broke the rules, at least not so blatantly. I crept closer to get a better look at him. He was tall and slender, with a mop of shaggy brown hair that covered half his face, obscuring his features. He wore a navy blazer, like he had just come from brunch, only I hadn't noticed him inside. He reached down and pulled another ball from the bucket at his feet. Tossing it up in the air, he swung wildly. His whole body swayed in sync with his stroke, like he was putting everything he had into the effort. That's when I noticed that he was holding the club from the wrong end, like it was a baseball bat. The ball followed the exact same path as the previous ones, landing closer to the Mercedes, like he was deliberately trying to hit it. The graceful motion of his body seemed so at odds with what he was actually doing, with the intensity and passion inherent in every stroke.

A jolt ricocheted through me as I watched him reach for another ball. The pivoting of his hips, the flick of his head, the swing of his arm. I was certain I had never seen him before. But the electric sensation that I had, that I *did* know him, surged up and down my limbs like a live wire.

Before I knew it, my legs were propelling me forward, darting between the parked cars, leading me into the thick of trees beyond the lot where the ball had traveled, way off its target. Was it intentional? Did he mean to miss this time? Pushing the overgrown brush aside, I found the ball shimmering on a patch of mud, like it was waiting for me.

Just then, I heard the faint sounds of a smooth, velvety voice. A male voice. I whipped around, hoping it belonged to the guy, that I would get a better look at his face, but no one was there.

The voice grew increasingly louder. That's when I realized why I couldn't see who it belonged to: it was coming from inside my head, harmonizing with the melody like a siren call. Then, out of nowhere, words suddenly broke through, like clouds dissipating after a rain storm, clearing the sky.

I see your face all over the place
Like a haunting from above
The only way for this to pass
Is to let go of your love.

All the pent-up emotion trapped in the melody came pouring out in the lyrics, his voice hanging on to each word like it might be his last. Combined—the tune, the words, the voice—it added up to something that seemed to match the mood of the boy hurling balls into oblivion, like it was his anthem as much as mine.

And it was the first time I wanted to hear more.

Later that night, once my mother was in bed, I snuck out to the sunroom. Noah was long asleep and even though it was Sunday, my dad had gone to the office after dinner. It was the first chance I'd had all day to use the computer in private. My mother was already home by the time I walked back from the club, having ditched the rest of the Easter activities to keep a close eye on me. She didn't even trust me enough to be alone in the house anymore, and hovered nearby like a swarm of wasps for the rest of the day.

As the screen flickered to life, I went straight to Google and typed the lyrics into the search field. There was something about the way they danced in my head that made the melody not only bearable, but uplifting. It was like this mysterious voice, sweet as honey, was an organizing principle, turning the random chaos into something intelligible, something seductive.

I scanned the results, turning the white dimpled golf ball,

which I'd held on to all afternoon, around in my hand like it was a crystal ball. There were over five million hits in total. Yet not a single one yielded an exact match, or anything close to it. I clicked through the first few links. They led me to a bunch of random, unrelated websites. I tried to narrow down the results by inserting quotation marks and adding the term "song lyrics" to the search. When that didn't help, I retyped every combination of those four lines I could think of, just in case I was remembering them wrong. But I knew I wasn't. It was the only thing I was sure of. The voice was the clearest thing I'd heard since everything happened. Still, nothing came up, like the song didn't want to be found. Like it didn't exist.

Maybe I really was going crazy.

I gave up on the search and clicked over to Facebook. I didn't even bother checking my page and went directly to Derek's. I'd been stalking it daily since I'd been back, but there was nothing new. I logged on to iChat next and stared at the shadow of his name on my offline buddy list, like I could will him to appear, like the chime of him coming online would sound any second just because I wanted it to.

I rolled the golf ball under my palm, as the lyrics echoed in my head. The image of the boy standing on the Jaguar flashed through my mind, sending the same rousing shock through my body as when I first saw him, and I wondered if I'd ever see him again.

Tucking the ball into my pocket, I went out to the garden.

CHAPTER 7

A HIGH-PITCHED VOICE pierced through the music. It took a second to remember where I was: third period English. Lifting my head from the desk, I could make out the silhouette of Miss Porter looming over me. Her lips were moving but I didn't hear a word she was saying.

She tapped my shoulder and motioned for me to remove my headphones. I took out the left earbud and let it dangle against my hair, like a long, white, plastic earring. I forgot I was even still wearing them. I was listening to a new playlist I had put together last night. I had stayed up for hours scouring the Internet, trying to find the song, even though I knew it didn't exist, that it was a figment of my imagination. That's what led me to discover all these other songs. Music was usually just something I had on in the background, something I used to fill the silence. But last night, for the first time, I really listened to each song and what it was about—love and loss and heartache. Maybe it took getting your own heart broken to really understand the true power of music—and why people wrote it.

"Are you all right?" Miss Porter whispered, crouching down so that we were on the same level. The rest of the class was busily writing in their notebooks.

"I know I'm behind." I pulled my mother's tattered copy of *Mrs. Dalloway* from my bag. At least I remembered to bring it.

"I'm not worried about that," she said, smoothing over the front cover of my book. It was bent from being stuck between two others on the bookshelf in my parents' room for so many years. "I just wanted to see how you were doing."

She was the first teacher to come close to broaching the subject of my absence, like she was breaking some collective pact.

"I'm fine," I snapped. I knew she was only trying to be nice, that besides Annie, she was probably the only one in this entire building who was on my side. But her attention only made things worse.

"The assignment is on the board," she said, straightening up. "Just do the best you can, even if you haven't finished the book yet."

I copied the question into my notebook—*Describe how nature is an important theme in the novel and how it relates to Clarissa Dalloway*. Without having read a single page of the book, it was all nonsense to me. English was normally my best subject and it was my only AP class. Derek said I would have been better off taking economics or government. He said English was a big waste of time since novels were all just a bunch of made up stories that had nothing to do with the real world. I was beginning to realize that maybe he was right. If only I had listened to him. About this class, and about everything else.

Without my playlist to distract me, the velvety voice erupted in my head. It was deeper, huskier now, like footsteps walking over a gravel path. The lyrics came out haltingly, like candies pried from a child's hand, as if the singer didn't want to let them go, each word a part of himself he was reluctantly setting free. There was something brave, hypnotic even, about how vulnerable he sounded. It wasn't until there was a knock at the classroom door that I realized I had drifted off once again.

Miss Porter opened the door, where the hall monitor stood on the other side. He handed Miss Porter a small envelope with the school logo printed in the corner. I glanced up at the clock. There were still thirty-five minutes until the bell. But when the hall monitor interrupted class with a note, it always signaled news that couldn't wait—urgent news. Bad news. Like when the hall monitor delivered Amy Ming a similar envelope in the middle of chemistry sophomore year, and it turned out her father had had a heart attack.

Miss Porter read the name on the envelope, then glanced up at me. I could tell she was trying to be discreet, but it was too late. Everyone turned around all at once. That was my cue. I slid my books into my bag, pushed my chair back, and got up. Even with my head down, I could still feel the collective gaze of the class tracking me as I zigzagged my way around their desks to the front. I don't think I could have felt more exposed, even if I were naked.

"I didn't get a chance to finish," I said to Miss Porter, who was waiting by the door.

"That's okay," she said, handing me the envelope.

I turned my back and pulled out the neatly folded slip of paper. It was from Dr. Green. I was requested in her office. Immediately.

A blunt pain penetrated my gut. Dr. Green was the school guidance counselor. Only the druggies and the seriously disturbed kids were forced to see her. No one ever went voluntarily.

Her office was on the ground floor, next to the language lab. I had passed it many times over the last four years, but I had never been inside. I walked into the waiting area and stood next to a rotating rack filled with self-help pamphlets, absentmindedly spinning it around and around.

"Olive?" Dr. Green appeared in the doorway. I nodded. "Come on in."

Her office was small but orderly. The soft glow of a standing lamp replaced the institutional fluorescent lights, and a Persian rug covered half the vinyl floor. But with the cinderblock walls and the standard-issue paneled ceiling, there was no masking the fact that we were still in school.

She gestured toward the nubbly brown couch. I perched on the edge. I wasn't planning on staying long.

"I don't believe we've formally met," she said, settling into the armchair facing me. "I'm Dr. Green."

"I know." I shifted on the couch.

She crossed her legs and peered at me through her red horn-rimmed glasses. They were the same color as her shoes and skirt. She was famous for coordinating her eyewear with her outfits. "How's your day going so far?"

I glanced up at the clock, wishing I were anywhere but here. "Have I done something wrong?"

"Of course not. I just wanted to have a chat to see how you're faring."

"I'm fine," I said evenly, trying to control the tremor in my voice.

"You've been through . . . an ordeal. It's a lot to process in such a short period of time."

"But I'm okay now." It may have seemed short to her, but to me it felt like forever. "My doctor said so, too. I can get him to write you a note if you want." Everything in high school was taken more seriously when you had a note.

Dr. Green removed her glasses and leaned forward, as if she was letting me in on a secret. "I understand that your body has healed, Olive, but sometimes it takes the mind a little longer to process a trauma."

"Are you really a doctor?" I was never this bold, especially not with authority figures, but I was sick of people sticking their noses where they didn't belong. Plus, she was using that same tone my mother had adopted since the accident, the one where it sounded like she was talking to a two-year-old, or someone who was mentally challenged.

"I'm not a medical doctor, if that's what you mean. But yes, I have a doctorate in psychology," she said, gesturing to the framed diploma behind her. "You can call me Stacy, though, if it makes you more comfortable."

She wasn't wearing a wedding band and there wasn't a single personal item in her office except for the stupid diploma on the wall. How was she supposed to understand what I was going through? What insight did her "doctorate" give her into my so-called trauma?

"Olive, I have experience dealing with issues like yours."

I pulled at a loose piece of knotted wool on the couch. "I'm not really sure what you're talking about," I said, but I had a good idea I didn't like where she was going.

"I'm talking about your suicide attempt."

"I," I started. "It was . . ." My breath caught. It felt like all the air had suddenly been suctioned out of the room. By now it was obvious that's what everyone thought. But it was different being confronted like this, straight to my face, as if it were an undisputed fact.

"You let out a cry for help and I want you to know that it's been heard."

She reached for my hand but I jerked it back. "No. It was an accident."

"I can't make you talk to me, Olive. That's not productive for either of us. But you do need to talk about what happened with someone. And more importantly, to talk about *why* it happened so that it doesn't happen again." She paused and stared right at me.

Talking about that night with Dr. Green—or anyone else— was definitely not going to help. In fact it was the surest way to guarantee that I'd feel even worse. She reached down and retrieved a glossy orange pamphlet from her desk drawer. The caption on the cover read DO YOU EVER FEEL ALONE? in big red letters, above a picture of a teenage girl staring dejectedly out a window. "There are a number of therapists and support groups listed here," she said, handing me the pamphlet. "Take a look and discuss the options with your parents."

I shoved it between the yellowed pages of *Mrs. Dalloway* and left without saying another word.

I thought I'd feel better once I was out in the hall, away from the pitying stare of Dr. Green. But the idea of going back to class made my stomach churn. My classmates' stares would be judgmental, which was the only thing worse than pitying.

I roamed the empty halls, enjoying a brief moment of anonymity, until I remembered it was Annie's free period, which meant she was in the darkroom working on the yearbook. The darkroom was completely out of the way, in the basement, next to the music and art studios. I hadn't been down there in a while. The last artsy class I took was theater, and that was back before I met Derek. When I wanted to take ceramics this fall, he said it was stupid to waste an elective on art, that to college admissions officers, it looked almost as bad as a failing grade.

"Finally," I said as the darkroom door swung open.

"Get in fast." Annie cupped her hands around her eyes. "The light's killing me."

I followed her down a short, narrow corridor, through another door, and into the darkroom itself. The pungent odor of sulfur and processing chemicals hit me at once. Surprisingly, they didn't make me feel queasy like everything else these days. If anything, the foreign mix smelled strangely appealing.

"Isn't it supposed to be completely dark in here?" I asked,

looking up at the dangling red bulb that dimly illuminated the black walls.

"That's only if you're printing in color. For black and white you can use a red safelight."

While the design and layout of the yearbook was all done digitally, Annie was a purist, adamant about preserving the art and romance of photography, and insisted on shooting exclusively on film.

As my eyes adjusted, the objects in the room began to take shape. A sink, beakers, various canisters, and a wide, sunken area carved into the counter containing three large metal trays filled with liquid. It looked more like a science lab than an art studio.

"Why the sudden interest?" she said, placing a blank sheet in the first tray.

"Just curious," I shrugged. It was the first time I had ever been in here, a fact I was slightly ashamed of given it was basically Annie's second home. She'd been taking pictures since she got her first camera when she turned twelve. While I loved seeing the finished product, I never thought to see how it was all done.

She turned around to face me, not buying it. "Are you going to tell me why you're really here?"

"Okay fine." I hoisted myself up on the counter next to where she was working. "I couldn't face going back to class."

I told her about the envelope, how I had been humiliated in front of the whole class and summoned to see Dr. Green. I told her how smug Dr. Green had been, acting like she knew everything about me. I left out the part about her accusing me of trying to kill myself, and my so-called cry for help. "Can you believe her?" I asked when I was through.

"That's just how shrinks are." Using a pair of tongs, she transferred the dripping wet paper from one tray into the next, like a game of musical chairs. "Don't take it personally."

But it *was* personal. It was about as personal as it could be.

After a few minutes, Annie removed the paper from the last tray. I followed her to the other side of the room, where she clipped it to a clothesline. It dangled like a flag, next to a bunch of other drying prints.

"What are these?" Each sheet on the line contained rows of smaller images, like a tic-tac-toe grid. My eyes strained to make them out in the dim light.

"Contact sheets. They're all the pictures from a single roll, and I pick which ones to enlarge so I don't waste time developing the bad eggs," she said, taking one down. "Here, take a look."

I stepped in closer to get a better view. They were miniature pictures from the school Halloween pageant last fall. Everyone looked so small, like they could fit in the palm of my hand. I scanned the page until I came across one of me and Derek. I was sitting on his lap, dressed as a cheerleader, wearing the shortest skirt I'd ever worn in public, clutching a pair of blue and gold pom-poms. Derek went as a quarterback, complete with the black streaks smeared under his eyes and the shoulder pads that made him look all muscle-y and twice his actual size. The costumes were his idea. He said it was supposed to be an ironic twist on the typical "American Dream," but deep down I knew it was just an excuse for him to pretend he was an athlete for the day. Sports were the only thing he wasn't very good at. They were also practically the only thing his father ever talked about. Derek's sister was his dad's favorite, and it wasn't because she was his only daughter; she was the only star athlete among his children. Staring at the tiny image, I remembered how self-conscious I had felt in that skirt with my pale, exposed thighs, and how just like Derek, wearing a costume wasn't enough to mask who I really was. The sheet slipped from my hands as a crushing realization popped into my head: Betsy Brill was a cheerleader, a real one who didn't have to fake it.

"Ugh, I'm sorry, Ol." Annie came up behind me and picked up the fallen print.

"Don't," I said, and snagged it away just as she was about to tear it in half. "Have you seen him again? I mean . . . with her?"

"With who?" It was a small relief that she had no idea who I meant.

"Betsy Brill." The way she leaned into him that day at lunch kept replaying in my mind, how she flipped her flowing blond hair and whispered in his ear. They barely knew each other. She had no right to be acting like that, like he was hers. "She was sitting next to him that day in the cafeteria."

"Oh please, that doesn't mean a thing. If it did, then I guess I've dated practically the whole school, and we both know *that* would never happen."

Maybe she was right. Maybe it was all in my head. But I

had every reason to be upset because there was more she didn't know. More I still hadn't told her about that night . . .

"You know what sucks?" Annie said, jumping up on the counter next to me. "That you didn't get amnesia when you died. Isn't that supposed to happen? If I could have magical powers, I'd erase all your memories of Derek O'Brien, just like this." She reached over and palmed my head, giving it a gentle squeeze. "Zap!"

I gave her a weak smile. But the truth was I didn't *want* to forget about *him*. Just what happened.

"Is that from Dr. Green?" Annie asked, pointing at the orange pamphlet poking out of my book.

"Why?" I asked, pushing it further back into the pages of *Mrs. Dalloway*. The glossy paper it was printed on made me think of those giant orange traffic pylons that signaled danger.

"Just curious," she said, mimicking me from earlier as she hopped back down off the counter. "And you know, maybe talking to someone isn't such a bad idea."

"Please, not you too." I felt my back tense up. "And I *am* talking to someone," I insisted.

She gave me her trademark look, the one with the head tilt and the right eyebrow raise. "You know what I mean."

"I swear your parents have brainwashed you. Not everything needs to be talked to death."

"No pun intended, I assume?"

"Maybe you should consider becoming a *comedienne* if this photography thing doesn't work out for you."

"Maybe *you* should," she teased back, laughing.

"Sorry it's taken me so long to check this place out," I said, lingering by the door. It was a whole different world in here. It reminded me of being out in the garden at night, under the cover of darkness.

"You're forgiven." Annie tugged on the earbuds that still dangled around my neck. "And you're welcome here anytime," she added. It was like she understood that I wanted to come back without my having to say it.

As I made my way out of the basement, I felt both lighter and stronger than I had in weeks. Positive thoughts were cycling through my head when I got to the third floor. I rounded the corner and was almost at my locker when something stopped me dead in my tracks.

Betsy stood with her back against Derek's locker, her foot pressed into the mustard-colored metal door, accentuating her long, lean legs. Derek was facing her, running his fingers through her perfect blond hair. With his other hand, he gripped the bent knee that suggestively poked through a gaping tear in her skin-tight jeans. They were both laughing, lost in their own world.

My arms went slack. My bag dropped to the floor. *How could this be happening?*

Derek stepped in closer. As his lips brushed up against hers, a biting chill ran through my veins. The song sped up in my head, playing at warp speed. The lyrics jumbled and overlapped until they were incomprehensible, just a bunch of gibberish. It felt like I'd been catapulted down the rabbit hole, where everything I'd always believed was turned upside down, where nothing made sense anymore.

My legs felt wobbly, like I was fainting standing up. I couldn't move or breathe or even feel my heart beat. All I could do was watch as their lips parted, as Derek reached for Betsy's hand, as they walked down the hall in the opposite direction, away from me, like I didn't exist.

CHAPTER 8

"MRS. DALLOWAY SAID she would buy the flowers herself."

I re-read that first sentence at least ten times. I was incapable of focusing, even though the line was highlighted in pink with three exclamation points beside it, courtesy of my mother. Apparently she was already obsessed with flowers when she was a teenager. Her notes were scattered throughout the book, next to doodles of misshapen hearts with things like *MC + HB Forever* scribbled inside them. Those were my parents' initials. They'd been together since they were fifteen. My mother's handwriting was different back then, all squiggly and loose, like a schoolgirl in love. I wondered when it had changed, when it had become so exact and formal the way it was now, and if it meant that her feelings for my dad had changed, too.

I used to think that love lasted forever. Now I knew that wasn't true.

Every time I closed my eyes, I saw Derek kissing Betsy. The image was seared in my brain. The Derek I knew didn't believe in PDA; he was much more private. He never gazed into my eyes or kissed me or even held my hand when we were at school. He saved it all for when we were alone, when he couldn't keep his hands off me.

I opened my eyes and tried to start over but the memory still burned. Derek caressing Betsy, playing with her hair. I sprang up and tried to shake it off, but looking around my room, all the reminders of Derek stared back at me. They all seemed to be taunting me—for being so foolish, for believing in happily ever after in the first place.

Anger roiled inside me and I swiped the dried roses off the shelf. The flowers were so brittle, the petals practically disintegrated into dust mid-flight. Crouching down, I pulled a floral hatbox out from under the pink bed skirt and placed it on the bed. The hatbox originally belonged to my mother. She had given it to me when I was little, to store all the clothes and makeup she'd handed down for dress-up. Now it was where I kept my most treasured keepsakes from my relationship with Derek. But what was the point of keeping them now?

I flipped off the cover and turned the box upside down. Everything came tumbling out—the cocktail napkin from our first date at Maggiano's, the ticket stubs from our first movie, programs from all the debate matches I had attended over the last two years. I tore it all up, shredding every reminder of our happiest moments.

I flopped down on the bed, the adrenaline still coursing through me. Staring up at the pink princess canopy, all I could think about were the countless times I had lain here with Derek. The way the billowing fabric draped down used to make me feel so protected, especially with him next to me. Looking at it now, I felt like I was suffocating, which only made my anger flare more. Reaching up, I grabbed a fistful of fabric in my hand and pulled with all my strength. One of the bedposts snapped in half, bringing down the entire canopy in one fell swoop. A deflated pink parachute. It looked exactly the way I felt.

About twenty seconds later, my bedroom door came flying open. My mother appeared, a frantic look on her face. She was wearing her gardening apron, holding a spatula. Chocolate icing dripped onto the remnants of a debate program. "What is going on in here?"

"Nothing."

"Nothing?" She picked up a piece of the broken bedpost. "You call this nothing? I'm sure half the neighborhood heard the commotion."

"That must be very embarrassing for you," I said, squaring my arms across my chest.

She let out a deep sigh. For the first time I noticed lines forming on the edges of her pursed lips. "I know this has been a difficult time, but enough is enough. You're moody and erratic. You won't talk to me. You hardly leave this room, and now this?" she said, waving her arm across the debris, the shredded memories. "You're not the same, Olive. I cannot and will not allow this to go on."

"Or what?" I said, digging my toes into the carpet. She was right about one thing. I wasn't the same anymore. I never did things like challenge authority, talk back, tear down bedposts. Or crash cars. But I had nothing left to lose, no one to pretend for.

She shook her head and surveyed the damage. "Is that the brochure from Dr. Green?" she said, noticing the bright orange paper poking out from my pile of schoolbooks.

"How do you know about that?" I asked as she bent to pick it up.

"Because she called me after your meeting. She's concerned, and frankly so am I."

I waited while she flipped through the pamphlet, hoping that once she was done, this conversation, this topic, could somehow be forgotten, swept under the rug the way things usually were in this family. The photo of the depressed-looking girl on the cover stared back at me. She had long brown hair that covered half her face and was wearing an oversized gray sweatshirt over baggy faded jeans. As I caught a glimpse of my reflection in the mirror on the back of the door, I realized we looked almost identical. It wasn't just our clothes or the style of our hair. It was the slump of our shoulders, the low hang of our heads, the blank expressions on our faces.

"There are some very good options in here," she said, reviewing the resource list on the back page.

"Can you let me be the one to pick?" If there were no choice about getting "help," getting to choose would at least make the whole thing a slightly easier pill to swallow.

The kitchen timer went off. The sweet smell of warm chocolate wafted into the room, announcing that her cake was done. My mom was normally so precise about these things, but she didn't budge as the buzzer continued to fill the silence.

"Fine," my mother finally relented, handing me the brochure.

"But if I don't see any improvement, I'm getting involved, no questions asked." She lifted a piece of the torn canopy with her free hand and turned to face me. "You loved this bed."

A few nights later, Annie drove me to my first meeting.

"Are you sure this is it?" she asked, pulling up to an old, dilapidated building on Hollywood Boulevard.

"Yup." It matched the address I had written out on a yellow Post-it, which was now stuck to the dashboard.

"I can't believe your mom went for this," she said, putting the Beetle into park. "What did you tell her?"

"The truth: that it's a support group." After reviewing the orange brochure, there wasn't anything I would willingly subject myself to. Every option was geared toward suicidal teens. Knowing my mom wasn't going to back off until I went *somewhere*, I scoured the Internet until I landed upon a group for people who'd had near-death experiences. From what I could tell, it had two things going for it. First, it was in Los Angeles, miles away from anyone I knew. And second, even though it was for people who had died, it had nothing to do with suicide.

Annie gave me her raised eyebrow look.

"Well it *is*," I insisted, even though I wasn't sure what kind of support the group actually provided. And now, taking in the seedy neighborhood, with motels offering rooms by the hour and liquor stores on every corner, I was beginning to regret my choice. "I thought Hollywood was supposed to be glamorous, with movie stars and stuff."

Even though L.A. was only thirty miles away, it may as well

have been three hundred. I hadn't been into the city since I was little, when we used to come see shows like *The Lion King*. But I never saw much more than the inside of a theater. Vista Valley was my whole world, and I didn't have any reason to leave. Until now.

"You're such a tourist," Annie said, rolling her eyes. "You're thinking of the fake Hollywood, fabricated on studio lots in the valley, on the other side of those hills." She gestured toward the hilltop beyond the community center.

"So, you're saying this is the *real* Hollywood?"

"Yup, where dreams are shattered."

"How uplifting. Well then, I guess it's a fitting location for a group of people who've risen from the dead." The fake Hollywood that came nicely packaged through my television was suddenly sounding very good to me. "How about we say I went and go get something to eat instead? You can give me a tour of your old haunts. My mom'll never know the difference."

"But you'll know the difference," she said. "I'll admit, it's a bit odd, but who knows? This group might just be the perfect thing for you. I mean it's not everyone you meet who's died and lived to tell the tale."

"Well then maybe you should go, so you can hear all their exciting stories," I said, fiddling with the gold heart around my neck. It had been such a part of who I was for so long, of who I wanted to be, that I forgot I was still wearing it.

"Come on, Ol," Annie said. "We've already come this far. Aren't you at least curious? I'll come in with you if that makes it easier." She turned off the engine.

"No, if I do this, I have to do it alone."

In all the weeks since the accident, I hadn't thought much about what it was like to die. But there was still a small part of me that wondered if maybe everything happened for a reason, if dying was all wrapped up in my destiny, which would soon be revealed. And it was that part of myself that led me here, to this group, hoping to find some answers.

"Just don't go too far. I'm not promising I'll stay for the whole hour," I said, unfastening my seat belt.

"I'll be at Amoeba Records down the street. Just text me when you're ready. And Ol? Is it corny for me to say I'm proud of you?"

"Totally corny," I said as the car rumbled back to life.

The foyer was dark, as if the entire place was abandoned. I glanced back through the cracked glass of the double doors, but Annie was already gone.

"Can I help you?" A gruff, old security guard stepped out from the shadows.

What kind of community center needed security? "Um . . . I'm looking for a meeting?"

"The Near-Death Society?" He shifted his eyes, assessing me up and down, as if I was some kind of ghost.

I nodded, kicking an imaginary pebble on the floor. Hearing it out loud, the name sounded so lame. It felt humiliating being associated with it, even in front of a uniformed stranger.

"Down the hall, room 109 on your right."

I walked down the dimly lit corridor, to the green painted door marked 109. The door creaked as I walked in. About twenty people, all seated in a circle, turned their heads at once, just like at school.

"Hello!" A bald, bearded, middle-aged man stood and retrieved a chair from a nearby stack. He had more hair on his face than on his head. He unfolded the chair and squeezed it in next to his own, widening the circle. "Welcome. Please, join us."

I tentatively made my way around the circle and perched on the edge of the seat.

"I'm Stuart," the bald man said. "And you are?"

"Olive." My voice came out dry and raspy.

"Is this your first time? I don't believe I've seen you here before." I nodded. He was sitting so close I could smell his stale coffee breath. "This is a safe place, where we share and support one another. Our motto is there's no such thing as the impossible. I think most of us in this room are living proof of that."

I looked around the circle at the group. They were all so much older than me, with lined faces and graying hair.

"If you don't mind my asking, how did you find out about us?"

"From my guidance counselor." Technically, Dr. Green was the reason I ended up here, even if she had no idea that this group existed.

"I'm so glad to hear we're being mentioned in schools! As you must know, a near-death experience can happen at any age. Surveys estimate that more than twenty-five million people worldwide have had an NDE in the past fifty years. Even so, it can feel like you're traveling down a lonely road after going through something so life altering. It's a subject a lot of folks aren't comfortable talking about. That's why we started this group, oh, what is it—about fifteen years ago now, Mary?" He looked toward a plump older woman, who nodded in agreement. Her silver hair was streaked with the most artificial shade of cherry red I'd ever seen. She reminded me of those weird psychics who hocked their services on late-night infomercials. "How this works is pretty simple. We make our way around the room so that everyone has a chance to speak and share their experience. Do you have any questions?"

I shook my head no.

"Well, feel free to pipe up at any point along the way. It's amazing the conversations that get started in here. So, where were we?" He drummed his fingers on his knee. He turned to an Indian man two seats over on his other side. "Ravi? Would you like to continue?"

Ravi cleared his throat and described the experience of leaving his body and traveling across the country, ending up in Philadelphia. "I found myself in my Auntie's closet. I knew it was hers from the scent of her clothes." He inhaled deeply as if he were still there, smelling her things. "When I woke up in the morning, I called Auntie and described everything I saw, down to the number of shoe boxes stacked in the corner. Sure enough, it was all accurate. I had really been there while my body slept in bed next to my wife."

"Thank you for sharing, Ravi," Stuart said when he was done. "This was, what, your third experience?"

"My fourth, actually," he said. "I seem to always end up in some relative's closet. I'd hate to read into that too deeply." He chuckled.

The rest of the group laughed along with him like it was the funniest thing they'd ever heard.

"How is it a near-death experience if you didn't actually die?" I didn't mean to blurt it out but I felt gypped, like this group was not as advertised.

"The term *near-death experience* is used to describe all sorts of transcendental occurrences, from literal deaths to out-of-body and teleporting experiences," Stuart explained. "Once you've had one of these encounters, it can happen again. In fact some of us can actually *make* it happen through our intentions. Like Ravi, we can train our subconscious to leave our bodies and release our souls. Some say that once you've traveled to the other side, part of you stays there, beckoning you to come back. Does that make sense?"

I politely nodded, realizing what a mistake I had made in coming here. These people were all certifiable.

"But I gather from your question that you did, in fact, die," Stuart said.

I felt heat rise to my cheeks as I looked around at everyone's expectant faces. Was I the only one? I realized they weren't going to leave me alone until I gave them an answer. "Yes."

"What was it like?" The question came from across the circle, from a petite, mousey woman sitting next to red-stripe Mary. Her eyes were bugging out of her pale face, like I just told her we were going to Disneyland or something.

"I don't know," I shrugged. "I can't really remember." It was the truth. It was almost as if time had stopped for those two and a half minutes and restarted again when I woke up in the hospital. But even if I did remember, I wasn't about to share it with a roomful of strangers who seemed to get off on that kind of thing.

"That's very common," Stuart said. "Of course it raises the question of whether your mind can still operate when your brain and heart have stopped. But new studies are proving that the answer is yes, which many of us in this room can attest to. Sometimes the collective power of our souls can help bring this memory back. We have a ritual that can help trigger the process. May I?"

Everyone in the circle locked hands as Stuart reached for mine.

Freaked, I glanced up at the door. All it would take was a mad dash across the room and I'd be out of here. I didn't want to remember. I never wanted to think about that night again. Suddenly, out of nowhere, the image of a collapsed stop sign and chunks of red metal flashed through my mind. I blinked hard to force it back as the invasive sounds—the crackle of fire, the grating screech of fingernails on a chalkboard—raced inside my head, colliding with the melody, like a distorted, scratched record, like they were competing, pulling me in different directions.

Just focus on his voice, I told myself as the lyrics in my head soared above the other noise. They were as loud and clear as the first time I heard them that day on the golf course. It made me think of the boy hitting balls from the roof of his car. How he looked courageous and free, just like I wished I could be.

As I was working up the nerve to leave, the door creaked open. A figure appeared in the doorway, causing me to gasp and nearly fall out of my chair. It was like I was having an out-of-body experience right there, on the spot. Only as I pinched my leg, I knew I hadn't gone anywhere. I was still in my body, in this windowless room, with these lost souls.

And him.

The boy who was hitting golf balls in the parking lot, the boy I was just thinking about, the boy I never thought I'd see again walked into the room. Even though I never got a good look at his face, I had no doubt it was him. He was wearing the same navy jacket, the same black jeans, and had the same wavy dark hair that swept across his forehead. But the thing that made me most certain was the way he moved, with a mix of grace and confidence, just like he had that day at the club.

My heart raced as I tried to stop myself from reading anything into it. The old me would have said it was fate; that there was a larger purpose behind everything, that perhaps we were meant to meet again. But whoever I was now knew better than to chalk it up to anything more than a coincidence. A meaningless coincidence.

With a sharp breath, I quickly averted my gaze as he sauntered toward the back of the room. Lifting a chair from the pile, he pulled it up just outside the circle and plopped onto it backward, his legs spread wide like he was straddling a motorcycle.

Now I was close enough to really see his face. His gray eyes were the color of steel, a thin layer of stubble blanketed his jawline, and his jagged nose looked like it had been broken and left to set without medical intervention. There was something so perfect about its imperfection. Despite the fact that the larger sum of his traits made him seem older, there was still something youthful about his features. It was as if whatever he'd been through in his life had aged him. But underneath, there was still a trace of the person he used to be. Looking at him was like looking at a reflection of myself. I looked the same way.

"Welcome back, Nick."

Stuart's voice snapped me out of my trance, reminding me where I was. Just a few minutes ago I wanted to escape. But now I found myself sitting here, across the circle from the mysterious golf boy. The mystery boy named Nick.

Nick shifted in his seat so that it tipped forward, balancing on its two rear legs. His right knee poked through a tear in his jeans. My thoughts snapped back to Derek's hand on Betsy's knee, jutting out through a similar hole.

"I wasn't sure we'd see you again," Stuart said. "What brought you back?"

"The donuts, of course. Best ones in town," Nick said, with a completely straight face. Only his accent, his completely unexpected English accent, made it seem like he was being sarcastic.

Just then Nick looked up at me, as if he both noticed me and sensed that I was in on the joke. I quickly glanced away, biting down on the inside of my cheek so hard I tasted blood.

"Why don't we take our break now." Stuart clapped his hands together. "We'll reconvene in ten minutes."

I made my way to the snack table by the entrance. Sure enough, two boxes of donuts were laid out on a white plastic tablecloth, next to a large thermos and a stack of Styrofoam cups. I hesitated for a moment before reaching for a chocolate éclair.

"Eat at your own risk," said a voice behind me.

Without turning around, I knew it was Nick. It was more than just his accent and his deep, gravelly voice. It was as if I could *feel* him behind me before he even said a word. I wondered if that's what happened when two people who'd died and came back to life got near each other, like the pull between two magnets. Of course Nick hadn't said that he died, but somehow I was willing to bet he wasn't here because of a weird, closet-hopping dream.

I took a deep breath and turned around. Something about him made me nervous. "I thought they were the best in town?"

A half-smirk edged up the corner of his mouth. "They probably were the day they were baked. Last week." He took the donut from my hand and tapped it against the table. "See? Hard as a rock," he said, handing it back to me. "Still want to give it a go?"

"I think I'll pass and take my chances with the coffee," I said, reaching for the thermos.

"Sorry, didn't mean to kill your appetite."

He walked around to the other side of the table, his arm grazing my backside. I flinched, like an electric current had jolted through me. Coffee sloshed over the cup's edge, onto my hand.

"Whoa, careful there." He set the cup down and inspected my skin where a small red burn was emerging. "Does it hurt?"

The sting evaporated beneath his touch. "I think I'll survive."

"That's a relief." He released his grip. "It'd be a little ironic actually dying here, don't you think?"

"Or maybe fitting . . ." I joked, quickly turning back to the table.

I reached to refill my cup but he blocked my path. "Sure you can handle it?"

Was he being sarcastic again, like he was with the donuts? His face was serious, but it was hard to tell.

"Yes, I think I can handle it," I spat back, my voice clipped.

"It usually takes longer for me to piss someone off but I guess I'm out of practice."

"It's not you," I said. I was suddenly tempted to tell him that I saw him at the club that day, hitting balls into oblivion. But something held me back.

"Goodness. It sounds like we're breaking up and we've only just met." Was he flirting or was that just his English accent playing tricks on me again? "Here, let me." He refilled my cup with fresh coffee, securing this one with a lid. "All right," he said, his voice softer now, like he was revealing a piece of the real him. "Let's start over. I'm Nick, and you are . . . ?"

"Olive," I said, taking a sip from my cup. The coffee was lukewarm, but it felt soothing against my cheek where I had bitten down on it.

"Nice to meet you, Olive. First meeting?"

"Is it that obvious?" I asked, taking another sip.

"No, it's just that I'd remember you." A shiver went up my spine as that almost-smile appeared on his face again. "We kind of stand out when the median age here is fifty-two, don't you think?"

I nodded and felt myself deflate a little. Yet another reminder not to look for meaning where there wasn't any. "How long have you been coming?"

"Long enough to know these meetings are bullshit. Most of these people don't know the first thing about death." A thick piece of hair fell into his face. He flicked it back with a quick jerk of his head, revealing his eyes. They had small flecks of green, only visible up close.

"Then why bother coming back?"

He shifted his gaze toward the floor. He was wearing an old, scuffed pair of red Converse. The laces on his left foot only reached halfway down his shoe. "It's what I deserve."

Nick snapped his head up and looked right at me. There was something haunting in his expression.

"Break's over." Stuart came around with a small plastic trash bin for our empty cups and used napkins.

Nick leaned in close. "Wanna get out of here?"

Even though it was only a whisper, his voice swooshed through my head like the melody, as if my ears had just popped after a long flight and I could suddenly hear again. Was he serious? We'd only just gotten there.

"We'd like to get started," Stuart said, clearing his throat.

"You coming?" Nick was already on his way out the door.

Everyone else had already returned to the circle. Our two empty seats stared back at me. It wasn't the kind of thing I would ever do, take off with some strange guy in the middle of Hollywood. So why did I want to say yes so badly? "I can't . . ." I finally said, and headed back toward my seat.

When I looked back, Nick was already gone.

CHAPTER 9

"READY FOR DESSERT!" Noah announced, pushing his plate away, just like he'd been doing since he was a toddler.

He still had those big round brown eyes and the same dimpled chin that he'd had since the day he was born. I was one of the very first people to see him, even before my dad, who was still clutching my mom's hand when Noah came out. It was strange to think that Noah was born in this house.

That definitely wasn't the plan. My mother always made sure to make that point whenever the story came up, which it did a surprising amount. She didn't want to give the wrong impression and have anyone mistake her for one of those crunchy home-birth moms who doesn't shave her armpits. Of course, all it would take was one look at my mom, in her sweater sets and pearls, to know she could never be *that* mom. She had been so determined to get every last thing done Before the Baby Came (it had become her mantra for the last eight weeks of her pregnancy), that she was able to ignore her contractions while she ironed a stack of onesies. Once her water broke, I was the one who called my dad. I was only ten, but I knew I had to do something while my mother insisted she wasn't going anywhere until she finished ironing. Looking across the kitchen table at Noah now, I couldn't imagine him being capable of making that kind of call.

By the time my dad got home, it was already too late to get to the hospital. An ambulance came and Noah was delivered right here, in this very kitchen. Derek was convinced that witnessing all that—the blood and pain and everything that went with it—must have scarred me, and that it was the reason I was afraid to have sex. Only I knew it couldn't be, because being there for Noah's birth was one of the very best memories I had.

"Wait for your sister to finish," my mother called from where she stood hunched over the counter, poring over paint samples.

"But she never finishes anymore," he said matter-of-factly, picking at my barely touched shepherd's pie.

"That's so not true." I kicked Noah under the table and forced down a few more bites.

"Ow, why'd you do that?"

Shut up! I mouthed. Ever since I went to the meeting last week, my mother had finally started to back off. Luckily, she remained too consumed with paint chips to notice. She was preparing to redo the kitchen. Again. She always gave at least one room in the house a makeover right around this time every year. She took spring cleaning to a whole new level.

"Hmmm, I can't decide," she said, holding two practically identical shades of white up to the wall, which was currently painted "canary." I remember because she roped me into this same process the last time she redid the kitchen two years ago. "Which do you like better, eggshell or minced onion?"

"Minced *onion*? That's a color?" I looked down at the fan deck displaying a dozen more shade options that all looked the same to me. "Why not do something really bold and go for white dove?" I said, reading the name off the closest chip. It didn't really matter which one I picked. She had already made up her mind anyway.

"I think minced onion would be lovely," she said, completely missing my sarcasm.

"Where's Dad?" I asked, desperate to change the subject.

"He's working late tonight." She dropped the samples in order to remove a pound cake from the oven. Hints of lemon and rum filled the air.

"Again?" I asked. She'd said it like it was just this once, like it didn't happen every night.

"You have to tell me how you like this, Noah. I'm testing a new recipe."

"Is he on a big case or something?" It was obvious she didn't want to talk about it, but I didn't care. It seemed like the only time I saw my dad anymore was from my spot in the garden, under the cover of darkness.

Her hand faltered as she cut the cake, the slice falling into a pile of crumbs. "Look what I've done."

"It still tastes the same," I said, popping one of the warm crumbles in my mouth. I felt bad for rattling her. "See? Delicious."

"Here, have a proper piece." She cut into the cake again, a smile spreading across her face.

"I've gotta go," I said, wrapping the slice up in my napkin as a car honked outside. "That's Annie."

"Is your meeting tonight? I could have sworn it was tomorrow." She double-checked the calendar on the fridge.

"The meeting is tomorrow. It's Senior Carnival tonight." That was its official name, but everyone called it "Spring Fling."

"That's wonderful!" My mother's face brightened. "I'm so happy you're going. Here," she said, shoving another slice of cake into my hands. "Take a piece for Annie."

"This is for you." I hopped in the car and handed Annie the cake. It still felt hot, even through the festive checkered cloth napkin. "From my mom."

"There's going to be tons of food there."

"You try telling her that," I said, pointing to the house, where my mother was watching us from the open doorway.

"Right." Annie rolled down the window and waved at my mother with her piece of cake in hand. "Thanks! Smells great, Mrs. Bell!"

"She's ecstatic you got me out of the house," I said as my mother waved back, beaming. "She was seriously starting to think I've become the world's biggest loser."

"Oh come on, the world has much bigger losers than you." Annie put the car in gear and pulled away from the curb. "Thanks for doing this."

"In and out. One hour, right?" I was filling in for Jason Gaits, the yearbook's assistant photo editor, who bailed at the last minute for a Magic: The Gathering tournament. Annie needed to cover the event for the yearbook, and I owed her for driving me to the meeting. And for being the only person who still treated me the same as before.

"Have you considered the possibility that we could actually, you know, have a good time?"

"At school?" I stared out the window, at the neighborhood whizzing by. "Fat chance. You know what everyone thinks of me."

"First of all, who really cares what those dork-bags think? Pretty soon we'll never have to see any of them again. In the meantime, we can just make fun of everyone acting like drunken fools. You know that's my favorite pastime. Especially when you get to capture it on film, for all posterity. Think what these pictures could be worth in thirty years. That's what I call power."

"Derek would never be caught dead doing something embarrassing. He still talks about that picture of Obama smoking a joint and how he'd never make such a dumb mistake. I mean he used to . . ."

Even though I hadn't spoken to him in weeks, Derek was still at the forefront of my mind and still kept popping up as my frame of reference. I rolled down the window and let my arm trail in the wind. I was wearing his favorite jeans, the ones that flared a little at the ankle. He never said they were his favorite in so many words, but he liked the way they hugged my butt, and I wore them whenever I wanted him to notice me.

"Oh, pulease! Like that picture really hurt Obama. Getting

high is probably the only thing that could help Derek. Talk about stiff and BO-RING."

"That's not fair." I still felt the need to defend him. He was like a phantom limb whose tingly nerve endings I could still feel long after they'd been cut. Maybe it was that I hadn't seen him or Betsy since that day by our lockers, or simply that more time had passed, but the possibility that we could still be together loomed even larger in my mind. Lots of couples broke up and spent time apart before getting back together.

"I wish Derek wasn't your guide for how to behave in the world." She shot me a look, once again nailing my innermost thoughts.

I looked up at the sky, now dark. The moon was fat and rising, casting a wide glow across the neighborhood. I wondered where Nick was now, if the same moon was shining down on him too. When I closed my eyes, I thought about him whispering in my ear, of how it made my body tingle. Trailing my fingers up my neck, I could practically still feel his breath on me. But the memory disappeared the second my fingers grazed over my necklace. The one Derek gave me. Reaching back, I unhooked the clasp and dangled the chain out the window. Watching it sway in the wind, I imagined the gold heart slipping off onto the road below, the crunching noise it would make as the tires rolled over it. All I had to do was let go, just like the voice was telling me to. But then I thought about Derek and the last two years. About my own heart, and about that night.

I tightened my grip and put the necklace back on.

● ● ●

We parked in the teacher's section. Annie had a special pass since she was technically working the event. The sound of music and voices rose above the school from the football field behind it, where the carnival was taking place. .

"Here, take this." Annie handed me a bulky carrying case from the trunk.

"This weighs like a million pounds. What's in here?"

"Film, lenses, extra batteries."

"Couldn't you have gone digital for once?" I said, slouching under the bag's weight.

She took her camera out of its case, strung it around her neck, and opened the shutter. "Think fast!"

"Hey!" I raised my hand to cover my face as the bright flash went off. "You know I hate having my picture taken."

"If you think you're getting out of being in the yearbook when your best friend's the photo editor, think again," she said, snapping another one.

"The last thing I need is any lasting evidence to remind me of this year."

"You say that now, but the year's not over yet. . . ." She started across the parking lot as fireworks exploded into the sky behind the building. "Come on, good times await."

The football field had been completely transformed. A few dozen booths lined the perimeter with things like dunk tanks, kissing stands, and ring toss contests to raise money for prom. There were popcorn, corn dog, and cotton candy stations, and a giant jumping bouncy castle set up in the middle of the field.

My stomach knotted as the sound of stifled voices and giggles rose from behind the bleachers.

"Hold on," Annie whispered. She climbed onto the seats and aimed her camera between the first two rows.

"What are you doing?" By this point I was so used to the stares and whispers I was sure they were aimed at me.

"This is where the real action is."

"What the—?" a male voice protested as the flash went off. Ten seconds later, Jeff Baker and Christina Larter, two kids from our class, came running out. Jeff's shirt was half buttoned and Christina's hair had fallen out of her usually tidy ponytail. She was part of a clique that Annie and I called the PCs, which stood for the Ponytail Clones. They all had the same shade of blond hair and wore their ponytails at the exact same point near the top of their heads.

"Hook up at your own risk," Annie said, snapping another shot.

"Give me that." Jeff lunged at her, trying to knock the camera from her hand, but he was so drunk he tripped over his own feet. Christina fell right on top of him in a fit of sloppy laughter.

"I didn't know they were together." I felt the sudden tug of envy as I glanced back at the two of them, rolling around on the ground without a care in the world.

"Eh. That's why they call it Spring Fling."

Maybe that's all that Betsy was too, I thought with a glimmer of hope. Derek's spring fling.

We made our way around the field, stopping at each booth

so Annie could take more pictures, until she turned and handed me the camera. "Here, why don't you take a few."

"It'll be a complete waste of film," I said, backing away. I thought about all the blurry, out-of-focus pictures I used to take on our trips to Arizona for my mother's family reunions. They never made it into the albums.

"I have, like, a million rolls. Another perk of being photo editor." She placed the strap around my neck. "Trust me, it's easy."

Knowing Annie wasn't going to take no for an answer, I held the camera up to my face and looked through the little peephole. "I don't even know where to press. See? Total waste."

"Not so fast my little naysayer," she protested as I tried to hand the camera back. "Just relax and have fun with it." She positioned my finger on the correct button then showed me how to focus the lens and adjust the zoom. "And remember, it doesn't have to be perfect."

That was the problem. I wasn't happy when things were imperfect. As much as I hated to admit it, maybe I wasn't so unlike my mother after all.

I aimed at the cotton candy booth just ahead, fiddling with the lens until Jill Rosen's face came into sharp focus. I sat next to Jill in math but had never noticed that she had so many freckles. I shifted the camera a bit to the right and snapped. Click. The shutter closed on Jill's outstretched pink tongue making contact with the fluffy mound of candy just as another round of fireworks erupted in the sky.

"There you go. See? Not so hard. Finish the roll and I'll help you develop them."

"Only if I can get a few of you," I said, zooming in on her face. "Don't think you can get out of it just because you're the editor."

"Then you'll have to keep up with me." Annie ran ahead, weaving through the thick crowd.

As I took more pictures, I felt my whole body relax. There was something comforting about the camera covering my face like a mask, while granting me this special window onto the world. I was usually so busy worrying about what other people thought of me that I didn't ever stop to notice them. Looking through the lens, I began to really see things—two hands touching, a stolen glance—like I was suddenly given a front row seat to other people's private moments.

We reached the end of the field and started back on the other side when a large, cheering crowd drew our attention.

"Try to get some shots of this," Annie said as we got closer. A heated pie-eating contest was underway.

There were so many people crowded around the stand that I couldn't make out the competitors. Following Annie's instructions, I kept snapping away as I inched closer and closer to the front of the crowd. I was almost there when Derek's face suddenly appeared in the frame. He was standing at the center of the booth, judging the contest. His smooth, clean-shaven skin, the dimpled indentation above his upper lip, his blond eyelashes were so vivid and clear through the lens, it felt like I could reach out and touch him.

My finger hovered over the shutter release. It was the closest I had come to him since everything happened. But I couldn't even take the picture.

Sensing what was happening, Annie appeared right behind me. Without saying a word, she took my arm and led me away from the crowd, to the other side of the field. We stopped in front of the bouncy castle. "Take off your shoes," she said, kicking off her vintage Doc Martens. "We're going in."

"I'm not in the mood." I hadn't been in a bouncy castle since I was five and I didn't even like them all that much back then. "We've taken a lot of photos. Can't we just go?"

"You need to cut loose and forget about that nerd-jerk once and for all." She stood over me with her arms crossed.

"And a bouncy castle is the way to do that?"

"It's a start. Besides, if you won't talk, you've got to let it out somehow."

I thought about the day I tore my room apart in anger, how even that didn't make me feel any better, how memories were deeper than anything you could touch or see. I began unlacing my sneakers.

"Yay!" she squealed. "I promise this will make you feel a thousand times better."

I poked my head in to make sure it was empty before crawling through the narrow opening. I struggled to gain my balance on the uneven surface. It was like trying to walk across a waterbed. At least the inflatable walls blocked out the sounds of the carnival, reducing the cheers from the pie-eating contest to a distant, muffled drone.

Just as I managed to get my footing, Annie dove in, causing the ground to swell like a wave.

"Hey!" I yelled as I toppled over. "You just knocked me down."

"That's the whole point! Now repeat after me: Screw him!"

"This is dumb," I said, trying to regain my balance.

"Come on, what do you have to lose? Just try it. Screw him!" Annie said, launching up into the air like a rocket.

"Screw him," I muttered, flinging myself into one of the walls.

"I can't hear you!" she yelled.

"Screw HIM," I said, a little louder.

"Now say it LIKE YOU REALLY MEAN IT!"

"SCREW HIM!" I screamed at the top of my lungs, hurling myself up so high my hands practically reached the ceiling, the castle's bold yellows, reds, and greens blending together as I tumbled down onto my back. I just lay there floating on the wobbly floor when I heard the sound of muffled giggling. I thought it was Annie until I turned my head and saw Betsy and her cheerleading posse peering in through the entrance. They were all in uniform: micro-mini skirts, midriff bearing tank tops, pom-poms and all.

"Oh, don't mind us," Betsy said, her hands poised on her small hips. "I'd hate to interrupt your little routine."

Another round of giggles followed.

Lying on the teetering ground, a giant wave of humiliation crashed over me and I suddenly felt seasick. I glanced down at my legs quivering on the castle's shaky ground. They looked so big from that angle, especially compared to Betsy's legs, which seemed to go on forever.

"I'm sorry, but we don't speak skank," Annie yelled back to Betsy. "Can you translate?"

Betsy just stared at her before curling her upper lip and doing an about face. Her friends followed suit. I lay motionless watching them retreat, their long, perfectly shiny ponytails swaying in sync. All I could think about was how many times I had tried to make my thick, unruly hair look just like theirs, but had never succeeded. Looking at Betsy's equally perfect round and compact butt, I tugged on my button-down shirt, wishing it covered more of me. There wasn't a single pair of jeans that could make my butt look like hers.

"You can't let her get to you," Annie said once they were gone.

"She's my replacement," I said flatly, staring up at patches of the dark sky poking through the top of the castle. "My upgrade."

"Sometimes I just want to shake you. Do you even hear yourself? You're a thousand times better than Betsy Brill, but that's not even the point because you can't see it."

"No, I'm not. My life is over," I said emphatically, propping myself up on my elbows.

"If you think your life is over, then do something about it." She went to put her boots back on and gather her bags. "Maybe you were given a second chance for a reason. Maybe this is your opportunity to start over. Did you ever consider that?"

I knew she was only trying to help but her words cut deep. I suddenly felt very tired, like I could slip into a long, permanent sleep. "No," I said. "I'm not like you."

"That's right, you're not. And you're not like Betsy or Derek or your mother or anyone else you think has control over your life. You're the one in charge. You're the only one who can change your destiny no matter what you might think. The sooner you figure that out, the sooner you can start living for real."

We drove home in silence. The moon was even brighter now, exposing all the fault lines in the pavement along the way. When I was little, I would avoid the cracks in the sidewalk and step over them, convinced it would keep me safe. But now I knew it was useless. The cracks were everywhere, and there was no escaping them.

The house was dark when I came in. I had no idea whether my father had come home yet, and I didn't care. Before heading out into the garden, I stopped to do my nightly check of Derek's Facebook profile. I nearly fell out of my chair when a new picture—of him and Betsy—appeared at the top of his page. A sharp pain pierced through me as I stared at the two of them, cheek to cheek, all smiles. It was just like the pictures he and I used to take. Betsy had only just posted it a few moments ago. It was as if she had done it for my sake, like she knew I still obsessively checked his page and wanted to send me a clear message that Derek belonged to her now.

But my heart stopped when I noticed another change. There, in clear black print, his relationship status now read, *In a relationship with Betsy Brill.*

My stomach clenched and my heart sped up in my chest. I felt like I was on the verge of throwing up. It hurt all over and nowhere in particular. I sat back and caught my reflection in the window. My hair looked all knotted and covered half my face. I looked just like the girl in that horror movie *The Ring.*

I was terrifying. No wonder Derek could barely look at me anymore.

I ran down the hall, past my bedroom, and into the bathroom. I flicked on the light and searched the medicine cabinet for the blunt scissors my mother always used to cut Noah's hair. The shelves were practically empty, devoid of the collection of old prescription bottles and Advil and cold medicines that normally accumulated there. I felt a dull jab in my gut. Yet another sign that my mother didn't trust me.

I finally found the scissors, hidden in the back of the second drawer next to the sink. I grabbed a thick chunk of hair and began to cut.

In the mirror's reflection I watched the long strands float down, like feathers in suspended animation, daring me to care.

But I didn't. I no longer had a reason to.

CHAPTER 10

THE LAST BELL of the day finally rang. I sprang from my seat and was first out the door. There were still almost four hours until the meeting, but being on the move made it seem like time might go by just a little bit faster. I was sure Nick hadn't given me a second thought; that is, if he even remembered who I was. And there was no guarantee he'd even show up, especially given the fact that he spent a grand total of about twelve minutes at the last meeting. Still, the thought of seeing him again allowed my mind to escape while the rest of me was trapped at school. For those few minutes that we spoke, I didn't feel like I was playing the role of Olive Bell the way I had to here at school.

Out in the hall the bell reverberated against the metal lockers. Classroom doors swung open like dominos. Students streamed into the corridor, surrounding me like an army of marching ants. Instinctively, I reached up to tuck a lock of hair behind my ear but felt nothing but bare skin. I glanced up, afraid of the intense stares I had become accustomed to. But no one was looking. Maybe I was finally old news now; maybe chopping my hair off wasn't such a disaster after all.

"Boo!" Annie grabbed me from behind and yanked out one of my earbuds.

I jumped, nearly dropping my books. "Jeez, you scared me!"

"I still can't believe you cut it all off," she said, touching my empty back where my hair used to fall. It was like a blanket had been yanked off me during the night. I couldn't decide if I felt lighter and free, or naked and exposed.

Just then Derek rounded the corner. It was pointless trying to avoid him anymore. It just made the times that I did see him hurt even more.

I quickly buried my head in my locker. Derek used to make fun of Annie's short hair behind her back, saying she looked like a "lesbo"—his word, not mine. Even though my hair wasn't boy-short like Annie's, I could still practically hear him laughing about my new look with Betsy.

"Can you not make a big deal of it?" I hissed.

"How can I not make a big deal? This is, like, the boldest thing you've ever done! Not to mention you look freakin' awesome."

I stared at my reflection in the mirror tacked to the inside of the door. My face looked so big and round framed by the short, blunt cut. I'd made sure to even it out into a semi-stylish bob. At first, I looked like a crazy person, with long, uneven strands sprouting out at every angle. I could tell my mother wasn't into my new look from her reaction ("Oh, you cut your hair"), but short of praise, she let it go. Looking at it now, I tugged down on the edges, willing them to magically grow back, to reverse my actions. "It was an impulse. I wasn't thinking."

"Maybe you shouldn't think more often."

The back of my head throbbed like the wound was still fresh. If I had stopped to think, I would never have done a lot of things. I angled the door to try to catch a glimpse of Derek through the mirror, but he was already gone.

"I seriously can't wait for you to meet someone else," she said, following my gaze to Derek's locker. "It's the only thing that will make you forget him once and for all."

My mind immediately went to Nick. But instead of feeling excited by the possibility of seeing him tonight, I suddenly felt terrified. I had almost told Annie about him so many times this past week, but now I was relieved that I hadn't. I'd already built him up in my head more than I should have. Telling Annie would elevate him to some super status and only guarantee disappointment.

Annie was looking at me expectantly. What did she know about moving on anyway? "Is that how you've gotten over all *your* exes?" I asked. The words came out sharper than I'd intended.

Annie reached into her locker. "I have to return this," she said, holding out a book as if she didn't hear me. But I knew she had, and that I had gone too far.

"I didn't mean that—"

"I'll meet you at my car in five," Annie said, cutting me off before I could finish.

I let it go as she hurried down the hall toward the library. I knew that if Annie didn't want to talk about something, there was no point trying. Like the time her parents went through a rough patch freshman year. She had told me enough to know that they were fighting, and that I shouldn't ask any questions. It was the main reason I knew I could count on her to not push me about that night. Annie was always private, especially when it came to her parents. They were this tight, happy little three-some that existed apart from the rest of the world. I used to think it was because she was an only child, but I came to believe it was really that her parents were so much cooler than every-one else's. They were interesting and fair and you could say anything to them without worrying they'd take it the wrong way. Maybe it was why Annie didn't care about boys and love as much as I did. Because she had so much love at home. It wasn't that my parents didn't love me. I knew they did. They just didn't know how to love me in the right way, in a way that didn't make me feel so alone.

I slammed my locker shut, trying to focus on the fact that soon enough I'd be miles away from everything I was trying to forget, when I came face to face with Derek. He appeared out of nowhere, like he'd dropped out of one of the ceiling panels. He looked up at the exact same moment and just stared at me. It was the first time he had really looked at me since everything happened, without turning his head away or averting his gaze. It was like he really wanted to see me. His lips began to move as he took a step closer. The air became heavy with the odor of chalk and stinky sneakers. It felt like the yellow walls were closing in on me. I had been desperate for Derek to talk to me, to acknowledge I still existed, for some sign of hope that I could cling to, but now that the moment had actually arrived, I took off in the other direction.

Annie was dancing wildly in the driver's seat when I got to the car. She lowered the volume when she saw my expression. "You look like you've seen a ghost."

I put on my sunglasses and took out my iPhone. "Mind if I plug this in?"

"Be my guest," she said, detaching hers from the adapter and swapping mine in.

I cued up my play list, turned the volume loud enough that we couldn't talk, and leaned back in my seat as we drove down Vista, aka Derek Memory Lane. What was he trying to tell me out in the hall? Just thinking about it gave me a queasy stomach.

I rolled down the window and tried to focus on the road ahead. It had been repaved when I was in the hospital. They redid it every year to fill the same potholes that kept coming back. Even though they only appeared on one part of the road, the city applied a fresh layer of asphalt to the whole boulevard, making it into one long, perfect strip, like a tarmac. But the more I stared at the inky surface, with its dotted lines the color of sunshine, the more I saw the gaping holes it was trying to cover.

I rolled the window back up and turned to Annie. "Let's go into the city early today."

When we got to L.A., I asked Annie to show me around her old neighborhood. We had plenty of time to kill, and it was only ten minutes away from Hollywood. I felt bad about what I'd said earlier about her nonexistent exes. Even if Annie seemed to have forgotten it, I wanted to somehow make it up to her. It got me thinking again about how Derek used to call her a lesbian. It wasn't just because of her hair, but how she never flirted with, or showed any sign of interest in, boys. I told him he was just full of himself because she never flirted with *him*. But now I was beginning to wonder if Derek had somehow been more perceptive about my best friend than I was.

"This is my old school." Annie slowed down as we approached a quaint, red brick building. It looked like the kind of school you'd find on the East Coast, surrounded by tall trees and a grassy lawn.

"Wait, this is the infamous Potter School for Girls?" I asked as a group of students came out a side door in matching plaid skirts and white shirts. I recognized the uniform from Annie's albums.

"The one and only," she said, with a hint of wistfulness in her voice. Whenever she talked about it, the school always sounded like this magical oasis, where you didn't have to worry about what to wear or who to impress. It was so small that there weren't any cliques and everyone was friends, even with their teachers, whom they called by their first names. I wondered if feeling so safe and protected back then is what made Annie so confident and different now. Maybe by looking the same as everyone else on the outside back when she was little, she was free to be different on the inside. There was clearly no one else like her in Vista Valley, but we didn't have any schools like this.

"This is where you met Jessica, right?" I knew that it was,

but I suddenly wondered if there was more to their friendship than Annie was letting on, not just to me, but maybe even to herself. I glanced at her from the corner of my eye to gauge her reaction. She just nodded and continued driving, until the school was just a red dot in the side view mirror.

We got an early bite at Annie's favorite diner. It was where she and her parents used to go for Sunday brunch before they moved. She said it was the best place for people watching, a place where young hipsters stumbling home from a Saturday night out in Hollywood and local families like hers intersected. With its torn vinyl booths, old-fashioned jukebox, and tattooed clientele (both young and old), it was a far cry from my family's Sunday brunch scene at the club. I couldn't imagine my mother ever setting foot in a place like this.

"See you back here in an hour?" Annie said, checking her watch. This time we got to the community center with ten minutes to spare.

Flipping down the visor for one last glance in the mirror, I pushed my hair forward so it covered more of my face. I wondered if I'd ever get used to the person who now stared back at me. "Wish me luck," I said as I hopped out of the car.

"Luck for what?" Annie called out after me, but I pretended I couldn't hear her and ran through the cracked double doors. If I stopped now, I might never make it inside.

The security guard nodded as I hurried past him to room 109.

There were still a few empty seats as I made my way to the

circle, with most of the people from last week in their same spots. But there was no sign of Nick. What did I expect given how little he seemed to want to be here last time? It was stupid to think that he'd come back just for me. But that didn't stop me from holding my breath every time the door creaked open. Or from deflating a little more each time it wasn't him. I had the sinking fear that he wasn't real, that maybe he was just a figment of my imagination, like the song running through my head.

"Let's get started," Stuart said, once all the movement and chair scraping had come to a stop. "We'll go clockwise tonight, starting with Michael."

I glanced toward the exit, hoping to see the door swing open, but it didn't. No one else was coming.

A man two seats over cleared his throat. He looked like he was around my father's age. He was dressed like my father too, in a suit with a fancy-looking leather briefcase tucked under his chair. I wondered if he had a wife and kids at home just like my dad, if he stayed up late at night drinking scotch while everyone else slept. "Pure bliss," he said. "That's the best way I can describe what it was like."

He closed his eyes and let out a long, deep exhale, like he was reliving the moment right there. I could never imagine those words coming out of my dad's mouth. I shifted to dislodge my thighs from the sticky plastic seat and wondered if Michael had been more like him before he died.

"I felt this overwhelming sense of cosmic unity," said the woman to Michael's left. It was hard to tell how old she was. Her dark hair had silver and white streaks running through it, but her skin was smooth and wrinkle free. She could easily have been one of those people who turned prematurely gray at thirty or a sixty-year-old health freak.

Now it was my turn. My heart began to race as I glanced around the room. Beads of sweat formed at my temples as all eyes turned to me. It suddenly felt hot and stifling. I didn't know what to say. I didn't belong here. I was nothing like these people. All I had to do was get up and make it across the room and out the door. Annie would be waiting for me on the other side. But a buzz swarmed into my head. It was so dizzying I wasn't sure I could get up.

"Olive?" Stuart finally said after a sustained silence.

Just one step at a time, I told myself as I peeled my legs off the chair. They felt leaden and heavy, like I was stuck in quicksand. Zeroing in on the red letters of the exit sign above the door, I bolted. I kept running down the darkened corridor, like I was stuck in a bad dream that would drag me back if I stopped for even a second.

The dying sunlight filtered in through the mottled double glass doors at the end of the hall. I was almost there. Just a few more steps to go when—

Bang.

I barreled into someone.

"Whoa, are you all right?"

It was Nick.

I doubled over, struggling to take in deep, heaving inhales, but seeing him only made it worse.

I felt his hand on my shoulder. "This way."

I straightened up as he guided me over to the wall. "Stand here and close your eyes," he instructed.

I leaned into the wall, my palms outstretched against the cool cement surface. "That's it," he said as I bowed my head and closed my eyes.

"Now." He drew in closer, his lips almost brushing against my ear as he whispered. "I'm going to count to ten and all that matters are the numbers. Nothing else, okay?"

I nodded.

"Good. Here we go. *One. Two. Three...*"

His voice was so soft and commanding that my humiliation started to give way to an overall sense of calm, like he was hypnotizing me.

"*Six. Seven. Eight...*"

I was concentrating so hard on his voice that I realized it was the only thing I was hearing. Miraculously it had taken the place of all the buzzing in my head.

"*Nine. Ten.*"

When I opened my eyes, Nick was standing next to me, wearing the same navy blazer, the same red sneakers, and the same pair of ripped jeans. Seeing him again felt both natural and completely unexpected. It was like an almost-vu, where I almost but couldn't quite remember experiencing this same feeling before.

"You cut your hair," he said, studying my face in a way that made me uneasy and excited at the same time. I nodded. "You look more like yourself."

The hint of a smirk edged up the corner of Nick's mouth.

It made him look even cuter, if that were possible. "So, are you going to turn me down twice in a row?"

"I have no idea what you're talking about." I wasn't trying to be coy. I just wished I knew what he was really thinking beneath his crooked smile and seductive voice. As much as I wanted to take him at face value, experience taught me that was a mistake.

"There's only one way to find out," Nick said, glancing toward the street. It was dusk now, hints of moonlight casting a shadow through the front doors. My heart raced with indecision. I thought about the person I used to be, and the new one—whoever she was—I so desperately wanted to become. The person Nick already seemed to recognize even if I didn't.

"Fine," I said, almost in defiance, telling myself this was different. This wasn't about dating and happily ever after and all the things I was looking for with Derek. This was about adventure; this was about escape. "Let's go."

CHAPTER 11

WE HADN'T EVEN walked one block when I was seized by a nagging discomfort, a feeling that I was doing something very wrong. The guilt took up residence at the base of my gut but I still couldn't stop, like Nick had cast some spell over me. When he wasn't looking, I fished my cell out of my bag and sent Annie a text: *Got a ride home. Don't worry.*

The phone was already beeping with her response as I slipped it back in my purse. I ignored it and switched the ringer to vibrate. I hurried to catch up to Nick, who was now a few paces ahead. Without warning, he stepped off the curb and started across the middle of Hollywood Boulevard. Not even the cacophony of honking horns or tires coming to screeching halts made him slow down. He just kept going like he was Moses or something, parting the Red Sea. When he glanced back and saw that I wasn't right behind him, he put his hands up to stop the traffic and gestured for me to follow.

He pulled a set of keys from his back pocket. Over by the curb, a forest-green Jaguar beeped twice. My eyes widened with recognition. It was the same car he had been standing on at the club that afternoon. Up close I could see it was scraped and dented all over. Even the parking job (three feet from the curb with the rear, semi-detached bumper jutting out into the street) seemed like an invitation to be hit.

Nick walked around to the passenger side and opened the door for me, but I took a step back. Even though I'd seen him at the club, he was still a stranger, and from what I had to go on so far, a very unpredictable one. Every sensible molecule in my body was telling me not to get in the car. But the part of me that couldn't sleep, the part that lay awake at night on the damp grass listening to a song in my head, was telling me something completely different.

"We can just stay around here if you want," he said, reading my hesitation.

"No, it's okay." I put my hand out to stop him from closing the door and got in.

As he walked around to the other side of the car, I kept waiting for my senses to kick in, to convince me to get out while I still could. But the only thing I heard was the voice sweetly singing in my ear, telling me to let go.

Nick revved the engine then peeled out into the traffic, igniting another discordant round of honks. His face remained calm and his shoulders relaxed as he expertly weaved in and out of lanes. The only sign of effort was in the fast twitch of his hand as he shifted gears, like a seasoned racecar driver. The further down Hollywood Boulevard we went, the seedier it got. Sleazy lingerie stores, tattoo parlors, and cheap motels lined every block. The sidewalks were littered with trash and grime, evidence of the thousands or maybe even millions of people that had walked up and down them. There was something about the dirt that made the area seem more alive, like it wasn't pretending to be something else. Even the street signs and billboards were tagged with colorful graffiti. It looked like it had all been painted by the same person. I pictured the artist scaling the surrounding buildings and street lamps in the middle of the night like a ninja, but instead of a sword tucked into his belt, he had an array of spray paint cans. I had never seen anything like it, except in movies. There was never any graffiti in Vista Valley. The one time it did happen, the whitewashed buildings were scrubbed clean and picture perfect within hours, as if nothing had ever transpired. It was as if filth wasn't permitted to exist there. My mother was captain of the people who made sure of it.

A few blocks later, Nick took a hard right onto a quieter street. The traffic thinned out and the Jaguar was practically the only car on the road. He tightened his grip on the stick and pressed down harder on the gas pedal. The sudden jolt of speed pushed me back against my seat. Storefronts, billboards, and street lamps whizzed past, blurring together into a Technicolor dream. It felt like we might launch into the air at any minute. I turned to Nick, whose eyes were fixed on the road. "So how do I know you're not some crazy ax murderer who's about to kidnap me?"

"You don't," he said, matter-of-factly. Something flashed in his eyes. There was no hint of the playfulness that had been in his voice a second ago. I studied his face, trying to read him. It felt like I was walking on the razor's edge between flirtation and danger. "But the way I see it, we're defined by the risks we take."

Was that a dare or what he actually believed? The street suddenly got darker and much quieter. The stores and restaurants gave way to run-down homes and dilapidated brick apartment buildings. "So you admit it's risky hanging out with you?"

"The question you should really be asking yourself is whether the risk is worth it." In that moment I realized what I was most afraid of. Not that Nick was some deranged killer, but the opposite: that he was as good as he already seemed, that he could sweep me off my feet and make me lose all sense of time and place, just the way Derek had. That was the risk that scared me even more than death. "However, judging from the fact that you got in this car, I take it that you think it is."

The caution and distance I had detected in his voice were now gone and I wondered if maybe I had imagined them. "So where are we going on this risky little adventure?"

"That depends." That same smirk edged its way back up the right side of his face. It felt like a signal, the green light that said I could relax again. "Do you have somewhere you have to be?"

I checked the clock on the dashboard. It was a little after eight. The meeting would just be getting out. Noah would be getting ready for bed, my mother was probably in the greenhouse, and my father wouldn't be home for hours. Nobody would notice I was gone. "No, I don't."

"Good, then how about we just drive," he said. "See where the road takes us. How does that sound?"

"Like the best thing I've heard all day." I settled back in my seat and got comfortable. With the fancy dashboard, the leather seats, and the dark road that blended into the night sky, it felt like we were flying above the world in our own private plane. I had no idea where we were but I wasn't scared. If anything, I felt safer than I had in a long time, even as the speedometer shot past fifty miles an hour. Looking through the rearview mirror, I could see the very last bits of daylight receding in the distance. For the first time since everything happened, I felt like I had stepped out of my life, put it on pause. Even my brief encounter with Derek that afternoon had faded into the background, just like the sun in the mirror. "Just as long as the road doesn't take me home."

"I think that can be arranged," he said, flicking the hair off his face. "I know the feeling all too well."

A warm sensation gushed through me. Given where we met, I was certain he understood me better than anyone I knew. Even more than Annie. He might be the only one. It wasn't just that he'd also had a near-death experience. It was more than that. Even though he never said it, I could tell that dying hadn't been a magical experience for him either. He seemed to have one foot in and one foot out of this world, just like me.

The dark sky stretched out before us as Nick zigzagged down a series of residential streets before turning onto a main thoroughfare. This one was different from Hollywood Boulevard. It was also run-down but it wasn't sleazy. Just poor. And all the street and store signs were written in Spanish, as if we had crossed an invisible border into another country. A cluster of high-rise buildings shot up in the distance. They appeared out of nowhere, like a mirage, especially compared to the low-lying architecture that surrounded them in all directions. They seemed so far away, but before I knew it, we were sandwiched between two towering skyscrapers.

The tallest building in Vista Valley was my school, which stood above the rest at a measly four stories. The fourth floor was added a few years ago to accommodate a growing student body. I remembered my mom being in a tizzy about the whole thing, on the phone all day and night trying to figure out a way around "Expansion-Gate."

Leaning my head against the glass, I craned my neck up to get a better view. From that angle, the buildings seemed to go on forever, extending up into the sky like an urban bean stalk. "It's a ghost town around here," I said.

"I know. It kind of makes you feel like you're the last person on earth." He glanced over at me. "Or the last two people."

His half-smile reappeared, like his mouth was conspiring against him. I met his eyes then quickly looked away, certain that I was blushing so hard I was glowing in the dark.

"Have you never been down here before?"

I shook my head no.

"Then you haven't seen anything yet."

He made a sudden U-turn. The sound of squealing tires bounced off the corridor of bright, empty buildings like we were driving through a tunnel. Two blocks later he turned onto a street lined with tents and cardboard boxes. Every square inch of sidewalk on either side of the road was overtaken at least two rows deep. Nick was right. This was something I had never seen before. Something I didn't know existed.

Dozens of homeless people wandered aimlessly in front of their makeshift homes like zombies. I kept waiting for Nick to speed up, to step on the gas, to get us out of there. But instead, he slowed the car to a crawl and opened the windows.

"Welcome to Skid Row," he said.

I stared out at the roaming hordes. We were close enough that I could hear the slow shuffle of their feet, smell the urine embedded in their dank clothes. Men and women with matted hair and hollowed, glassy eyes. They didn't seem to notice our presence even though we were just an arm's reach away.

"They're like the living dead," I said. "How do people end up like this?"

Nick shrugged. "I guess something happens that makes them fall off and get stuck between the cracks."

The way he said it sent a shiver up my spine, like he was really talking about himself. It made me think of the first time I saw Nick, hitting golf balls from the top of this very car. I was about to bring it up, but when I glanced over, something held me back. The way he was looking out at all these sad, homeless people made me suddenly realize what I recognized in him that day: it was his pain.

When the tents and boxes began to thin out, he sped up and zoomed away. Even though they were now behind us, I knew I'd never forget the haunted look in their faces.

"What's that?" I asked, pointing toward a massive stainless steel structure up the street. With its large slabs of curved metal protruding at odd angles, it looked like an alien spacecraft.

"That's Disney Concert Hall. Not to be confused with

Disney*land* or Disney *World*. It's home to the L.A. Philharmonic and one of L.A.'s most distinguished landmarks."

I felt a burn rising in my cheeks. With his accent, I couldn't tell if he was being sarcastic or making fun of me for not knowing. Either way I was embarrassed for being so ignorant, for never having heard of it before.

As we rounded the corner, an elegant crowd spilled out onto the sprawling front staircase. Women in fancy gowns and men in black tie milled about with cocktails in hand, the glistening building rising up behind them.

Nick turned to me, a twinkle in his eye. "How about we crash a party?"

I looked down at my faded jeans, my chipped toenails poking out of my flip-flops. "Um, I can't go in there like this."

"Sure you can. All you have to do is act like you belong," he said, driving around to the other side of the building, down a back alley where several catering trucks were parked. At the end of the row, he made a sharp turn and diagonally wedged his car to fit between the last two vans. "Besides, I think you look great."

That was all it took for me to unbuckle my seat belt and follow him inside.

We went through a back door that landed us in the kitchen. Harried chefs handed off hot trays of hors d'oeuvres to a rotating slew of waiters. I looked nervously around, waiting to be yelled at or caught, but Nick kept going with his head held high like everyone worked for him.

We emerged into the main lobby, where the party was in full swing. Up close the women looked even more glamorous, like they had walked off the pages of a glossy high fashion magazine. Their diamonds and rubies sparkled under the warm glow of the crystal chandeliers that were evenly spaced across the low ceiling above.

I had never been anywhere like this before. How could I act like I belonged when I didn't know how? Nick clearly did, with his raised chin, his confident stride. He was right. It wasn't about the clothes you wore, but something else, something deeper, something I didn't possess. It was in that moment that I realized I felt more comfortable on Skid Row than I did in here. That was the world Nick and I had in common. I didn't know this other world he was caught between, the one he apparently came from, but it was clear it was not the same as mine.

"What's the occasion?" I asked, looking around at the mingling crowd.

"Who knows, probably some benefit to build schools in Africa."

"That's nice," I said, realizing that the kind of "benefits" we had in Vista Valley only benefited ourselves, not those truly in need. Things like school bake sales to raise money for prom, or the fall drives my mother organized to pay for the public flower gardens.

"What would be nice is if these people gave a shit about the poor right under their noses," Nick scoffed. "Think about the irony of all these jokers in black tie stuffing their faces when there are dozens of starving people just down the street."

A flash of heat spread across my face. I felt as if I was the one who had just been scolded. Before tonight, I never realized that there were so many starving people right here in this country, right here in this state, that deprivation of that magnitude wasn't just a problem in places like Africa.

A waiter passed, balancing a tray of hors d'oeuvres. Nick reached over and grabbed a few. "Here," he said, handing me a white spoon filled with slimy, steely gray balls.

"Oh, no thanks," I said, waving it away.

"Why not?" He shoved one in his mouth.

"I don't have much of an appetite these days." But I was also a little confused by what we were doing here, how Nick could go from judging everyone to eating their food in practically the same breath.

"Maybe you're just eating the wrong things." He licked the spoon clean. "Try it. What's the worst that can happen?"

"What is it?"

"Beluga caviar. Also known as fish eggs harvested from a two-thousand-pound sturgeon somewhere in the Caspian Sea. This fish came a very long way to reach your taste buds, Olive."

"Is that your best pitch?" The thought of willingly ingesting fish eggs made my stomach churn. "Because you're going to have to try a little harder, preferably without any reference to fish or their eggs."

"Fair enough. How about, it's a rare delicacy enjoyed by kings and queens the world over, and this mouthful," he said, eyeing the serving in his outstretched hand, "is probably worth a mere hundred."

"Dollars?" I asked, my eyes bulging. "For one bite? You'd think they could spring for a cracker at that price."

Nick laughed. The way his face tightened I got the sense

he didn't do it that often. "That would pollute the pure taste. Even metal would, which is why it's served on a spoon made from mother of pearl. But don't let me force you. I'd be happy to have yours."

"Fine, I'll try it." I took the spoon and popped the whole thing in my mouth, bracing for my gag reflex to kick in. But the smooth, Jell-O-y texture felt surprisingly cool and soothing against my tongue. My throat relaxed as my mouth exploded with the salty, indescribable flavor, like I was experiencing the sense of taste for the first time. It gave me chills. "Wow."

"What did I tell you?" Nick said. "All it takes is a little trust."

The only problem, of course, was knowing how to trust the right person. And to trust myself to know the difference. I still barely knew him, but I was drawn to Nick in a way I had never experienced with anyone before, not even Derek. Already it was so powerful it was unsettling.

"Another bite?" Nick asked as the caviar-toting waiter made another round.

As tempting as it was, I knew I needed to hold back. I wasn't ready for more. "I'm good for now." A lone egg swirled around my mouth. I tried to catch it with my tongue but it was too slippery.

"Then come on," he said, tugging my arm. "I want to show you why we're really here."

He led me down the corridor, through the center of the party. Reaching a set of double doors, he pushed them open and gestured for me to go through first. I walked in to find myself standing before the massive, empty concert hall.

"This way." He raced down the center aisle, taking the steps two at a time, past all the empty rows to the stage at the bottom, behind which stood a massive organ made of curved wooden pipes. It reminded me of the circular Elizabethan theaters we had learned about during the Shakespeare unit in English. There was something even more intimidating about being in this grand, vacant space alone with him than out in the party with the crowd to distract and hide behind.

When I didn't follow, much less move an inch from the spot where I was standing, Nick looked back. "Aren't you coming?"

I started to make my way down, the chatter of the party becoming more distant as I descended each step. When I reached the stage, Nick helped me up. The strong grip of his hand pulsed even after he let go, like an undulating blood pressure cuff had been wrapped around my forearm.

"This is the main attraction. The acoustics in this place are unbelievable. It's a shame we're too late to hear the orchestra."

He marched over to the center of the stage. Taking a deep breath, he reached his arms up above his head. "HELLO!" he belted at the top of his lungs.

The sound traveled evenly around the room as if he had yelled through a bullhorn. I was startled, not so much by its intensity but because it had happened at all. Nick was so hard to read, and I didn't know what to expect next.

"No, that won't do," he said, when the ghost of his echoing voice finally faded. "Don't go anywhere."

He walked across the stage, down a set of four back stairs, and disappeared through a door, leaving me standing there, on the stage, alone.

I stared up at the rows of empty seats and the balconies stacked above. I tried to imagine how it would feel to be in front of an actual audience, to have hundreds of pairs of eyes trained on me, watching my every move, when it hit me: I already knew. I experienced it at school.

A high-pitched, scratchy noise emerged from above. A few seconds later a thumping electronic beat suddenly filled the void, blasting from what felt like a million invisible speakers. Nick came running back through the door, up the steps, and across the stage to where I stood waiting.

"Now, this is the way to experience this place."

His body bounced to the music. Soon, I was moving, too. It was unavoidable. The strong, steady beat was like a force field, propelling us up, up into the air with every pulse until we were surfing on cushions of vibrating sound. It was the same way I felt when I heard the voice sweetly singing in my head: transported somewhere else, somewhere magical, somewhere full of hope.

The music suddenly stopped and was replaced by a stern, gruff voice that seemed to be coming from the ceiling. "What's going on? Who's been in here?"

"What are we going to do?" I whispered, my heart racing.

"Make a run for it."

"But he has your music."

"It's replaceable." Nick shrugged.

"Hey, you two over there." The security guard, a paunchy middle-aged man busting out of his uniform, appeared at the side of the stage.

Nick looked back at him, then calmly surveyed the hall. He grabbed my hand and whispered in my ear. "Okay, let's go!"

We bolted back up the center aisle, through the double doors, around the winding corridor until we were back in the thick of the party. It reminded me of running away from the grounds-keeper on the golf course the day I first saw Nick. I couldn't help but feel the two incidents were somehow connected. That maybe everything was connected to Nick.

He elbowed through clusters of people, jostling drinks and trays along the way, until we made it to the kitchen and back out into the alley the way we had come in. My heart pounded like crazy against my ribs even once we were safely outside. But before I could catch my breath, I noticed a tow truck backing in toward Nick's car. "Look!"

We started to move at the exact same moment. Within seconds we were both running in an all-out sprint. We made it to the car just as the tow truck driver was about to connect it to his flatbed. Ignoring the driver's string of profanities, Nick revved the engine and peeled out.

"Where to next?" he said once we were safely on the road.

I looked at the clock. I couldn't believe it was only eleven. It felt like I had lived more in the last few hours than I could in a year at home. "I should probably be getting back."

"And where's home?"

"Have you been to the valley?" I asked, knowing full well that he had. And that I'd finally have a chance to casually mention that I'd seen him before.

"You mean the expanse over those hills," he said, pointing

toward the Hollywood sign, which was barely visible at night. "Can you be more specific?"

"I live in Vista Valley." I paused, waiting for him to interject, to say he knew exactly where it was, that he'd been there before, but he didn't. "It's about thirty miles northeast of here," I continued. "Ever been?"

"Nope," he said with a straight face, with not even a flicker of recognition. "Never heard of it."

I swallowed hard and tried to focus on what a great time I'd had with him, to ignore the other questions that burned in my mind, like why he was lying, or what he was trying to hide.

There were hardly any cars on the road at that hour so it only took forty minutes to get back.

"Thanks for an interesting time," I said when he pulled up to my house. *An interesting time?* I could be such an idiot sometimes. I bit down on my lip. It was still salty from the caviar.

"No, thank *you*," Nick said as I got out of the car. "For being good company."

I listened to his idling engine as I walked up the path to the front door. The left side of my head started to tingle from where he'd counted in my ear, back when this adventure all started. When I got inside, I pressed up against the closed door and peered through the peephole as he drove away. It was strange. When I was with Nick it felt like the rest of the world melted away, like time expanded until there was no time, just infinity, with no end in sight. But now that I was back home and he was gone, it felt like I had dreamt the whole night.

CHAPTER 12

"FINALLY," ANNIE SAID, flinging open the door to the darkroom. "I was wondering if you were ever gonna surface."

It was already lunch and the first time we had seen each other all day. "I told you my mom was taking me to the doctor this morning. Remember?"

"You know that's not what I'm referring to," she said, starting back down the hall. She had texted me a bunch of times while I was out with Nick, but I didn't respond until I got home. "But first tell me what the doctor said."

"It was just a follow-up to check my head and make sure it's healing okay." I felt it throb just talking about it.

"And is it?"

"Yeah. He said I might experience some phantom pains because the nerve endings are raw from where the stitches were, but he doesn't need to see me again." I had almost asked him about the song, if it was a phantom too, but my mother was there. She had miraculously gotten off my case in the last few weeks, and I didn't need to give her a reason to get back on it.

Besides, I wasn't so sure I wanted the song to go away. Not now that it reminded me more of Nick than anything else.

"Well, that's good. About not needing to see him again." Her voice was cool and distant.

"Come on, don't hate me," I said, following her down the corridor toward the darkroom. Even when I was being evasive about something, I had never avoided Annie before, at least not deliberately.

"On one condition," she said as we walked into the darkroom. "You tell me who kept you out all night and don't say no one because you are in the best mood I've seen you in since the *Hailey's Clinic* summer marathon."

"Very funny," I said, turning away so she couldn't see the shade of red I was sure my face was turning. I could always tell I was blushing from the prickly sensation that came along with it. "Why are all the lights on?" I asked, ignoring her other question. I had been hoping they'd be off. It would be easier to evade Annie in the dark. I wasn't ready to talk about Nick yet. I had attempted to Google him the second I got home last night, but without his last name, I had nothing to go on. Every search yielded millions of results except for the one I was looking for, just like with the song.

"I'm working on layouts for a yearbook meeting for which I'm already supremely late," Annie said, checking the time on her phone. "But stop changing the subject. You kind of freaked me out, Ol. It's so not like you to just disappear like that, especially in a strange city."

My mind raced with the other things that happened last

night that weren't at all like me either. Ditching the meeting, getting in Nick's car, going to Skid Row, and crashing the party at Disney Hall. I could practically still taste the caviar when I swallowed. I walked over to the table where several mock year-book pages were laid out and picked one up. It was labeled *The Way We Were*, an infamous section that appeared in every edition. It was supposed to be a comedic homage to the graduating class with "before" and "after" shots to show how much we had all transformed since the beginning of high school. "I didn't disappear. I texted you when I got home."

"Oh please," Annie said, pulling her black leather portfolio carrying case from the wall cabinet. "Are you really going to be like that? You're talking to me, not your mother, you know."

My stomach tightened into a ball of guilt thinking about the various secrets I had been keeping from her lately. "It's not what you think." I hoisted myself up on the table, letting my feet dangle freely below. "I was just out with this guy I met in the meeting," I said, trying to sound as nonchalant as possible.

"I knew it!" Annie screamed, slapping her thigh in excitement. "You are so busted! I demand that you tell me everything immediately!" She jumped up next to me on the counter, right on top of a series of contact sheets she had carefully laid out.

"I thought you were late." I pulled the pages out from under her so they wouldn't bend and noticed they included some of the pictures from Spring Fling.

"I am." She didn't budge, and I felt her eyes probing into me.

"Hey, I took this one!" I said, pointing to the image of Jill

Rosen licking the cotton candy, an explosion of fireworks in the background. The way the colored flames fanned out behind her head made it seem like I had included them on purpose. "And it's not even terrible."

"It's really good, actually. That's why it's in there. You're a natural. But STOP. CHANGING. THE SUBJECT!" She crossed her arms over her chest. "I'm not leaving until I hear more."

"There's really not that much to tell," I said, avoiding her probing stare.

"You were out until midnight and there's nothing to tell? How about his name, for starters."

I let out a sigh. "Okay, fine. It's Nick. We met during the break at the meeting last week and talked a bit, probably because we were the only two people there under the age of forty. I told you, the group is a bunch of old weirdos." It felt strange talking about Nick, to even say his name out loud, like it might make him—and the memory of last night—disappear.

"Are you kidding?" Annie sprang from the counter. "That's, like, insanely romantic. Almost tragically romantic. Meeting at a group for people who died? Wow. So what's his story?"

"I don't know. We didn't really get into that stuff." Even though it was what linked us, I bristled at the thought of Nick dead.

"I see," Annie said, raising an eyebrow. "Now I really understand why you were ignoring me."

"Believe me, nothing happened." Just thinking about kissing someone else, someone who wasn't Derek, still made me uneasy. I knew it was over, that he was with Betsy now. I was starting to accept that. I also knew that being with Nick made me feel more alive than I had in a long time. But as much as my stomach flipped when I was near him or how my skin tingled from his touch, the idea of kissing him frightened me more than anything. I wasn't sure that would ever go away. All it took was coming back to school, to my old life, to remind me of that. "And he doesn't think of me that way."

"Oh, really," Annie said, not buying it. "Then what kept you out all night, Cinderella?"

"It wasn't all night." My voice got quiet and I felt defensive, like I was letting her down. I still didn't know anything more about Nick than I had when I got in his car, at least not anything I could put into words. I just knew that when I was with him I forgot about Derek, about that night, and school, and Dr. Green, and my dad swirling his half-empty glass of scotch. I forgot about everything. But that's not what I told Annie.

"Okay, mysterious one," she said, collecting her things. "I just hope he's not another blond-bot."

"Stop it," I laughed. "He's not. And I'm telling you. We're just friends." My stomach fluttered thinking about the way Nick's dark hair fell over his ears and into his face. "Oh, and he has an English accent."

"Get out," Annie said, then nodded knowingly. "No wonder you're being all coy. Nothing like a man with an accent."

"Annie!" I yelled, playfully pushing her toward the door. "Enough!"

"Now you're kicking me out of my own darkroom?"

"You can continue grilling me after school."

"What's after school?" she asked, stopping by the door.

"You're taking me shopping." The idea sprang up as I spotted a picture of me from freshman year. Except for my hair, I still looked the same, even if it felt like everything else had changed. "I'm sick of my boring old clothes."

"Wait, did I just hear correctly? *You* want to go shopping? Okay, Miss 'there's not much to tell,'" she said, attempting her best impersonation of me. "I can read between the lines." She turned off the lights. "Aren't you coming?"

I stepped back into the darkened room. "Is it cool if I hang out here until the end of lunch?"

"Be my guest." She rummaged around her oversized vintage Prada bag, one of her infamous flea-market finds, and tossed me her keys. "Just make sure you lock up. I'll meet you after school. Don't forget!"

"How could I forget? It was my idea."

I watched her retreat down the narrow corridor. Once she was gone, I shut the door, launching myself into sudden and complete darkness. The room was so well sealed not even the light from the hallway could seep in through the cracks. Reaching my arms out in front of me, I blindly felt my way across the room, banging my right knee up against one of the table's legs.

"Ow!" I yelped, rubbing my leg before hoisting myself back up on the counter. The cold, metal surface gave me goose bumps. I lay down and stared up toward the ceiling. The room was so dark, there was no visible proof that it existed, of where the space began and ended, like all the walls had vanished and I was at the epicenter of a massive black hole. We had learned about them in physics last year, how their gravitational pull was so strong that not even light could escape their grasp. Mr. Kahill had explained that once something entered a black hole, there was no going back, that it would remain suspended in time, forever. It was one of those pieces of information you don't realize you've retained until it finally starts to make sense. Because it's how I felt now, swallowed up by the darkness, suspended in time.

Fractured images of Nick flashed in my mind, like pieces of a puzzle. The stretched skin across his knuckles as he changed gears; the quick flick of his head to clear the hair out of his eyes; his partial grin; whispering in my ear. But no matter how hard I tried I couldn't see him whole.

The notes started up in my head, like raindrops on a windowpane. As the voice kicked in, they flourished into long, deep, fluid chords, an orchestra of guitars. The sound was so rich and grand. It made me think of dancing with Nick in Disney Hall, of being carried off to a soothing, dreamlike place where anything was possible. I stared into the darkness, listening, waiting to see where the melody took me, when the bell started clanging right above, like a violent intrusion. And an unwelcome reminder that I hadn't been swallowed up by a black hole. I was still in school.

I slid off the table and made my way to the nearest wall to guide me around the room and to the door.

"Ow!" I yelled as I banged the same knee again.

I hobbled the rest of the way to the door and flicked on the lights, revealing I had walked right into the cabinet Annie had left open. Various boxes and supplies had scattered on the floor. As I began stuffing everything back in, I noticed a camera peeking out of a partially zipped case on the shelf. It definitely wasn't Annie's. She kept hers with her at all times, like a true photojournalist. Plus, her case was covered with hip pins and stickers. This one was unmarked except for a piece of masking tape stuck to the top with *Property of VVH Photo Club* written in red Sharpie.

I had never stolen anything before. Not even a piece of five-cent bubblegum from the 7-Eleven on a dare when I was ten. But this camera didn't technically belong to anyone. Besides, I was only borrowing it, I told myself as I carefully lifted the camera off the shelf and slipped it in my bag. I didn't even know why I was taking it. But I could worry about that later, I thought as the second bell began to ring and I made my way to class.

"Here, I found these." Annie met me at my dressing room with a pile of clothes stacked so high I couldn't see her face. We were at Bleu, the trendiest boutique in the mall. I had passed it a million times, but this was the first time I had ever ventured inside. It was Annie's idea, of course. I think she liked it just as much for its French name as she did for its clothes, because it reminded her of Jessica.

"Bring the whole store, why don't you," I said, lifting a sexy black sheath off the top. "And you're crazy if you think I'm wearing this in public, let alone trying it on."

"I am the public," Annie said as she began hanging the items on top of the ones I'd already chosen. Each one was slinkier and more revealing than the last. "Look around. No one else is back here."

"Still." I adjusted the shirt I had just tried on and stood in front of the mirror. "What do you think?"

She looked at me flatly. "What do I think? That we might as well be shopping at Kmart if that's what you're going to pick. I thought you said you wanted a change."

I looked at myself again. The shirt fit loosely on top and landed halfway down my thighs so that it covered both my boobs and my butt, just the way I liked it. "This is different. It's striped. You know I don't own anything with stripes."

"Oh boy," Annie said, shaking her head. "We have a lot of work to do. Will you at least humor me and try some of these on? What's the worst that can happen?"

"Fine. But I get to try my picks too. I can alternate."

"Deal. It's my turn. Start with this."

She handed me a flirty sleeveless dress in cobalt blue. "This is way too small," I said, checking the label.

"That's another thing. Enough of wearing things three sizes too big. I think that's your main problem."

I sighed and went back in the fitting room. I unzipped the back and stepped into the dress but it got stuck on my hips. Of course it did. This was already so humiliating. "It doesn't fit," I yelled over the curtain.

"I'll be the judge of that." Annie parted the curtain and came right in.

"Hello! I'm half-naked in here," I protested, flinging my arms across my chest.

"Please, you're wearing a bra. And, duh, it's not gonna fit like that," she said, throwing her hands up in the air. "The waist is cinched. You have to put it on over your head. Haven't you worn a dress before? Wait, don't answer that." She waited as I stepped out of the dress and slipped it on the other way. "And side note? We're hitting a lingerie store next. Time for a little upgrade in that department too."

My stomach twisted into knots. My mind flashed to the night of the accident. "My bras are fine. No one's going to see them anyway."

"Okay, okay, one thing at a time." Once the dress was on she zipped me up and spun me around to face the mirror. "Take a look at *that* girl."

"It's too tight," I said, pulling at the stretchy fabric that clung to me like a magnet. "And way too short."

"Are you crazy? You look great. It's time you embraced your god-given gifts and showed them to the world!"

"Unzip me, it's my turn," I said, pulling something I had chosen from the rack.

I came out a minute later in a long, gray dress. Compared to the blue number, it felt like I was wearing an oversized bathrobe. "Okay, maybe this isn't the greatest either."

"Yes, progress!" Annie said, fist-pumping the air.

After alternating between our picks a few more times, something happened. I began to see myself differently. It dawned on me that maybe I was clinging to a style that defined who I used to be: the quiet girl who stayed out of the spotlight and followed the rules. But that girl didn't exist anymore. She was dead and

I couldn't bring her back no matter how hard I tried. "You're right," I said, dumping the rest of my selections onto the reject pile. "These are way too big. Hand me that one."

I emerged from the changing room in the little black dress that I had originally discarded. It was shorter than the others I had already tried on, but the way it hung without sticking to my body made it seem like my legs went on forever. The front dipped down into a low V that landed in the middle of my chest, accentuating my cleavage. As I stared at my reflection in the mirror, I kept waiting to wince or to run back into the dressing room to take it off immediately. But I didn't. Instead, I tucked my hair behind my ears, stood a little straighter, and smiled. Annie stared at me, mouth agape. "Don't you have anything to say?" I asked her.

"Yeah," she finally said, flicking my bra strap. "Get rid of this."

I reached back, unhooked the clasp, and let it drop to the floor. I had never gone braless before.

"Wow. Now I really am speechless."

"What, am I turning you on?" It just slipped out of my mouth. It was the first time I'd said anything like that to her before, and I wasn't so sure how she would take it now that I was beginning to question her sexuality. It wasn't that I thought Annie was into *me*. It was that I didn't know how to have that conversation.

"I think you can turn anyone on in that dress," she said, without a hint of discomfort. It made me realize that maybe she didn't need to have any conversation. Maybe *I* had changed and was now seeing things I had been blind to before.

"Okay, I'll admit, it doesn't look half bad, but where would I wear something like this? It'd be a total waste sitting in my closet."

"Olive. You don't buy a dress like this for an occasion. You create the occasion for the dress."

I thought about Derek and how I never got dressed up for him. I always thought our senior prom would be the first time. Then I thought about all the fancy women at Disney Hall, how this was exactly the kind of dress they would wear, for no occasion at all. I started to fantasize about wearing it one day for Nick. "Then help me pick some shoes to go with it."

Barefoot, I marched out into the store. The lightweight chiffon tickled my thighs with each step. The more I moved, the more comfortable I felt, as if the dress was made of feathers that would lift me up, up, and away.

"Work it, girl," Annie said, following close behind.

I paraded across the room like a model on the catwalk. When I got to the door, I kept going, strutting my stuff out in the main mall. I didn't know what possessed me but I couldn't stop.

With the tags still on the dress, my hasty departure set off the store alarm. Within seconds I had the attention of all the passersby. There, among them, standing in front of Tasty Delight Frozen Treats, were Derek and Betsy. He stood holding her purse and a large collection of shopping bags as she ate her yogurt. They were both looking at me. I could just imagine how much fun he was having; he hated the mall and he definitely despised shopping. His mother still picked his wardrobe from a catalog at the beginning of every school year. Betsy tried to whisper something in his ear but Derek leaned away from her, still staring.

I felt my throat tighten and my knees begin to buckle. I closed my eyes and pictured Nick standing next to me, his soothing voice calmly counting in my ear. When I got to ten, I opened my eyes again. My throat was back to normal and I took a deep breath. "Take a picture. It'll last longer," I yelled across the way before sashaying my hips, spinning around, and flitting back into the boutique with Annie in a fit of laughter.

CHAPTER 13

"I CAN WAIT with you," Annie said when we pulled up to the community center. There were twenty minutes until the meeting started.

"That's okay. I need to catch up on some homework," I said, patting my schoolbag, which contained *Mrs. Dalloway*. I had been carrying it everywhere even though I never cracked it open, as if just having it on me would make the words seep into my brain via osmosis. But it clearly wasn't that easy.

"Right, homework . . ." she said with a knowing look. "Is the assignment Nick?"

"Annie!" I flipped down the sun visor but after one glance in the mirror, immediately flipped it back up. I hated looking at myself close up, where there was no hiding the patches of uneven skin, the blemishes from having tried to scratch away too many chicken pox when I was seven. That was one of the reasons I was always so nervous when Derek used to kiss me with the lights on. I hated the thought of him seeing me up close, so exposed. "How many times do I have to tell you we're just friends?"

"Yeah, friends with 'benefits' when he sees you in that." I was wearing one of my new outfits from our shopping spree. It wasn't all that different from my usual T-shirt and jeans, but the look had been Annie-fied, which is to say everything was much tighter. "He's going to have to fend off all those middle-aged guys who will be drooling all over you. They'll think they've died—again—and gone to heaven."

"Ewwww, gross. And on that lovely mental image, I'm leaving," I said, opening the door.

"Wait. Am I picking you up?"

"No, I'm good." A small pit began to form in my stomach as the words came out of my mouth. I didn't even know if Nick was going to show and now here I was jinxing it. It was entirely possible that I'd never see him again. What on earth was I thinking? I could easily end up stranded in the middle of creep-ville.

"Yup, just what I thought," she said, revving the engine. "I expect a FULL report mañana, hot mama."

My heart raced as I watched Annie's car disappear down the road. I suddenly felt extremely foolish for telling her to leave. All I had to do was dial her number, and she'd be back. Within ten minutes, we'd be on the freeway. I could sneak back into my room while Noah fell asleep in front of the television, while my mother finished washing her gardening tools, while my father still toiled away in his office, all before the meeting even ended. I leaned against the scaffolding, gripping it with both hands to try to steady myself. With the torn posters tickling my fingers beneath, I slowly began to count until my pulse slowed, just the way Nick had taught me last week. Was it only a week ago? In some ways it felt like yesterday, but in others like another lifetime.

I shook it off, put in my headphones, and decided to take a walk. I wasn't in the mood to deal with Stuart and crew, especially after my dramatic exit the previous week. I crossed to the other side of the street to see if by some unlikely miracle Nick was already here, parked in the same illegal "spot" as last week. I kept my head down and counted the number of steps it took to get there—*ten, eleven, twelve*—telling myself the whole way that if his car was there, then everything would work out, that I would end up happy. I used to play this game waiting for Derek to call me when I couldn't reach him. It always worked. Well, almost always.

Thirteen, fourteen, fifteen . . .

I heard a nearby car honk twice, but I didn't look up. Maybe I was attracting the wrong kind of attention and should have worn my old clothes. I wasn't used to being noticed like that. When people described me, they would say things like: "Olive Bell is nice" or "Olive Bell is quiet," but never "Olive Bell is cute" and certainly not "Olive Bell is sexy."

The car honked again, this time with four long, persistent beeps. I yanked out my earbuds and turned around to give the driver a piece of my mind. "Hey!—" I stopped midsentence as the car—a beat-up green Jaguar—pulled over and the driver's window opened. Nick sat behind the wheel.

"Oh, it's you," I said sheepishly.

"No, please, carry on. I'm dying to know what you were going to say."

"Do you always honk at people like that?" I countered, relaxing a bit as his wry smile poked through.

"I'm sorry, I didn't mean to startle you."

The melody hovered, like a low-settling fog. It was as if each strum of the guitar was a breadcrumb that led me here to this place, to Nick.

"It's okay."

"Last I checked, the meeting's in the other direction."

His jawline was covered in a thicker layer of black stubble, which made him look older—and even more handsome. But combined with the way his dark hair flopped over his eyes and into his face, it also gave the impression that he was hiding from something or someone.

"I'm not in the mood," I said, trying to cover the fact that I was really out here looking for him. "Besides, aren't you the one who said they're bullshit?"

"I'm sorry I'm such a bad influence." Even with the accent, I could tell he really meant it, that he wasn't teasing this time.

"No, you were right. Those meetings can't help me."

"Then care for some company?"

He reached across the seat and opened the passenger door. My stomach flipped and a chill went up my spine. I didn't know if it was nerves or a warning sign or both. But I got in the car.

Within a few minutes, we had left the congested Hollywood traffic behind and were cruising through a different neighborhood from where we'd driven last week.

"You definitely know your way around. Do you live near here?" It occurred to me that he knew exactly where I lived—

he had even seen my house—while I had no idea where he was from.

"Not even close. I'm all the way over on the Westside."

I assumed he meant the west side of Los Angeles, but that didn't mean anything to me. "I didn't realize they talked like Brits over there."

Nick threw me a sideways glance and flashed his crooked smirk before shifting into higher gear. "And she's cheeky too."

My actual cheeks began to burn as I wondered what he meant by "too." I wasn't normally this sassy, except with Annie, but Nick somehow brought it out in me. "But seriously, if you live here, why do you have an accent?"

"My father's English. Mum's American. We moved here just after I was born, but they shipped me back to the Mother Country for boarding school. Acquiring the accent was the best way to survive. After ten years there, I suppose it stuck."

"How old were you when you went?"

"Eight."

"Wow." I tried to imagine what it was like being sent away, so far from home, at such a young age. "Was it lonely?"

"You get used to it." His foot faltered on the pedal and the car momentarily slowed down.

"When did you move back to L.A.?"

"I haven't." Something flashed across his face and his expression darkened. "I'm just here until the autumn."

"What happens then?"

"I go back." He said it like it was some sort of sentence.

"Back to England?" My stomach tightened, waiting for him

to answer. Even though I was supposedly going away to college then anyway, I didn't want to think about Nick leaving.

"Yes." He released his foot from the gas pedal to change gears. "To Oxford."

Picking up speed, he stared at the road. A silence settled over us. A ball that felt about the size of a marble lodged itself at the base of my gut. It reminded me that no matter how much I wanted to escape from the rest of the world when I was with him, it still existed. It was also a reminder that there was more to the story that Nick wasn't telling me.

"My turn," he said a few minutes later. "What's your story, Olive . . . ?"

"Bell," I supplied.

"Olive Bell. It has a nice ring to it, pun intended."

"Never heard that one before," I teased. "I still don't know your last name, by the way."

"That can be your next question. It's still my turn." His voice was now light and playful. "You don't want to argue with a man behind the wheel." He made a wide figure eight across the empty lane on the other side of the road. I should have been afraid, but I wasn't. It was the calmest I had felt since the last time I was with him.

"So tell me, what's it like being Olive Bell?"

"Let's see . . ." I tapped my fingers on my knee, pretending to think. "I'm a senior at the very prestigious Vista Valley High, which is precisely two point three miles from my house, which is about three point eight miles from the hospital where I was born. And that about sums up my fascinating life."

"I bet that doesn't even scratch the surface," he said, with no hint of irony. My stomach fluttered from the way he looked at me, his gray eyes flashing beneath his bangs.

"Trust me," I said, thinking about the fact that Nick had spent at least half his life on another continent, while the most adventure I'd ever experienced was with him. "I've barely been anywhere else."

"Then let's fix that."

We cruised down the freeway, heading east, in the opposite direction of home.

"Just let me know if we leave the state." I pressed the recline button and leaned back in my seat. From that angle, all I could see were the retreating city lights growing smaller and smaller in the side mirror, and the still faint crescent moon rising.

"Deal," he said, and stepped on the gas.

I closed my eyes and sank deeper into the plush leather seat. Concentrating on the steady rhythm of the humming engine, I tried to ignore the other questions that smoldered in my mind, like who Nick was and whether I could really trust him. Almost fifteen minutes passed before I realized that neither of us had spoken a word since we left the city. The radio wasn't even on to fill the void, but it wasn't awkward. It was the opposite: a comfortable silence. The kind where you get lost in your own thoughts without losing your connection to the other person. The kind you normally shared with someone you've known a long time, not someone you've just met. The kind of silence I suddenly realized I had never experienced with Derek.

Nick made a left off the highway onto an unmarked dirt path. Following it a few hundred feet down to where it ended, he stopped and turned off the engine. The dashboard lights slowly faded, pitching us into complete blackness.

"We're here."

We started down a thick, ragged path of overgrown brush. I so desperately wanted to reach out and grab onto his arm, but the sound of twigs and branches snapping beneath our feet stopped me. It reminded me of the haunting noises that invaded my brain, like the crunch of broken bones, rupturing any sense of calm. A small part of me still wondered if Nick was really some masterful serial killer who had lured me to the middle of nowhere, if I had willfully ignored all the signs until it was too late.

A few hundred yards down, we came to a wide clearing illuminated by the moon, directly above. Once my eyes adjusted, I could make out the distorted shapes of branches ahead and the soft, expectant expression on Nick's face as he waited for me to catch up. It was definitely not the look of a mad killer, but of someone who could steal my heart.

"Where are we?"

"The real California." He stopped by a cluster of trees and lay down on his back. He patted the cracked earth to his left, an invitation to join him.

Up close I could see the branches were burnt and bent, the remains of a wildfire. I lay down, careful to keep a few feet between us. I couldn't tell what I was more afraid of—his next move or how I was feeling. It was almost like lying down in my own backyard, only the blooming flowers were replaced by blackened wood, my own jagged breathing by Nick's steady breath.

"Why here?" I asked. The face of his gold watch caught the moonlight. There was a hairline crack on the glass at the left side, where both hands were frozen on the number nine. I wondered how it broke, what had happened at nine forty-five and why Nick still wore it.

"So that you can say you've been somewhere, a place of your own. And I thought you would like it. Out here nothing's hidden. It's kind of *jolie laide*."

"What does that mean?" I had taken a year of Spanish for my foreign language requirement but didn't speak a word of French.

"It literally means ugly-beautiful, but there isn't really a proper English translation for it. It's what this place is, though."

I wrapped my arms around my chest as another chill ran through me. Was that what I was, too? Ugly-beautiful? Only I wasn't sure what the beautiful part was.

"Beneath the palm trees, this is what L.A. is really like," he continued. "A desert. The trees don't just naturally grow there. Practically nothing does." He gathered a handful of dirt and let it sift through his fingers. "This is what's real, all around us. This is the way things are really supposed to be."

I thought about my neighborhood and the lush green lawns that spread out before each house, block after block. The even rows of palm trees lining Vista Boulevard and the sprinkler systems that went off like clockwork every morning to keep the illusion in place.

We stared up at the open sky. It felt so much bigger than the pocket of night I was used to from my tiny patch of grass. I imagined looking down at Vista Valley from an airplane, where the view revealed that everything was divvied up into neat allotments. Our town was just one of hundreds like it. It was like discovering that there were so many more planets in the galaxy than the eye could see, that life encompassed so much more than the subdivision I was born into. I turned my head so my cheek was touching the cool, dry earth. Under the shroud of darkness, I stared at Nick. It wasn't just his physical features that defined him. It was everything: from the way he moved to his battered car to his frayed jeans and his broken watch. He clearly didn't care what anyone else thought of him, like he was used to being the only one around, the way we were in the vast open desert.

I reached into my bag and took out the camera. Like my copy of *Mrs. Dalloway*, I had been carrying it around every day, since the day I had taken it. But this was the first time I was inspired to use it.

"You're a photographer?" Nick asked, propping himself up on his elbows.

"Hardly." I was glad it was dark because I felt my cheeks start to burn again. "I just . . . borrowed this from someone."

I got up and walked over to the tree looming precariously next to us. The branches were gnarled and twisted, but up close, intricate patterns, like interweaving veins, emerged beneath the charred top layer. I removed the lens cap, zoomed in, and adjusted the aperture. As more moonlight filled the small glass frame, I understood what Nick meant. And he was right. It was ugly-beautiful.

When I looked back, he was lying down and his eyes were closed. Without thinking, I aimed the camera toward his face, zoomed in as close as possible, and clicked.

He opened them a minute later, after I had already screwed the lens cap back on and the camera was dangling from the strap around my shoulder. But it still felt like I had been caught in the act, like I had stolen something from him.

CHAPTER 14

"OH NO," I muttered as I made my way up the walkway. My father's Buick was already in the driveway. He had beaten me home. The engine was even still crackling.

I fished my keys out of my bag and gently pushed open the front door. I held on to the doorknob to minimize the noise until it latched shut. I made my way inside, still clutching my phone. Nick had taken it from my lap and keyed his number into it when he dropped me off. I tiptoed down the dark hall and peered toward the kitchen. All the lights were off. *Maybe he's already asleep*, I thought, relaxing my shoulders and continuing toward the kitchen.

"Olive?" my father's voice called out.

I nearly tripped over myself as I flicked on the lights, revealing my father sitting at the table, in the dark, his right hand gripped around his nightly glass of scotch.

"Are you, like, waiting up for me or something?" I asked, standing by the door. Knowing that he regularly came home so late made me feel like I somehow had license to question him before he had the chance to question me.

"I must have dozed off." He cleared his throat to get his voice back, then took a sip of his drink. His tie was loosened around his neck. His jacket hung from the back of his chair. He always wore a full suit, even on the hottest days of the year. How many times had he sat here like this, in the dark, after the lights went off? "You look like you're in a good mood. Where were you?"

I didn't realize I was still smiling, but relaxed my cheeks when I saw the numbers on the stove clock flash 1:57. It was much later than I thought. Had I really been out with Nick practically all night? "I fell asleep at Annie's," I said. "We were studying for midterms." It surprised me how easily the lie rolled off my tongue.

My father's face lit up. "I'm glad to hear that you're getting back into your school work. You're a smart girl. I have no doubt you'll be caught up in no time."

The truth was, I hadn't actually opened a book in days. But it wasn't like before, when I first came back and was too shell-shocked to do pretty much anything. Now I couldn't concentrate for a different reason. Because of Nick. Every time I tried to read *Mrs. Dalloway* or do a math problem set, I'd find myself doodling his name across the page. It was as if the song was also conspiring against me, pulling me further and further out to sea, away from my regular life here and toward him.

"How about you?" I asked. I didn't want to go any deeper into the topic of my homework. "Why are you still up?"

"I'm working on a closing and lost track of time." He rattled the ice cubes around in his glass. "One second it was six o'clock and next time I looked up it was already one in the morning. I was just having a drink to wind down." He said it so casually, like it didn't happen almost every night. Maybe he had his own reasons for lying. Just like I did.

"So, how does it feel to almost be a high school graduate?"

He posed the question the way a distant relative might, in an effort to strike up conversation. Lately it felt like we were barely part of the same family. This was practically the first time we'd talked since the drive home from the hospital. He was never around but I wondered if that even made a difference. "Okay, I guess. Thankful it's almost over."

"Can't wait to get out into the real world, huh? I remember that feeling."

"I guess." That wasn't the way I meant it, but I didn't bother correcting him. I hadn't thought much about the future since the accident. I no longer knew what it looked like, no longer knew what I *wanted* it to look like. "Not that college really counts as the real world."

"That all depends," he said, gazing outside. With the kitchen lights on, the windowpane reflected his image, like he was staring into a mirror. "Sometimes it's the other way around."

"What do you mean?" I came into the room and pulled up a chair.

"I almost dropped out of college before I even started." He got up and walked over to the counter to refill his glass. He was so relaxed, it seemed like he was almost about to whip out a glass for me, too. My dad was usually so lawyerly, when he wasn't being all Father Knows Best. But tonight was different;

tonight he was acting more like a friend. "I had this hippie English teacher in high school, Jerry Cooper. He insisted we call him by his first name, which, in those days, was considered countercultural." It still was, at least in Vista Valley, I almost said, but I didn't want to interrupt him. "At the end of senior year, he pulled me aside and gave me a copy of *On the Road*, you know, the classic by Kerouac." I had no idea what he was talking about but nodded anyway, eager for him to get to the point. He sat back down with his refreshed scotch. "So Jerry told me to read it before making any decisions about my future. He knew my plan was to go to law school and become a lawyer, just like my father, but he thought I should explore becoming a writer." He paused to take a sip of his drink. "I thought he was crazy. I'd only written a story here and there, nothing that would make me give up everything, but I was also flattered, so I decided to read the book. I devoured it in one day. It was a Sunday. I remember because the banks weren't open. I waited until the next morning to empty my account, buy the cheapest car I could find, and hit the road, just like Kerouac. I didn't tell a soul. Not even your mother, and I skipped out just two days before high school graduation."

"Are you serious?" I wondered if the alcohol was slurring his thoughts. He didn't sound anything like the person standing right in front of me, also known as my father. I had no idea that he'd ever written *anything*, much less that he was apparently good at it. "How long were you gone?"

"Almost two months. I drove across the country, mainly through the South. I'd stop in towns along the way whenever I ran out of money, which was every couple of days. I picked up odd jobs here and there, bussing tables, milking cows. Whatever I could get to make ends meet and get me to the next town." He sat back down and stared out the window again, like his mind was somewhere else, maybe back in one of those towns.

I couldn't picture my dad pulling on a cow's udder. Every time I tried, he was wearing a three-piece suit. "Why'd you come back?"

"My parents eventually tracked me down with the help of a private investigator. They threatened to cut me off if I wasn't back in time to start college." He paused to finish off his drink. "And your mother was waiting for me. We were married by the end of that year."

"What if they never found you? What would have happened?" My breath stuck in my chest, like I had suddenly been plunged under water. I knew what would have happened. He wouldn't have married my mother. I wouldn't exist.

"I don't ask myself those kinds of questions. It was too long ago."

For the first time in my life, I felt sorry for my father. For being forced to come back, for believing that a book could really change his life forever. Even I knew that it took something much bigger than that.

"I like your hair like that." He swept a stray piece out of my face. It reminded me of when he used to tuck me in at night back when I was little. He'd always make sure to pull my hair out from under me and fan it out on my pillow so it wouldn't get tangled while I slept. "Is it the new style?"

"Not exactly." I reached back and felt for the bald patch around the wound, but it was no longer bald. Wispy strands had grown in around the ridge of uneven skin. It was practically long enough to pull into a ponytail again. "Mom hates it."

"Did she say that?"

"She doesn't have to."

He let out a deep sigh and closed his eyes for so long I thought he might have fallen asleep. "I'm sure she'll come around."

I didn't believe him. My mom had barely been able to look at me since the accident. At least not in the way she used to. With pride.

"And she means well," he added after a long pause, like he was trying to convince himself more than me. His voice was heavy and he looked tired. The etchings of deep wrinkles settled across his forehead in a permanent state of concern. His hair had even started to whiten on the sides. "It's probably best we keep this conversation between us."

Yeah, obviously. "Okay."

He stood up, the chair scraping loudly behind him. He headed for the door and turned around. "You coming?"

"Not yet." I tightened my grip around my phone. Just thinking of Nick holding it a few minutes ago sent a tremor of excitement through my body. "I'm going to grab a snack."

"All right, but don't stay up too much later. You have to be up for school in a few hours."

I let out a wry smile. Little did he know that I had been staying up long after him for weeks. After he left I turned out the lights, sat in his vacated seat, and stared out the window into the garden. I reached for the almost empty glass he had left on the table. It was wet from condensation and contained mostly melted ice. When I took a sip, it had the vague and acrid taste of poison. My dad's confession had made me realize that my dad was really just a person, like me. That he also had a life he wanted to escape.

As I stood to leave, my father's suit jacket slipped off the back of the chair. A piece of paper from the front pocket fell to the floor. There was just enough moonlight streaming in to make out what it was—a receipt for the Biltmore Hotel in downtown Los Angeles. From tonight, check-in at 7:13 P.M., checkout at 12:48 A.M. I waited for confusion or anger or even guilt for finding it to wash over me. But if anything, I felt relieved that I wasn't the only one in this house keeping secrets. Even if his secret could destroy our family, or whatever was left of it.

I picked up the receipt, crumpled it in my hand, and went out to the garden.

My throat tightened as I passed the greenhouse.

Trailing my hand along the glass, I walked around to the south-facing side, where a string of plants sat perched on a shelf. All the orchids were headless, brown, and seemingly dead, except for the one on the end, which was in full bloom. As I examined the three small, delicate petals blossoming from its stem, the lecture my mother gave Derek the time she walked in on us in the greenhouse came rushing back to me. "Every flower has three sepals," she had explained, pointing them each out. "And this one here is the labellum." She had tickled the petal at the base of the flower, like it was a pet, adding, "It's also sometimes called the lip."

"I thought your mom was going to have an orgasm in there," Derek had said later that night when I walked him to his car. "I can't wait to touch your labellum." I had stood motionless on the sidewalk, mortified by how humiliating my mother could be, as he patted my behind and pecked me on the cheek before driving off. But now, something angry bubbled up inside me. Without thinking, I picked up a pebble and whipped it against the window, nicking the corner. It was barely visible, but making a crack in the glass house somehow made me feel better.

I ran to the back of the garden, away from the greenhouse, and held my breath as I waited for a light to go on in the house. The stone had made such a loud pinging sound when it bounced off the glass that I was sure my dad, who was still awake, or my mom, who had supersonic hearing, would have noticed. But nothing happened.

Lying down on the ground, I inhaled the sweet smell of freshly cut grass. Spears of moonlight poked through the dangling leaves overhead. It was hard to believe I had been staring up at the same night sky with Nick just an hour earlier. I thought of him sprawled out on the cool, desert ground. Of how much further his legs stretched out than mine, the curve of his uneven nose in profile, the flash of his intense eyes, and the face of his broken watch. The images whirled and collided, as if I was viewing him through a kaleidoscope.

I swept my arm across the empty patch of grass to my right, half expecting Nick to still be there next to me. The song whistled back in like it was being carried by a distant wind. I closed my eyes and listened carefully when the notes took a sudden, unexpected turn. They sounded rushed, more urgent, lost even, until his voice broke through.

Your voice is like an angel
I can hear without sound.

They were new lyrics. I sat up and strained my ears to hear more, imagining they were Nick's words, that he was the one singing to me.

My leaden heart starts floating
Whenever you're around.

His voice rose above the roiling notes, reaching a breathy pitch that was simultaneously confident and vulnerable, like it encompassed the span of human experience.

I released my grip and smoothed out the wrinkled hotel receipt. A silent gust blew in and lifted the tissue-thin paper up into the sky. I lay back down and watched it recede into the blackness, like a kite without a string, when I felt my necklace snag on my hair. Lurching myself to my knees, I leaned forward and began to dig into the ground at the base of the tree, rustling free earthworms and stray stones caked in moist earth. I didn't stop until I'd carved out a perfect hole. The next thing I did was unclasp the chain, drop it into the ground, and fill it back up, burying the gold heart until there was no sign that it ever existed.

CHAPTER 15

"YOU HAVE TEN minutes left," Miss Porter announced. She was observing us from her desk at the front of the class.

I stared down at my blue booklet, then back up at the question written out on the board.

Virginia Woolf created Septimus Warren Smith as a double for Clarissa Dalloway. In what ways are they similar? In what ways are they different?

I still hadn't made it past page ten of Mrs. *Dalloway*, so I had no idea who Septimus was or what the question even meant.

I chewed on the end of my pen, watching everyone else busily writing away. Some people had even filled up the entire blue book and were almost through their second. I used to be like them. But now, my booklet was empty.

It was midterm week. I'd managed to scrape by the exams in my other classes, especially the ones that were mostly multiple choice, like American history and bio. But there was no faking an essay based on a book I'd never read.

Miss Porter's chair scraped against the linoleum floor as she stood up. With her hands clasped behind her back, she walked up and down the aisles, peering at our progress.

"You should start wrapping it up now," she said, glancing over students' shoulders.

I looked down at the blank page then back up at Miss Porter. She was one row away. Without thinking, I turned my pen around and started writing. She stopped when she reached my desk. She was standing so close I could smell her perfume. It was a light floral bouquet that didn't make me want to gag like the sickly sweet perfume my mother doused herself with five times daily. I hunched further over my blue book and tried to cover the page with my forearm. I didn't want her to see what I was writing. Not now anyway. Not in front of the whole class. To my great relief, she resumed her stroll a few seconds later.

"Please put your pens down and bring your booklets to me."

There was a series of moans and the typical pleas for just a few more minutes as people started to shuffle toward her desk. I hung back until the line thinned out before adding mine to the neat pile.

I was almost to the door when Miss Porter called me back. "Olive, I'd like to talk to you for a minute."

My shoulders slumped and I turned around. She lifted my booklet off the stack and opened it to the first page. Apparently she had noticed me, after all.

"Is this a poem?" Miss Porter asked.

I shook my head. They were the lyrics from the song. I was barely aware that I had written them down. They just rolled off my pen as naturally as air being exhaled from a lung. I was just relieved that I hadn't scribbled *Olive + Nick* across the page inside little hearts, the way my mother had.

"It's beautiful." She closed the book, returning it to the pile. "But it wasn't the assignment."

"I know," I said, looking down at my feet. I thought about my conversation with my father the other night and the stories he had written when he was in high school. I wondered what they were about, and if he still had them.

"Have you even read the book?"

I shook my head again. There was no point lying. It was already patently obvious that I hadn't, because if I had, I would have been able to fake it enough to fill half a blue book.

"I'm not trying to scare you, Olive, but I need you to be aware of the consequences. If you fail the midterm, you won't pass this class. And if you don't pass, it's highly likely that you won't get into college. I'm rooting for you, Olive. I want you to succeed. I really do. But you have to try to meet me halfway."

I used to wonder how the usual problem kids felt when they were called out like this. I always assumed it was shame or humiliation that lurked beneath their blank, defiant expressions, because otherwise how could they live with themselves? But I was starting to see things another way. It was too hard to care about this kind of stuff anymore, even with my future at stake.

"I'm going to give you another chance. You can make up for the exam by writing a ten-page paper on the same topic. You have until the end of the semester to turn it in."

"Thanks." I knew it was the right thing to say since she

was being so kind. But I felt so removed, like I was floating on a cloud, looking down at my life. From that vantage point, all this effort to get good grades just to go to college and do the same thing there all over again seemed pointless, like a way to avoid really living. I was starting to realize that I had spent my life trying to make *other* people happy—Derek, my parents, my teachers. But what was the point? If nothing else, surviving death had taught me that, and spending time with Nick confirmed it. He was the first one to show me that there was more to life than what went on within these walls. And he was all I could think about.

"Can you hear me?"

I was taking a drink from the outdoor water fountain by the front entrance when Derek tapped me on the shoulder. The school day was over and I was waiting for Annie to finish a yearbook meeting.

"What's that?" Startled, I straightened up and removed an earbud.

"I'm glad to see those things aren't glued in." He lifted the loose earbud dangling from my neck and began twirling it around his finger. "I was just saying leave some for the rest of us," he said, gesturing to the water fountain. He was standing close enough that I could smell his Old Spice deodorant.

"Oh, yeah, sure," I said, taking a step back so he could take a drink. It felt so strange to be standing here talking to him after such a long silence. Six weeks to be exact. What was even stranger was that I hadn't thought about him once all day.

"And that was a joke. Are you okay?" He asked it casually, like we still hung out all the time.

"Yeah." I instinctively reached up for the heart around my neck, forgetting that I had buried it. I dropped my hand back by my side. "Why?"

"You look like you have a headache."

"What do you mean?"

"You always kind of squint your eyes and get this cute indentation on your forehead when your head hurts. It's right here," he said, pressing his finger above my left eye.

I waited to feel some jolt or sense of excitement at his touch, but I didn't feel anything except confused. "Well, I feel fine."

"It also happens when you're concentrating hard. Or sometimes when I kissed you. . . ."

My heart lurched in my throat. Why was he suddenly talking to me like this? I looked around, waiting for Betsy Brill to show up and link her arm around his. It was the first time I had seen them apart since they started dating, officially that is.

"What were you humming?"

I didn't know which song it was, the one from my playlist or the one in my head, so I shrugged. "It's just something Annie gave me. I don't know what it's called."

"You're becoming such a rocker chick." He leaned against the water fountain and stared me up and down. With his short, close-cropped politician hair and his steady, unwavering expression, he almost seemed like a stranger, not the boy I had spent the last two years obsessing about.

"I don't know about that." I ran my hands along the outer,

gauzy layer of my new sundress. I had paired it with a faded denim jacket, one of the few items from my old wardrobe I could salvage. I had swapped out my usual flip-flops for a pair of silver ballet flats. "Can I have it back?" I asked, motioning to the cord Derek had wrapped around his finger.

"What's the rush? Betsy's at cheer practice," he said, as if that was the only reason I felt uncomfortable. "Look, I really need to talk to you, Ollie."

His voice got soft, the way it did after a fight or when we were fooling around, and I felt something inside me soften too. I was just about to respond when my heart started beating a million times per minute. It had nothing to do with Derek or Betsy or whatever it was he needed to say. It was Nick. And the fact that his beat-up old Jag was pulling up the school driveway. There was no mistaking the car, or Nick, as he got out.

"I have to go, okay?" I quickly unraveled the earbud from Derek's finger. I had never spoken to him like that, so dismissively, but I suddenly felt that I had no choice.

I looked back over my shoulder only once as I cut across the grass toward Nick. Derek was still standing where I left him, watching me.

"What are you doing here?" I asked when I reached Nick's car.

"Is this a bad time? I can go if you're busy." He reached for the door.

"No, stay," I said, with less edge this time. "I'm just surprised to see you."

"Good surprised I hope?" He looked at me with his clear, gray eyes. They were even brighter under the sunlight. I realized this was the first time we had seen each other during the day.

"Yes, a great surprise," I said, getting used to the fact that he was really here, that he wasn't just a figment of my imagination.

"Seeing as I don't have your number and *someone* never texted me, I had no choice but to ambush you."

My face flushed. It had been three days since I'd seen him. I'd been dying to call and had pulled up his number at least a dozen times before chickening out because I didn't want to seem desperate. I knew where desperation could lead, and it wasn't to a good place. "Wow, I've never had a stalker before."

"I find that hard to believe." I bit my lip as his gaze shifted toward the water fountain. It took everything in my willpower not to turn around.

"Here you are." Annie came huffing over with all her bags hanging off her small frame. "I thought we were meeting by the lockers."

"Need a hand?" Nick said.

"No, I'm good." Annie snapped her head around at the sound of his accent. "Wait, are you Nick?"

That was Annie. Miss Subtle. I waited for that tiny ball of nerves to form in my stomach like it did every time she and Derek interacted, but it didn't. I wasn't nervous about what Nick thought about her, or the other way around.

"Indeed I am," he said.

"This is Annie. She's my best friend," I said. "Also known as the Bag Lady."

"Camera equipment," Annie explained, tilting her head toward the bags weighing her down.

"Ah, another photographer," Nick said, extending his hand. "Very pleased to meet you."

"I'm not going to need a lift," I said, quickly changing the subject. I wasn't even sure Annie picked up on Nick's comment, but I hadn't told her about taking the camera yet.

"Yeah, I figured," she said, eyeing the Jaguar. "Nice ride."

"It gets the job done." Nick walked around and opened the passenger door. "Shall we?"

We said goodbye to Annie and I climbed into the car. She gave me a big thumbs up when Nick's back was turned. She also mouthed something along the lines of "he's hot" but I pretended not to notice. We could have a debriefing session later, when Nick wasn't three feet away.

"It just occurred to me that you're the one who should be driving," Nick said as he turned the key in the ignition. "This is your territory, after all. Switch?"

I caught a quick glimpse of Derek through the side mirror. He was still by the water fountain where I had left him. Betsy was now with him, dressed in her cheerleading uniform. Only he wasn't paying any attention to her, or the fact that she was trying to kiss him. He was too busy staring straight ahead at Nick's car. At me. The back of my head began to throb. "No, you drive."

"So, who is he?" Nick said when we were a few blocks from school. We hadn't yet spoken, aside from my telling him which way to go from the pick-up/drop-off lane.

"Who?" I asked, even though I knew exactly who he meant.

"The one who's got you all rattled."

My heart sank. Was it that obvious? Derek had already ruined my life once. He was better left buried in the rubble of my past, no matter what he wanted to tell me. "Nobody important."

CHAPTER 16

"IT'S A LOVELY neighborhood," Nick said. We had been driving aimlessly for the last twenty minutes and were just coming up on Vista Boulevard. "Must be a nice place to grow up."

"You can't be serious." I threw Nick a sideways glance. And it wasn't because he used the word "lovely." With his accent, he could pull off words like that without sounding pompous— or like my mom. It was that judging by the places he gravitated to—sketchy Hollywood streets, Skid Row, burnt-out deserts— Vista Valley hardly seemed like it would rate high on his list of favorite destinations. But then again, I knew he'd already been here before. I just didn't know why.

"Why wouldn't I be?" he said as we headed down the town's main drag. "It seems to have everything. Green spaces, well-maintained homes, and even a quaint main street. It's picture-perfect. Like a postcard."

"You forgot boring," I said, gesturing to the whitewashed arches and shops lining the street, all in the same Spanish mission, colonnade style. "And fake."

"How so?" he asked, looking up. He seemed to really be interested. I still didn't know where Nick lived except that it was on the west side of the city. I assumed it was someplace fancy based on his car and his accent, his gold watch, and how comfortable he seemed in that crowd at Disney Hall, eating caviar like he had it every day. And then there was the whole boarding school thing. Wasn't that for rich kids?

"I don't know. Everyone here's the same. They all look the same, act the same, and go to the same school. Then they grow up, get married, and start the same cycle all over again. Vista Valley's like quicksand that traps you and pulls you under."

We stopped at a crosswalk in front of Maggiano's to let a group of freshmen girls I recognized from school pass. The girls looked like a younger version of the Ponytail Clones, as if they appeared simply to prove my point. "Nobody ever thinks or talks about the stuff that really matters. They just care about how things look on the surface."

"But you're from here so it can't be all bad." The way he said it took my breath away. If I weren't already seated, I was sure my knees would have given out on me. "And you don't look or act like anyone I've ever met."

You didn't know me before, I thought, but I held back, careful not to reveal too much of my past. That was one of the reasons I felt so comfortable with him. He didn't know anything about me except for the limited amount he'd experienced for himself. I could decide who I was as I went along—and he'd accept it.

With the big block letters of the Maggiano's sign looming so close, my mind flashed to Derek. The more I thought about what happened by the water fountain, the more uneasy I felt. It was something I hadn't felt in a while, but something I easily recognized: it was the feeling I got whenever there was something wrong with Derek. I'd detected a sadness in his voice and it stayed with me. I couldn't help but feel bad for him, despite everything that had happened. Looking down the rest of the block, at all the places I couldn't separate from my life with Derek, the feeling only intensified. It barely mattered that Nick was sitting right next to me.

Once the road was clear, I leaned over and yanked hard on the wheel. "Make a right here."

"Whoa. What was that?"

"That was me taking control," I said. Now that we were no longer driving down Vista, I felt I could relax again.

As we rounded the bend up Del Canto Canyon, Nick threw me a look and smiled. "Are you sure you don't want to drive? You seem to be on a mission."

The patchy brown hills peaked in the distance, a stark contrast to the lush gardens that surrounded us. We were just three short blocks away from Hyacinth Circle, where my old life had come to an end.

"Sure," I finally said as the new lyrics and melody took over, like his voice, whoever he was, was guiding me. What did I have to lose anyway? "I'll drive."

Del Canto was one of the few roads in the neighborhood that didn't have any sidewalks. Nick drove up a little further until we came to a clearing wide enough to pull over. Without exchanging a word, we unbuckled our seat belts, got out of the car, and switched places. Stretching my legs out to the pedals, I slid the seat forward until my right foot rested comfortably on the brake (or was it the gas pedal? How quickly I forgot), leaving a slight bend in my leg. Next, I adjusted the mirrors so that I could see in all directions and placed my hands in the ten and two positions on the wheel. That's what Bob, my driver's ed instructor, had taught me was the ideal placement. In many ways, this felt like my first time driving. I was taking all the precautions I hadn't the last time I got behind the wheel.

"Have you driven a stick before?" Nick asked.

"It's how I learned," I said, trying to find the clutch with my foot. "But not since I got my license, and that was almost two years ago."

"It's just like riding a bike. And besides, what's a few more dents in this puppy," he said, smacking the dashboard with a chuckle.

I was too nervous to laugh. Of all the adventurous things I'd done recently, this felt like the most daring. "I can't even remember how to put it in first," I said, fumbling around the gear shift.

"You can do it," he said, softer this time, like he knew what had happened, why I was afraid. Had he also crashed his car? Is that why he understood so well? Is that why he could calm me in a way no one else could, with the sound of his voice alone? He took hold of my hand and gently guided it to the right place. "I'm right here with you."

I focused on his voice as I attempted to shift out of neutral. The car stalled on the first couple of tries, but with Nick's encouragement, I didn't give up. Pretty soon, we were moving, even if it was only at fifteen miles an hour.

"There you go," Nick said. "You're doing great."

Picking up speed, I shifted into third and kept climbing up Del Canto until it snaked back down on the far side of the golf course.

The golf course.

I knew Nick had been here before. The question was how many times? And why wasn't he showing any hint of recognition? I followed the road until we reached an intersection. Going straight would take us back to Vista. Turning left led to Hyacinth Circle. And the entrance to the club was down the road on the right.

There was only one real choice. I turned right onto Flores Drive.

"Where does this go?" Nick asked.

I also knew that he had driven down this same street before, because it was the only way to get to the course parking lot. "The Vista Valley Country Club."

"Sounds impressive. Are you a member?"

I tried to detect some clue in his voice, but it remained calm and even. "Yes . . . well my family is."

"How about a tour?"

Was this really why he came to see me? So that he could find his way back to the club? It suddenly occurred to me that maybe I had gotten it all wrong and that Nick wasn't some royal aristocrat. His gold watch was broken after all, and his car, despite its luxury brand, was all banged up, one dent away from the junkyard. Maybe he only had access to country clubs and fancy benefits by sneaking in. The reason he appeared to belong anywhere, in any crowd, was that he didn't care what anyone else thought of him. Still, none of that explained why he had been here before or why he wanted to come back.

"Sure," I said, pulling up to the front gates.

The main clubhouse was empty. It was only four o'clock, before most members got off work. No one would be here except for the diehards who left the office early, or the rich diehards, as my dad called them, who didn't work at all and spent all day on the course. I knew what my dad meant, but now that I thought about it, it seemed like a pointless distinction because everyone who could afford to be a member here was rich—some were just richer than others. In fact pretty much everyone I knew had money, except for some of the teachers at school, or Lydia, who cleaned our house on Tuesdays and Thursdays. It was like a prerequisite for living in Vista Valley. There weren't any poor people, and certainly no one was homeless. I always thought it was because we took care of our own so that no one went hungry, but I was beginning to realize how naive I'd been to think that. There weren't any homeless in Vista Valley because they weren't welcome here.

"This is where the locker rooms, dining room, and snack bar are," I said as we walked down the corridor. I sounded like one of those ladies who worked in membership. I'd see them giving a tour sometimes when I used to come after school with Derek to "do homework," which always translated into going behind the cabanas to fool around. "The pool's out there," I said, pointing toward some double doors. "And the course is on the other side." But Nick already knew that.

One of the attendants came out of the men's locker room, pushing a cart of dirty towels. He was Hispanic, which meant he probably had to drive really far to get here every day. There were barely any Hispanic people living in Vista Valley, even though it was a so-called Spanish town, and the few who did live here weren't members of the club. Instead they worked there, cleaning the bathrooms, mowing the course, and preparing the food. Something about that seemed wrong to me now. How had I never noticed it before?

"There's really not that much else to see," I said. I didn't feel like being here anymore.

"Do you play golf?" Nick asked, as if he didn't hear me. It was the first time he had spoken since we'd gotten there.

"God, no," I said. "Unless driving the golf cart counts. That's my specialty." Or it used to be. "Why, do you play?"

Something flashed across his face. "Badly."

I thought about him swinging the club like a baseball bat from the roof of his car and almost chuckled. "Then you can give me a lesson in what not to do."

"They have pros for that," he snapped. His face darkened and suddenly he was somewhere else. His features appeared sharper and more severe. I almost didn't recognize him.

"I was only joking," I said, taking a step back.

"I just meant you could do far better than me," he said, with less edge. "Isn't there a pro here?"

"There's always a revolving door of pros," I said. "They're

all from the PGA and usually only stay for a few months between tournaments. Why, do *you* want a lesson?"

He gave me a weak smile, and I noticed something different about his eyes. They no longer looked gray, but colorless. It reminded me of what I had heard in Derek's voice earlier, and I felt a new tear in my heart.

"Our last one died," I blurted. "The golf pro, I mean."

Nick snapped his head up. "How?"

I shrugged. "I don't know the details, just that it happened at the beginning of the summer. I completely forgot with everything else that's happened since . . ." I said, my voice trailing off.

"Did you know him?" Nick asked. He was looking at me with such intensity that I felt guilty for not even knowing the guy's name.

I shook my head no. "I never even met him. He was only here a few weeks before he died. My dad took a lesson with him though," I said as the memory returned. "He said the pro helped him shave a few strokes off his game. Whatever that means."

Nick's shoulders relaxed and he smiled. Wherever he had gone, he seemed to be back and I felt my body relax too. That is, until I heard her voice.

"Oh shit." I saw her round the corner at the other end of the hall.

"What's the matter?" Nick asked.

"Shhh," I whispered, pressing my hand over his mouth. "It's my mom."

She was talking on the phone. Her telephone voice was always loud enough to suggest that the person on the other end of the line might be deaf.

"Follow me," I said.

We slipped out the nearest door and ended up by the second hole. I figured she was going to the locker room and that we'd be able to sneak back inside. But my mother's voice didn't disappear. It got louder, which meant she was still headed our way.

Nearby, a middle-aged foursome in clashing pastels and plaids were arguing about the scorecard. Spying their cart, I tugged on Nick's arm and motioned for him to hop on. It was our only way to escape.

Without hesitation, I powered up the cart and started driving onto the course.

"Hey! That's ours!" one of the cotton-candy men called out after us.

"Try to catch us!" Nick yelled back. I let out a full, deep belly laugh and pressed down on the pedal. I couldn't stop laughing as we zigzagged our way across the pristine carpet of grass beneath us on our slow-speed chase. When I looked back, my mother was standing at the edge of the course. It was too late. She had seen us, but I kept going anyway. I didn't want her to meet Nick. Not yet, anyway. It would only invite all sorts of questions I wasn't ready to answer, starting with where we met.

I drove around the entire course, past the twelfth hole and the driving range and all the places that I always associated with Derek. It felt like I was passing through a cemetery, with gravestones commemorating a past I was finally willing to let go of.

I glanced up as we got to the other end of the course, by the parking lot, but Nick's expression didn't give anything away. I wondered if he would ever open up and admit that he had been here before. But I had secrets of my own. And I knew that secrets didn't come out just because someone else wanted them to.

CHAPTER 17

"OLIVE?"

Even through the closed bedroom door, I heard my mother rattling down the hall, her gardening apron stuffed with every tool imaginable. Sometimes I wondered if she slept in that thing. Five seconds later there were three rapid-fire knuckle taps as the door came swinging open.

"There you are." She charged in as if she'd spent the last thirty minutes searching for me. "What were you doing?" Her tone was accusatory.

"Homework," I said, waving my unopened copy of *Mrs. Dalloway*. I slid my phone beneath the pillow. I'd really been texting with Nick since I got home from school.

My mother had been more on edge the past few days, ever since the incident at the club. Mr. Fitzgerald, the club's newly elected president, filed a formal complaint for the theft of his cart. Apparently I messed with the wrong foursome and now my mom was on overdrive trying to make it up to him with flower deliveries and cookie baskets. She was worried about her reputation and the fact that this might ruin her chance of being elected the club's social secretary.

She'd started to keep a closer eye on me again, voicing her concern that I was falling into the wrong crowd. Just as I predicted, she wanted to know who Nick was, or as she put it, "that scruffy guy I was running around with." I told her he was just someone I knew from school and that I had bumped into him at the club. She would never let me go back to another meeting if she found out that's how I knew Nick, or that he wasn't from Vista Valley. My mother was always suspicious of outsiders, probably because she had spent her entire life within the same five-mile radius. This bubble was all she knew.

I could tell she was also starting to question if the support group was helping. The last couple of days she'd started to ask more questions, like how many others were in the group and the kind of things we talked about. I told her that there were usually fifteen of us, and that we shared our stories with a group moderator. I knew my mother probably pictured fifteen depressed teens just like she thought I was, but I wasn't technically lying.

My phone sounded with a new text. It was from Nick. I had already given him his own special chime so that birds sang every time he called or texted.

We had been going back and forth, trying to stump each other by texting acronyms that the other had never heard of. Things that I thought everyone understood were completely foreign to Nick because he had grown up in England. It all started when I texted *IMHO* in reference to what I believed to be the best movie ever made (*Amélie*, starring the adorable

Audrey Tautou), and I couldn't believe he didn't know what it meant: *in my humble opinion.* (The fact that he had never seen the movie was an entirely different conversation.) I texted *LOL* in response to his confusion, adding *laughing out loud* in brackets, just in case that one hadn't made it across the pond. *Cheeky girl,* he fired back, and from there the challenge was born. I was completely mystified by Nick's latest—*TTFN*—and officially surrendered. I knew this incoming text would have the answer, and I couldn't help but sneak a look.

TTFN = Ta-ta for now, it read. Another text came in right after. *AKA: CUL8R*

I started to laugh, imagining Nick uttering those words: *Ta-ta.* I was about to respond, asking if he was secretly a sixty-year-old woman in disguise, but thought better of it when my mom loudly cleared her throat, reminding me she was there. "Sorry," I said, wiping the smile off my face. I thought she'd at least be satisfied that I was in a better mood these days, but clearly my happiness wasn't good enough for her. "Do you need something?"

"I was just coming to tell you that there's someone here to see you. Didn't you hear the bell?"

For a second I imagined it was Nick. For all I knew his latest text was sent from the front hall. But before I could ask who it was, Derek appeared in the doorway.

"Hey, Olive."

My phone chirped again with another text from Nick, but I slid it back under the pillow and hopped out of bed, smoothing out my clothes. "Oh, it's you."

Derek stood awkwardly behind my mother, who shot me

a pointed look. I knew that look. It meant *be polite*, because politeness was a virtue valued above all others in her universe. She scrunched up her nose and went directly to the windows. "You need some air in here," she said, flinging them wide open. "There, that's better."

"The front lawn is looking better than ever, Mrs. B. I keep telling my mother that she needs to learn your secrets," Derek said.

I rolled my eyes as my mother giggled like he was actually flirting with her, as if Derek and his family hadn't been ignoring us for the last two months. It was the same way she had reacted when Derek complimented her on her orchids that day in the greenhouse. He was good at finding people's soft spots and remembering them, another check in the politician box. "Shall I shut this?" she asked, her hand resting on the doorknob.

"No," I said at the exact same moment that Derek answered "yes." The ball in my stomach started to grow and harden as I put my hand out in front of the door to stop my mother from obeying him.

Once I heard her apron jangling back down the hall, I went to stand by the window. Derek's father's old silver Lexus was parked across the street, in front of the Millers'. He had been driving it since the accident. Derek always used to park in that spot, where stray purple wisteria petals couldn't litter his windshield. I had forgotten what a neat freak he was. Just then a red robin perched itself on the outstretched branch by the window and began to sing. It sounded just like my phone, like the bird was delivering a message straight from Nick.

"What's so funny?" Derek asked, stepping in closer.

I didn't realize I was smiling. For a second I had forgotten he was even there. "Nothing. So, like, what do you want?" It came out harsher than I intended.

"Can't old friends catch up?" He came up behind me by the window. His clothes still had that Downy scent, like they came straight from the dryer. "We're still friends, right?" When I shrugged and didn't turn around, he backed away and plopped down in my reading chair, right on top of a pile of laundry. "I think I left a book here."

A book? He had come all the way over for a book? Couldn't he have texted or just asked me about it in school? "Which one?"

"What happened?" he asked, gesturing to the broken bedpost that jutted out like a splintered spear. The canopy was gone but I still hadn't bothered to fix the rest. "Things get a little too rowdy?"

My stomach turned and I steadied myself against the wall. He was trying to be funny, but his voice said something else. I knew he saw me leave school with Nick last week, and what he was getting at. Was *that* why he was here? Was he checking up on me? "What book?" I asked again.

"Chem textbook. Can't find it anywhere."

"I haven't seen it," I said, trying to pull the clothes out from under him. I knew Derek well enough to know when he was lying. He'd never lose track of a book he used on a daily basis.

"Oh sorry," he said as the strap of a lace-trimmed tank top got caught on his shirt. I bit the inside of my cheek as he dangled it from his fingertip.

"Where's Betsy?" I asked, snatching it from him.

"I don't know. Probably the mall." He sank deeper into the chair and draped his left leg over the side. "I told her I had debate. I don't think she'd like that I was here."

"She'd probably like the truth more. It's just a book, right?" A tiny throb began to pulse beneath my scar, taunting me with thoughts about that night.

"You don't know Betsy." He looked up into my eyes. "She's not like you."

I pretended to search for his book, even though I knew I didn't have it. I had already done a sweep and gotten rid of everything Derek related. Or almost everything. I dug through the bottom drawer of my desk and came upon an old photo of us. His mom had taken it when we were hanging out in his backyard one Sunday afternoon at the end of last summer. We were tan and smiling. "It's not here," I finally managed to say.

"This feels familiar, doesn't it?" I could feel his eyes still trained on me. "Hanging out in here?" The weird thing was that it didn't actually feel familiar. It felt strange and uncomfortable. Like I was doing something I wasn't supposed to. "There's another reason I came, Wollie."

I froze and fixed my gaze on the rug. I hadn't heard Derek call me that in ages. He'd made up the nickname in honor of my second-favorite movie, *Wall-E*. He rarely used it though, only when he really wanted something.

He came closer and tugged on the ends of my hair, just like he used to when it was long. I wasn't sure where this was going. I wasn't even sure I wanted to know. Just a few weeks ago, this would have been the answer to all my wishes. But I didn't know what to wish for anymore.

"I've been wanting to talk to you for a while but I didn't know how. I guess I've been too embarrassed and figured you probably never wanted to see me again."

If he'd said this earlier, like the first day I came back, I would have stopped him right there. I would have told him that I understood exactly what he meant and that we could just put it all behind us. But that was before. Before eight weeks of pain. Before Betsy and before Nick. Before I had Annie's voice in my head telling me not to let him off the hook. Before I thought about the choices I'd made and if they'd really even been choices in the first place. And before I had any doubts or confusion about what I really wanted.

"I thought if I ignored it," he continued, "that it'd all go away. Turns out, you're pretty hard to ignore, Olive Bell. Especially lately."

I looked down at my yellow sundress. It was short and fitted and framed my shape perfectly, as if it was made to measure. But inside I still felt like the same girl in the picture in the drawer. I wondered if Derek thought I still resembled her, if he'd still be standing here if I did. At first it was hard seeing him with Betsy, but I had gotten used to it. Having him here alone in my room with all these unresolved feelings was much worse.

"So, what do you want now?" I may not have known what I wanted, but Derek always did. It was one of the reasons he was so successful. He set goals and went after them.

"I just wanted to make sure we're good." Something registered in his voice, something I'd never heard before. He straightened up and his gaze faltered. Maybe it was because he wasn't used to me being this direct.

"Good?" What did that even mean?

"Just . . ." His voice trailed off. "Everyone makes mistakes and can act stupid sometimes. It doesn't mean anything."

But I didn't know whose mistakes he was talking about—his or mine. Besides, mistakes counted for a lot. We both knew that.

There was a knock at the door. Even though it was open, for once my mother didn't come barging in. How long had she been standing there?

"Sorry to bother you two. I just wanted to invite Derek to stay for dinner." Her voice went up an octave the way it did when she was in the company of anyone outside the immediate family. "Your dad's working late so there's plenty."

She was acting like Derek's presence automatically meant we were back together. And like my dad didn't miss dinner every other night of the week.

"Wow, thanks Mrs. Bell. It's very tempting but I have to go." He glanced up at me and I felt my heart sink. What did I expect to happen, anyway? "But I definitely miss your cooking," he said, looking back at my mother.

A bird chirped. This time it was the one on my phone. "I better get that," I said.

After Derek left I marched out into the garden to find my mother. She was in the greenhouse, of course, potting a new batch of baby orchids.

"What was that all about?" I asked, standing at the entrance. My heart was racing.

"What was what about?" she asked. "And mind your tone."

"Then please mind your own business."

She pitched a handful of earth back into the bag. Only half made it in. The rest scattered on her red toenails. "I have no idea what you're talking about and unless you care to explain, I can't help you."

"That's just it. I don't need your help." I glanced back toward the cracked window where I had thrown the stone. A short, thin line shot across the bottom. With one kick, the whole panel would shatter. Maybe even the whole greenhouse would come crashing down.

"I honestly don't know where any of this is coming from," my mother said, throwing her gloved hands up in the air.

"How about for starters, stop inviting my exes for dinner. If you miss Derek that much, make your own plans with him."

"Exes? So you are seeing that other boy?"

"God, you can be so infuriating," I said, kicking a pebble across the floor.

"I'm worried. You haven't been acting like yourself since . . ."

"Since when, the accident? Why don't you just come right out and say it. That you think I deliberately caused it, that you think I wanted to die."

"I never said that."

"But you did." I thought about the knife rack and the medicine cabinet, the way she talked down to me, and how she didn't look at me like she used to. "You should just stick to your orchids. They're all you care about, anyway."

"That's not true." Her voice was clipped and distant.

"Isn't it? Why do you think Daddy's never here? Why do you think he always comes home so late?"

I stopped short of telling her about the hotel receipt. A well of tears gathered and pushed against the back of my eyes. I hadn't called my father "Daddy" in years. I suddenly wished he were here. *Don't cry*, I told myself, biting down on my cheek. I winced. It was still tender from biting it earlier. My mother picked up the can and resumed watering the plants. The slight tremor in her hand caused the water to splatter onto her feet.

"And for the record," I continued, "I can't go back to the way things were before, so you might as well save your energy and stop trying to make me."

Before she could respond, I booked it out of there, knocking the crate of baby orchids off the counter on my way. I stepped right on top of the scattered batch of earth, flattening the fallen plants underfoot. She could spend the next ten years trying to bring them back to life for all I cared.

I raced in through the kitchen, down the hall, toward the front door.

"Where you going, Ollie?" Noah called out from his room.

I didn't realize he was already home from soccer. Had he heard my outburst? Just in case, I turned around and went over to him. "Whatcha doin', bud?"

He was sitting on the floor, his hamster cage half disassembled around him. "I was trying to clean it but I don't know how."

I kneeled down beside him. "Where's Herman?"

"In here." He pointed to an old Nike shoebox with small breathing holes poked through the cover. At the sound of Noah's voice, Herman started scurrying about inside.

"All right, let's see." I surveyed the cage's various parts. They were caked in dirt and grime. "When's the last time this was changed?" I asked, eyeing the frosted water bottle attached to one of the grated sides. It was almost empty. What was left had turned an opaque shade of green.

Noah shrugged. "Mom used to do it."

"When did she stop?"

"When you went away."

Something tugged on my heart. I couldn't help but feel that I was responsible. Noah's room, like my parents', faced the garden. I peered out the window. The sun reflected off the greenhouse so that all I could see were the vague contours of a shadow flitting about inside.

"Sit tight. I'll just be a minute."

I went to the kitchen for cleaning supplies. When I came back, Noah and I got to work wiping down and scrubbing each part.

"This is quite a cage for such a little guy."

"Technically, it's called a habitat. And dwarf hamsters need a lot of space to run around. Even more than big hamsters."

I smiled. "When did you get so smart?"

He smiled back. "I don't know. I was just born this way."

We laid down the fluffy wood-pulp bedding and finally put in fresh food and water.

"Shall we?" I said, lifting the lid off the shoebox. I was about to reach in when Noah stopped me.

"You can't do it like that. He'll bite you." He put the lid back and turned the box. A small, makeshift door had been cut out and taped shut. "You have to do it like this," he said, removing the tape so the flap swung open.

Herman's tiny nose poked out from the dark hole first, his whiskers twitching. "It's okay, Herman. It's my sister. Remember her?"

Noah's voice spurred him on. His tiny white and brown spotted body followed and he walked out onto Noah's outstretched palm. I couldn't remember the last time I had seen Herman, if I had even really noticed him before.

"He really likes you," I said, watching them interact.

"Here, want to hold him?"

Before I had a chance to answer, Noah dropped him in my hand. He was so delicate I could crush him with one squeeze.

"He likes to be petted here," Noah said, tickling him under his chin.

I could feel his tiny body relax into my palm as I gently stroked his fur. He was almost purring. It reminded me of how I used to feel curled up against my dog Buck's warm belly. Even though he was a seventy-five-pound Lab, and Herman weighed no more than an ounce, the experience didn't feel all that different.

"He likes you, too," Noah said. "He just needs love."

I stayed with Noah for the rest of the evening and read him his favorite comic books, while Herman did laps on his wheel. I didn't leave until they were both sound asleep.

CHAPTER 18

I MADE IT to the end of the walkway when the porch light went on.

"Where are you going?" my mother asked, standing in the open doorway. She checked her watch. "It's almost dark."

"To study at Annie's."

"I don't see her car." Her knees were stained with dirt and there was even a smudge across her left cheek. Had she spent all this time cleaning up the mess I made?

"She's running late so I decided to walk a bit. She'll text when she's nearby."

I was learning how a simple lie could mask everything. Just like my dad. We were both living double lives. Only it was strange having that kind of power over my mother.

"Do you have your keys?" I could tell she wanted to say more, but it was as if something inside her had shifted since our fight, and she backed down. It was something I'd never seen her do. But I didn't feel triumphant like I expected I would. Instead, I felt sad.

"Right here," I said, patting my pocket.

She leaned further out the door and peered down the street, as if to make sure it was clear of predators. "Just be careful."

I didn't look back until I was halfway down the block. My mother was still standing there, watching me. Framed by the matching flower beds on either side of the door, her stance reminded me of the day I came home from the hospital.

The backlog of tears started welling up again. It wasn't just my mother. As much as I tried to push everything that Derek said out of my mind, I couldn't. Had he really been thinking about me all this time? Had he really been ignoring me because he felt embarrassed? If that was true, why was he dating Betsy, and why was he so public about it? It didn't make any sense.

It was cooler now that the sun had set, but the air was still thick and heavy from the day. It had been especially hot lately, but it wasn't uncommon to have heat waves in May. I glanced up to see if the moon was out, but I was now running too fast to focus. It felt good to move my body, to feel my blood pumping and the oxygen flowing through my lungs.

I was panting when I got to the corner of Lily Lane and Foothill Crescent at eight thirty, exactly as planned.

It was the twilight hour, when everything was coated in a glowing blue light and didn't quite look real, including Nick's Jaguar, which was just now rounding the corner. He came to a stop and pushed open the passenger door. I hesitated for a second, Derek's visit still fresh in my mind. He was clearly still with Betsy, so why did I feel guilty seeing Nick?

My phone chirped and I glanced down. "Did you just text me even though I'm standing right in front of you?"

"Indeed I did."

I smiled and read the message. *GR82CU*

"Do I need to translate that one?"

A warm feeling came over me, like the sun had suddenly been revealed after being blocked by clouds for hours. "It's good to see you, too," I said, and got in the car.

"How very MI5 of you," he said, pulling away from the curb.

"How what? Is that another obscure British text-ism?"

"It's the British secret security service. Sort of like the CIA." He made a U-turn and started heading toward the freeway. "You know, because of the cryptic pick-up spot. It's all very mysterious, Olive."

"Ha, it's definitely not that exciting." As we passed Baskin-Robbins on Vista, I recognized a group of kids from school sitting on one of the benches out front. Getting ice cream was one of the only things to do here on a Wednesday night. "I had to sneak out because I'm on thin ice with my mom."

"Not still on account of the great slow chase, I hope?"

I shrugged. "It's a little more complicated than that."

"Am I going to get you in even more trouble tonight?" He flashed his crooked grin, but from his profile, the way his right cheek muscle was flexed, it appeared as though his whole face was smiling.

"That remains to be seen." I pushed my seat back and propped my feet up against the glove compartment. We were on the freeway now, heading south toward L.A. I had no idea where Nick was taking me, back to Hollywood or the desert or maybe someplace new. It was right then that I knew there was no returning to my old life, a life spent accepting the status quo, a life trapped within the invisible boundaries of this antiseptic bubble. Not just because it was impossible. But because it wasn't what I wanted anymore. Not only was I not the same girl in the bottom-drawer photo anymore, I couldn't be. "I suppose it'll depend on your definition of trouble."

I cracked the window slightly, letting in a whistling warm breeze. It was a beautiful night.

Your voice is like an angel
I can hear without sound.
My leaden heart starts floating
Whenever you're around.

The song seeped in with the wind, but this time I couldn't hear the guitar. Only his voice, singing gently in my ear, a whispered lullaby. This was my life. At least right now, in this moment.

Forty-five minutes later, we exited the freeway onto Sunset Boulevard. Block after block buzzed with nightclubs and bars and restaurants. Practically every car surrounding us swayed and thumped as it cruised along, like the street had been converted into a giant concrete dance floor for moving vehicles.

"Is this the famous Sunset Strip?" I asked, rolling down the window.

"It is," Nick said, glancing up toward the looming hills above. "But we're just using it as a shortcut tonight."

"So I take it you have a destination in mind?"

"Indeed I do," he said, flashing that adorable half-smile. "But it's a surprise."

A shiver went up my spine. "For someone who spent the last ten years in England, you know this city pretty well."

"You just need the right person to show you."

"Lucky for me I already have that," I said. "The question though, is who was your excellent guide?"

Nick shifted into a higher gear. The sudden force of acceleration pushed me back against the seat. He didn't slow down even when we approached a sharp curve. I clutched the door handle as the tires hugged the pavement without so much as a squeak. Even though his gaze was fixed on the road, his mind had clearly gone somewhere else. Just like the time at the club. The question was where?

As the road straightened out, Nick glanced over. "Don't worry, she can handle it." He slapped the dashboard as if it were the side of a horse. I smiled weakly and relaxed my grip on the door. The problem was that I didn't know if I could handle it. Not his erratic driving, but the secret he seemed to be hiding.

When I looked out the window, the landscape had changed. I was already getting used to this, how the city could transform so drastically from one block to the next. Gone were the fancy bars and stores. Now, almost every concrete surface was tagged in black spray paint, and in some cases, bright, colorful graffiti like the kind we saw on our way to Skid Row. Were we going back there? After a few turns, Nick pulled into an empty lot.

"What is this place?" I asked, staring up at what looked like a bombed-out building. Wooden boards covered a gaping hole where the front door should have been.

"It's a church."

Nick didn't strike me as the religious type. And this didn't strike me as much of a church. I poked my head out the window. A stone bell tower stretched high above the steeple. It was practically the only thing that seemed intact. Most of the wall facing us was boarded up too. "What happened to it?"

"There was a fire a few years ago and it's just been sitting here since."

He led me to the other side of the building, where there was a gap between the boards just wide enough to slide through. Inside, it was just a big, empty, cavernous space. Clearly it had already been looted. No pews or pulpits or any sign that this was a place of worship remained, except for the stained-glass windows near the ceiling. They were probably too high for anyone to reach.

It smelled damp but the air was oddly clear as we walked through. Shards of tinted moonlight filtered through the colored glass. When we reached the pulpit, there was a low archway concealed on the other side. It looked like a secret passage. Nick ducked his head and walked through.

"Where are you going?" I whispered, even though we were the only ones there.

"To the top." He took another step and motioned for me to follow.

I crouched through the opening, where a spiral staircase coiled up from the ground. It was so narrow we had to walk up single file. I paused after my first step. The wooden stairs were so soft and damp it felt like they might collapse beneath me.

"Everything okay?" Nick was already halfway up. His voice echoed down the stairs, like a stone skipping across a lake.

"Yes," I called up, hoping the echo would mask the hesitation in my voice. I steeled myself and kept climbing, careful not to grip the banister too hard. It was just a long, twisted nylon rope, the kind you might find on a boat. Half the hooks meant to secure it to the wall were missing, so it drooped like a wilted flower just above the stairs. One wrong tug would have me swinging like a chandelier.

"I'm sorry," he said as I reached the top. I stepped out next to him on the wide stone balcony. "I should have asked if you were afraid of heights."

"I'm not," I said, realizing that wasn't what I was afraid of. I was afraid that Nick's heart belonged to someone else. And if it were true, that it could never belong to me.

He relaxed his shoulders. "Then come check it out." I joined him by the concrete railing at the edge of the balcony and looked down. We towered over the city and its flickering lights. The moving cars looked so much smaller from here, like they were toys that could fit in the palm of my hand.

"This is my favorite view," Nick said, letting out a sigh.

"I can see why." It was so different from the flat, fixed panorama I was used to from my bedroom window, the stagnant sea of identical homes, one after the other. This view was endless and full of possibility.

My arm brushed against Nick's as I shifted forward on my elbows. There was just a thin piece of cotton separating us, and I could practically feel his warm skin through my sleeve. It was like the charged cackle of static electricity. We weren't touching, but almost. Maybe it was better this way, standing on the edge, suspended in between, where you can't get your hopes up too high or your heart broken.

The sound of hundreds of car engines rose up from the streets, morphing into a quiet roar that was oddly calming, like white noise. It reminded me of the way all the discordant sounds in my head reduced down to a soothing hiss. Looking down at the city sprawled out below, I noticed there was no particular grid or pattern. It looked more like bicycle spokes sprouting from an amorphous center. None of the spokes were the same length; some jutted out at odd angles like they were broken, but somehow they all fit together.

Nick stepped up on the railing, pressing his entire body weight against it. By now, I was used to his risky stunts. But the way he was leaning, his waistline teetering over the ledge, made it seem like this time he was deliberately tempting fate.

"Are you sure that's safe?"

He knocked the railing with his knuckles. "Solid as a rock."

I came closer and also leaned into the railing. There was something about the warm, sweet air and the twinkling lights below that made me feel like I could do anything.

Maybe that's how Nick felt, too. Invincible.

I closed my eyes. It felt like I was floating, like I was being lifted up and carried away by the rising hum. Like I had experienced this feeling before.

A loose stone gave way beneath my foot. I snapped open

my eyes. For a second all I could see was the ground hundreds of feet below. Nick grabbed my arm and yanked me back as the rock plummeted to the street. He was squeezing me so hard it hurt.

"I'm so sorry." That same mysterious flicker crossed his face again. "You were right. It isn't safe."

The way he said it sounded like a warning. "It was just a pebble." I tried to meet his gaze but his hair flopped over into his eyes. "I'm okay. See?"

I twirled across the patio, my skirt billowing with the motion. It was the first time I could remember feeling genuinely feminine, and it wasn't because of what I was wearing. It was the way I felt when I was with Nick.

"Come on, sit down over here," Nick said, his face softening.

We settled into a spot on the ground under the cover of the clock tower, far from the railing. Leaning back against the cool stone wall, the giant brass bell gently swayed above. It felt like we were in a hot air balloon, with only the starlit sky around us.

I reached into my bag and quickly typed out a text without Nick's seeing. His pocket vibrated the moment I hit send, and I watched his grin reappear as he read the message. "You're welcome," he said, slipping his phone back into his pocket.

"You know, I still don't even know your last name," I said as the thought dawned on me. I couldn't believe I had even waited this long to ask. That was a remnant of the old me, the one who was afraid to rock the boat or ask for anything more than what was handed to me.

"It's Wilkins," he said after a long pause. "Any other burning questions you want to get off your chest?"

Now that I knew his full name, there were all sorts of things I'd be able to find out online, photos I'd be able to look at for as long as I wanted. But there was one thing, one question, that had long been lurking, and I didn't think Google could answer it. Even if it could, I wanted to hear it from him. "How did you die?"

The second the words came out of my mouth, Nick's expression darkened. He stood abruptly and went over to the other side of the tower. "If I wanted to talk about it, I'd still be going to those pathetic meetings."

I pulled my knees into my chest. His tone was stern and unwavering, and it made me wish I could take the question back. What was worse was watching him disappear, even while he was still standing right in front of me. Because it meant that our connection was gone too, that the invisible tether that linked us had been severed. And that's when all my fears flooded back, filling the gap. My fear that I couldn't compete with the world of mystery and adventure that he was used to, that I was just a boring suburban girl with no real life experience. And above all, my fear that getting closer to Nick would eventually break my heart all over again.

"Shhh." Nick pressed his finger to his lips and tilted his head back. "Can you see them?"

"See who?" I asked, looking up into the cavern of the dark tower.

Nick was back. The edge and distance in his voice were gone and I felt my whole body relax, every cell release a collective sigh of relief. I realized I couldn't really blame Nick for his reaction. I wouldn't talk about my accident with anyone either—not even him. It wasn't just the question of how I died that I wanted to avoid, but all the things that brought me to that point. I wanted to apologize, to let him know that I understood, but I feared I'd already said too much. It was enough to recognize that he was also haunted, that there was something unresolved about his experience too. And maybe most importantly, that he wasn't put off by my pain, like everyone else in my life. The least I could do was let him be.

"Take another look." He was still whispering.

I craned my neck up again. Once my eyes adjusted to the darkness, a smile spread across my face. At least a dozen green parrots were perched on a branch of a nearby tree that jutted through a gaping hole in the tower.

"They're sleeping," he said.

They were so still, they almost seemed fake. "What are they doing here? They look like lost pets."

"Some of them probably were, originally. Legend has it they escaped a fire at a pet shop a few decades back. Or that smugglers from Mexico released them into the sky when they got caught crossing the border."

"Which one do you believe?"

"It doesn't really matter," he said, staring up into the tower. "They're wild now." It reinforced the fact that it didn't matter where we had been before. What mattered was how it had changed us, how it had brought us together, and what happened next.

Hints of the birds' green feathers reflected off the bell's

dulled brass surface. A smaller parrot was perched just a few feet above our heads on a protruding stone ledge.

"He looks so young," I said, taking in his majestic red beak. His tiny heart was beating so fast I could see it thumping in his chest. "Look at his heart. Do you think he's having a nightmare?"

Nick shook his head. "Their hearts just beat much faster than ours. Especially the chicks'. Almost five hundred beats a minute." How did he know so much about everything? It seemed to come to him naturally. Not like Derek, who worked hard to be a know-it-all. "Most animals end up having the same number of heartbeats throughout their lifetimes. When all is said and done."

"How many?"

"About a billion, give or take."

I stared up at the small parrot, its bright green feathers fluttering with every breath. I wondered how many beats he had left. "And what about humans, how many heartbeats are we supposed to have?"

"Many more. Around three billion." His voice lowered. "In an ideal world."

I brushed my arm across my chest. It was pounding as fast as the bird's. Did Nick and I die because our hearts were speeding out of control? And did coming back mean the count started over from zero again? I started to wonder how you really measured a life. "Maybe time doesn't even matter," I said. "Maybe it's what you do with that time."

Nick sat up and leaned forward on his knees. Beneath the stubble, which was growing into a beard, and his feathery bangs, which hung almost to his nose, I saw something open up in his face. It was as if he wanted me to see it.

"I . . ." Nick started to say something but stopped.

My breath caught, suspended by the silence, waiting for him to tell me whatever it was he'd been holding back. Was he finally ready to confide in me?

"The parrots aren't always here," he finally said, regaining his voice. He sat up against the wall. "They migrate north every spring and find enclaves all around the city like this one before moving on. They only just recently came back."

"Oh yeah?" I let out a deep sigh. I couldn't tell if I was relieved or disappointed that he changed his mind. Or both. "When?"

"The same night I met you. This is where I came when I left the meeting. It's . . ." His voice trailed off, like he was finishing the thought in his head.

I had the urge to lean in closer, to touch him, when my shoulder began to strain under the weight of my messenger bag. If it hadn't, I didn't know what I would have done. "Don't move."

I took out the camera and began to unscrew the lens cap when Nick snatched it from me.

"Here, let me have a go." The way he said things, with his sexy accent and his funny English expressions, made my insides turn to liquid. "Quick, don't smile."

He turned the camera around and extended his arm so he could snap a picture of us. There was a clicking sound as the roll started to automatically wind back to the beginning. "Is this actual film?"

I nodded. "Black and white."

"Like a true artist. I'm not surprised."

I shrugged and looked up at the parrots again. I had never thought of myself that way, as an artist. Before, I would have been embarrassed or felt like a fraud. But when I was with Nick I felt like I could be or do anything.

"Do I ever get to see these?" he asked, handing me back the camera.

Before I had a chance to answer, the clock struck eleven. The bell clanged overhead, awakening the sleeping flock of parrots. They took flight through the tower's vaulted archways. The rapid fluttering of their wings was just like the flapping I'd been hearing in my head since the accident. Only now it didn't sound remotely terrifying. It sounded otherworldly.

Their red beaks let out what sounded like a distress call, a discordant, screaming cacophony, as if they were at war with the swaggering hunk of brass. But as they dispersed into the open sky, their squawks became less urgent, blending into a harmonious song they belted out in unison. With their bright green wings, they glided through the clouds as one, singing at a pitch I'd never heard before.

Nick leaned in so that our arms were touching. A sizzling sensation shot through me, taking hold of my entire body. It started in my fingers, spreading up my arms, across my chest, and down my legs, to the very tips of my toes. It reminded me of the way I felt the first time I saw him. Struck by lightning.

"You know what that is," Nick said, looking up at the sky. "That's the sound of freedom."

CHAPTER 19

THE RISING SUN was just starting to poke through the leaves of the willow tree when I sat up with a start.

Annie. I had completely forgotten about Annie. I promised I'd help her get the school gym ready for senior portraits, which were happening today. The assistant photo editor, Jason Gaits, canceled at the last minute, again. Something about needing to stand in line all night for the release of some new video game. Nerds, it turned out, were even less reliable than the general population. Apparently, now I was too.

I pulled my phone from my bag. There wasn't a single missed call or text from Annie, which made me feel terrible. It was so unlike her. Annie was never one to hold back feelings or bottle her frustration. Her silence spoke volumes. It meant she was really mad. Or worse, that she had given up on me.

I gathered my things and headed toward the house. It was only six o'clock, but the kitchen light was already on, which signaled my mother was up half an hour earlier than normal. I usually made it to my room with a few minutes to spare before I heard her stirring.

I hesitated before opening the door as a sinking thought occurred to me. The reason I didn't hear from Annie was that she must have come over to pick me up, only to discover that I was gone. My heart rate quickened. Did she ring the bell? Did my mother now know that I had lied to her about where I was going? But then I remembered that there weren't any missed calls from my mom either; nor had she waited up for me, so she mustn't have had any idea.

I crouched down and peered through the window. The kitchen was empty. This was my chance. The scent of baking banana muffins hit me the second I walked in the door, and it didn't turn my stomach. If anything, it made me hungry. I glanced at the timer on the stove to see how long I had before my mother would appear. Two minutes and thirty-eight seconds. I stopped in my tracks. Exactly the amount of time I was dead. I took it as a symbol that everything was turning around. *Maybe there really is such a thing as fate after all*, I thought as I hurried to my room to get dressed.

My mother was in the kitchen when I appeared a few minutes later, showered and dressed for the day.

"You're ready early," she remarked, glancing at the clock.

I breathed a sigh of relief, now fully convinced that Annie hadn't blown my cover. "Having a bake sale?" I asked as she placed a set of muffins in a tin. There were five identical tins waiting on the counter.

I already knew that she wasn't going to bring up my explosion in the greenhouse last night. I could always detect her mood within the first three seconds of a conversation. If her tone was clipped, then she was still harboring resentment. If it was warm, it meant all was forgiven. And if it was breezy, like it was this morning, then I knew that whatever residual frustrations she may have felt had all been channeled into the muffins. Baking was my mother's version of meditation. It was how she was able to sweep almost anything under the rug, no matter how lumpy the rug got.

She shook her head. "Just trying to salvage some rotten bananas. I can freeze whatever doesn't get eaten."

She was the perfect suburban housewife. The American Mrs. Dalloway. Watching her flit around the kitchen, I knew for certain that I would never be like her. It wasn't just because we were different, but because I didn't *want* to be like her. A sudden wave of compassion overcame me. I felt sorry for her— and for what I'd done to her plants. I reached for a piece of broken muffin that had fallen on the counter. It was still warm. "These are great," I said, taking a bite.

"Oh good!" My mother's face lit up. "So, what *are* you doing up so early?"

The funny thing was, I was up this early every day. She just didn't know it. "I'm helping Annie with senior portraits." At least that was my plan, to try to make it up to her. But first, I needed to apologize. In person. If she was ignoring me, a text or phone call just wouldn't cut it. "Mind if I take some with me?" It was the closest thing to a peace offering I could come up with at six thirty in the morning.

Now my mother was really beaming. She got out her Tupperware and loaded up a container. "One bin's good," I said as she reached for a second one.

"How did studying go last night? I didn't hear you come in."

For a second I forgot that's where I said I was going last night. It was getting hard to keep the lies straight. Before I had a chance to answer, my dad walked in, scanning the room for his briefcase. I hadn't seen him in a few days. Neither in the house nor from my perch in the garden. Noah darted in right after him, making a beeline for the fridge. Everyone knew to stay out of his way until he'd eaten his breakfast. He was never a morning person, even as a baby. As Noah poured milk into his cereal bowl, my father rummaged through his files, and my mother continued boxing muffins, I realized it was the first time all four of us were home at the same time, in the same room, since the night I came home from the hospital. That felt like a lifetime ago. I had gotten so used to our being apart that it felt strange being here together. Maybe because with each of us caught up in our own worlds, we weren't really together, and none of us was really present, not in a way that mattered. Not in the way I felt when I was with Nick.

It was six forty-five when I finally made it out the door. I calculated that it would take me twenty minutes to get to Annie's on foot, not that I really knew since I never walked anywhere. Nobody in Vista Valley did. But I knew someone would be up, if not Annie herself. Her parents sometimes started seeing patients as early as seven in the morning. Annie and I used to spy on them from her bedroom window, coming and going up the side path to her parents' offices in the back house, trying to see if we recognized any of them. Vista Valley was a small community, so we often did. Like the parent of some kid from school. A shop-keeper. Or the time we saw Señora Smith, our freshman year Spanish teacher, walking up the path. I used to feel sorry for them, wondering what could be so bad that they were willing to risk public humiliation just to talk about their problems. The sessions were supposed to be strictly confidential, but these things had a way of getting out. It had been a long time, though, since Annie and I had perched together in her window. Since I had even been to her house.

A chorus of birds started singing as I got to the corner of Annie's street. They flew out of a tree and started coasting along next to me, like they were my own personal escorts. I felt just like Amy Adams in that movie *Enchanted*, where animals and birds and insects fell in love with her and followed her everywhere she went. It also made me think of the night before, of standing next to Nick, our arms touching as the green par-rots flew out into the moonlit sky. Breathing in the sweet morn-ing air, everything around me seemed so vivid and alive. Not just the birds, but the way the sun cast shadows off the tree branches, the sound of a dog barking in the distance, the delicate curve of a rose petal that had fallen to the ground. All these details added up to something beautiful, something that reminded me of Nick.

Annie's mother answered the door. She was still in her robe, clutching a mug of coffee. "Olive, hi."

"Hi," I said, wiping a bead of sweat off my brow. "Is Annie home?"

"Come in, honey," she said, opening the door wider. "Annie's still in her room. You look like you could use a glass of water."

I followed her into the house. I'd forgotten how bohemian it was. Her parents decorated it with all sorts of eclectic things they had collected on their travels. Indian tapestries hung from the wall. African facemasks lined the mantelpiece. An old Chinese wooden door had been repurposed into a coffee table. Candid family pictures in mismatched frames were haphazardly placed in every nook and cranny, some on top of a pile of books that looked like it was on the verge of toppling over. I was also now remembering how much I used to love spending time here. How it used to make me feel like I had escaped and gone somewhere else. There was an ordered chaos to the place that made it feel lived in. Comfortable, like a real home. Just not mine.

When we got to the kitchen, Annie's mother poured me a glass of water straight from the tap. We only drank bottled water at our house.

"Thanks, Mrs.—I mean Dr. Irving," I said.

She gave me a look. "God, it really has been a while if you've forgotten that I will only answer to Nancy. Mrs. Irving is my mother-in-law. I'm not that old yet. At least, I hope not."

"You're not," I laughed, breathing in the delicate floral scent of the candle burning on the counter. Its flame cast a soft, pleasant glow against the orange-painted wall behind it.

"Coffee?" she asked, refilling her mug.

I shook my head no. She was acting like my coming over at seven o'clock on a Thursday morning was the most normal thing in the world. It was one of the reasons I knew she was a good therapist, that she actually helped her patients. Unlike Dr.

Green, who just wanted to remind you she was a doctor every chance she got.

"Do you mind if I go see Annie?"

"Not at all, honey. I'm glad I had a cancellation this morning so I got a chance to see you. Mitch is with a patient now, but I know he'll be sorry he missed you." She reached over and squeezed my arm. "You look really happy." She said it not in the pitying, trying-to-make-me-feel-better-because-I-must-be-crazy kind of way, but like she really meant it. Probably because it was true.

Annie didn't hear me approaching. She was too busy talking to her computer screen, which I couldn't see from the door.

"Hey," I said.

She turned with a start and immediately slammed her laptop shut. It reminded me of how I reacted when my mom came barging in unannounced, especially when I had something I wanted to hide. But I was surprised and a little bit hurt to see Annie react that way with me; I was supposed to be her best friend. "What are you doing here?"

"Sorry. I was going to call but I was worried you wouldn't pick up."

"You were right." She got up and started collecting things off the floor.

It stung, but it's what I deserved. "Were you talking to Jessica?" She was already dressed and was even wearing makeup.

"Yes."

"How's it going?"

"She's fine." I had meant how were things going between

them, but from her tone I could tell I wasn't going to get much more out of her. I purposely left the question vague because I didn't know how she'd take it. Annie still hadn't explained the true nature of her relationship with Jessica, and I sensed that there was more to it than she was letting on. Maybe she thought I wouldn't understand. But I did, now more than ever. Because love was love and when you felt it you wanted to share that feeling with the rest of the world.

"Look, I'm really sorry I wasn't there last night."

"Are you? Because I get the distinct impression that if given the choice, you'd do it all over again."

"What's that supposed to mean?"

"You don't look very sorry."

I caught my reflection in the mirror hanging above her desk. My cheeks were flushed from running, my hair was windswept, and my eyes were wide and clear. Annie's mother was right. I did look happy. But that didn't mean I couldn't also feel bad for letting her down. "I know I messed up. I was—"

"Just save it." She got up and started making her bed as if I wasn't even in the room. "I don't need to hear about how you forgot because you were with Nick and that it won't happen again. I guess I was just hoping that things would be different now that Derek was out of your life. All this time I thought he was to blame, but I was wrong. You're the one who has consistently chosen a guy over your best friend."

I wanted to dive into her bed and hide under the covers. Annie didn't throw insults or blame around just because. She only did it when she had good reason. And that's what made this all burn even more. "You're right," I finally said. "I was being selfish."

She was packing her school bag now, pulling books off her desk. But she paused long enough for me to know that I had gotten through to her. Remembering the muffins, I handed her the plastic container. It was still warm. "Here, I brought these for you."

"Freshly baked muffins. In Tupperware? Are you turning into your mother now?"

We stared at each other, Mexican standoff style, until we both busted out laughing.

"What?" I said, throwing my arms up. "It's a peace offering. And they're really good." I opened the container and shoved one in my mouth. "See?"

"Hey, those are mine," she said, grabbing the muffins from me.

"I really am sorry, Annie. I didn't mean to let you down."

"So, you were out with Nick?" she asked, ignoring my apology. I nodded. The memories from last night started flooding back just hearing his name. "From the look on your face, it seems like it might even have been worth pissing me off."

I laughed and felt myself blush. "Do you want to hear about it?" The truth was that I was dying to tell her, but I wanted to make sure she wasn't still mad.

"Go on," she said, dropping her bag and settling down on her half-made bed. "I want every single detail."

I hopped up next to her and started with how Nick had to pick me up a few blocks away so my mom wouldn't know where

I was going. I told her about the abandoned church, the stained glass, and the rickety spiral staircase. I described the breathtaking view, what it was like looking down at the city, and then how the green parrots awoke and flew out into the night. I also told her what it was like being around Nick. How it felt so natural, like I didn't have to try or pretend. How we didn't need to talk to fill our silences, how he made me see things I didn't even know existed. The only part I left out was the way Nick sometimes drifted off like he was somewhere else, and how a darkness settled over him when he did. I couldn't yet explain it to Annie, not when I didn't fully understand it myself. The last thing I said was something I wasn't even conscious of until it came out of my mouth. "I also feel pretty when I'm with him. Not just on the outside. It's like I feel happy being me."

When I finished, Annie just stared at me, slack jawed and completely silent. "Aren't you going to say something?" I asked.

"I'm sorry, I think I'm in shock. I've *never* heard you say anything remotely positive about yourself before, much less anything neutral. I'm glad that at least someone can make you realize how incredibly fabulous you are, and I don't just mean your looks," she said, taking a bite out of a muffin. "I definitely never heard you talk about Derek like this."

I felt a small twitch at the back of my head as I thought about how the evening had started: with Derek's surprise visit. That was the other thing I wasn't divulging. What he had said and the small seed of doubt he had planted. I could practically feel it burrowing through my body, trying to find a place to take root.

The song was gently playing now, but it was so quiet it was barely audible. I was only aware it was still there if I listened carefully. It was just looping back to the beginning again, to the first line. *The only way for this to pass is to let go of your love.* In that moment I was finally ready to accept what it meant: that *Derek* was the one I had to let go of. The question was, could I?

"Well, it's a good thing your brother's the one who came to the door last night," Annie said.

"He did?" I was genuinely surprised since Noah had been sound asleep when I left. But maybe he'd just been pretending like I'd been for the last couple of months. "Where was my mom?"

Annie shrugged. "Noah said she was in the garden. She must not have heard the bell even though I had to ring a few times before Noah even showed up. Anyway, he told me you went out so I left before your mom appeared and complicated everything. I figured you were with Nick."

A ball of guilt set up shop in my stomach. "You protected me."

"I did."

"Why?"

"Because I love you."

"You know this just makes me feel like a worse friend."

"Good," Annie said with a smirk. "It should."

CHAPTER 20

I HADN'T MADE it through half the morning when I got pulled out of history by the hall monitor. I had been summoned once again, this time by Dr. Green *and* Principal Kingston. A full-on intervention.

I ducked into the administrative office and took a seat on the bench next to Mrs. Shay's desk. As the school secretary, she took her position as the gatekeeper to Principal Kingston very seriously, like he was some kind of prison warden or something.

"They'll be with you shortly," Mrs. Shay snipped, peering at me through her weird glasses. They were the thick, multi-prescription kind that made one of her eyeballs look ten times larger than the other. Her nickname around school was "the Cyclops," and everyone always made fun of her behind her back. Only now, for the first time, I suddenly felt sorry for her. It couldn't be easy being an old, one-eyed spinster in this town.

After ten minutes that felt like an eternity, Principal Kingston finally emerged.

"Right this way," he said, ushering me to a black leather loveseat wedged into the back of his office. His infamous bushy, salt and pepper moustache fluttered with every breath.

Dr. Green was already seated in one of two mismatched oversized armchairs facing the couch. Aside from their clashing faded floral prints, like they'd been salvaged from a trash heap, the chairs were much too big for the space, pressing up against the round wooden coffee table between them. The whole room was small and cramped, with books and papers spilling out from every available surface, stale crumbs littering Principal Kingston's desk.

"Would you like a glass of water?" he asked, settling down next to Dr. Green. A half-filled pitcher sat on the coffee table. The water was still and slightly murky, like it had been sitting there untouched for days.

"No, I'm good." He was so close our knees were practically touching.

"Thank you for coming in to see us, Olive," Dr. Green said. "We're concerned. You've been back for over two months but your grades are still lagging."

"Miss Porter said I could make up for the midterm with an essay. I've already—"

"We're aware of that, but it's not just English," Principal Kingston interjected, reviewing a thick gray folder bearing my name. "Let's see. It's also math and social studies. Things aren't as bad in history, but you're still behind last term's average."

I looked down at my feet, pushing my toes into the ends of my ballet flats. His words washed over me as my mind went back to last night. I thought about what it was like leaning against the edge of the tower with Nick, how it felt like we were the only two people in the universe, how when I was with him, nothing and nobody else mattered. And I thought about what it would be like to kiss him, if his stubble would tickle when his cheek brushed up against mine.

Principal Kingston cleared his throat like it was a secret code, and Dr. Green took over. "We want to help you, Olive." Her condescending, shrinky voice felt like it was straight out of a guidance counselor manual, and I was half inclined to kick her. She was sitting close enough that I could claim it was an accident, but I was already on thin enough ice. Why couldn't the school replace her with someone like Annie's mom, who didn't make you cringe every time she opened her mouth? "We'd hate to see you miss out on college next year when it's well within your reach." She leaned forward, clasping her hands on her lap, and stared at me through her purple-rimmed glasses. They matched her purple pumps. "But remember, you have to *want* to be helped."

I felt a smile creep up the side of my mouth, thinking about what Nick would do if he were in my place, how he'd know the perfect thing to say to put her in her place.

"Is this amusing for you?" Dr. Green asked.

"No, of course not," I said, trying to look more serious. It was getting harder to even pretend to care about my future when all I cared about was Nick. I could worry about the rest of my life later, when he was gone, back in England. I felt my heart sink just thinking about next year, about Nick leaving.

Maybe he would change his mind and stay; maybe he would decide that he didn't want a future that didn't include me. Maybe we could just pack our bags and get in his car and see where the road took us, just like my father.

"What about the pamphlet I gave you?" Dr. Green pressed on. "Have you sought any help?"

"Yes," I said, mainly to get her off my back. What I did outside school hours was none of her business.

She raised her eyebrows over her glasses, like she didn't believe me. "With whom?"

"One of the support groups." I was being intentionally vague while still trying to answer her questions. The last thing I needed was for Dr. Green to get involved and mess things up. The meetings were my best cover for seeing Nick. "I've been going every week."

"I'm glad to hear it, but based on your performance, I'm wondering if you'd benefit more from some individual therapy to help you through this."

"No," I said, with a little too much emotion. "I mean, I think the group's really starting to help." My mind went back to the church and the parrots. I wished I could be one of them and fly out of this room.

"Well. we can revisit that later," she said, not fully convinced.

"In the meantime, I'm obliged to send Georgetown your transcript," Principal Kingston added, tugging on the end of his mustache.

"Fine," I said, looking at the floor, itching to leave. "Can I go now?"

● ● ●

There were twenty-five minutes until next period when they finally released me. I aimlessly wandered the halls, replaying the intervention in my mind. It sounded like they were trying to brainwash me to join their cult, to save me from what was sure to be a doomed fate without them. I read the veiled threat in their voices, but all it did was make me want to flee. What was the point of staying here? What was the point of anything? There was one person I knew would understand. I pulled out my phone and sent him a text.

Can u come get me?

I had barely pressed send when my phone buzzed with Nick's response.

where r u?

school.

right now? it's the middle of the day.

i know. and yes.

r u sure?

YES

It was the only thing I was certain of.

The beat-up old Jaguar was parked—if you could call it that—diagonally across the path leading up to the main entrance. I had waited for him in the darkroom where nobody, especially Principal Kingston or Dr. Green, could find me. When I got in the car, Nick reversed it back onto the street. The tires screeched as he turned left toward the freeway. I didn't start breathing until five blocks later, when I realized I had gotten away with it. I didn't trip some silent alarm, cross an invisible fence, or cause a commotion of any kind. Playing hooky was as easy as walking out the front doors.

Nick hit a button on the dashboard and an ambient, methodical beat filled the car. All four windows opened simultaneously, inviting in a warm breeze that swept up my hair, the view, and all sense of time. I closed my eyes and let the wind and music wash over me. Derek, school, and all my worries were suddenly five blocks plus a million miles away.

I pretended I was still in the bell tower with Nick, the parrots soaring overhead as the neighborhood sounds mixed in with the images in my mind—the beeping of a reversing car, the whip-whip-whip of a rotating sprinkler, skateboard wheels ca-thumping on the pavement. They were like the distant drone of a beeping alarm clock pressing up against a pleasant dream. Until they started to blend in to the sound of the squawking birds. The unfinished song. Nick's voice and the one singing to me. Until I could no longer distinguish between reality and what was playing out in my head. If there was even a difference.

It made me think about what Nick said last night as we watched the parrots disappear. And that he was right.

It was the sound of freedom.

CHAPTER 21

WE HAD BEEN driving down the 101 for almost half an hour when Nick exited and started up a steep hill.

"I love this part," he said when we got to a stretch of road that crested the top.

We were miles from Vista Valley now, but the suburban layout beyond the freeway below looked almost identical: little square boxes on square plots, one after the other, all perfect little planned communities. "It's like being on top of the world," I said, peering down.

"You're right."

Nick glanced over, his eyes lingering on mine. Whenever he looked at me like that, so intentionally, I felt my whole body light up. I wondered how many times that could happen, if it was limited, like the amount of power in a battery, or infinite, like the sun.

We drove down the other side of the hill, into a residential neighborhood. It was nothing like any of the places Nick had taken me so far. He had clearly been here before because he was as comfortable driving these windy roads as he was the gritty streets of Hollywood. There were no sidewalks, and the houses, which were large, gradually became even larger. The yards got more expansive, and the hedges lining each property even taller, until eventually all the homes we passed had disappeared from view.

"Where are we?" I asked. Now we were in the middle of nowhere, without another road, person, or house in sight.

Nick pointed to a discreet green sign with white cursive letters just up ahead. It read: *Welcome to Bel Air*.

Bel Air was legendary, like Beverly Hills on steroids, home to the rich and famous. "What are we doing here?"

"Patience, grasshopper."

I nudged his arm, smiling. "Is that one of your British-isms I'm supposed to decode?"

"It's American, actually. From an ancient television show my father watched as a boy."

"Oh yeah?" It was the first time Nick had ever mentioned his father, much less anyone in his family. "What was it called?"

"I can't remember," he said, with a hint of sadness in his voice. Only it seemed like he did remember, and that for some reason, he didn't want to talk about it.

He made a quick turn onto an even more secluded, hedge-lined road, and then stopped in front of a set of massive black gates. Reaching out his window, he punched a code into the keypad. Within seconds, the gates started to swing open. The car silently rolled onto a narrow, paved road, lined by tall trees, forest-deep. Once we were through, the gates closed behind us, swallowing us whole.

I stared up at the swaying branches. They stretched high across the road on either side and met in the middle like intertwining fingers, forming a natural canopy overhead. It felt like we had driven across a border into another world. Another universe, even. "Where are we?"

"Home," Nick said, stepping on the gas.

The trees escorted us down the path, like well-trained cadets. They were so thick and tall it was almost intimidating, as if they had arms that could reach out and snatch us. *Home. He just said home.* It was the last place I expected him to be taking me. Up until now, we had been meeting in neutral territory, at least where Nick was concerned. He already knew where I lived and went to school, and he'd been to the country club, all of which gave him a pretty clear idea of what my life was like. But this was my first official foray into his private world. It could only mean one thing: that the dark cloud that sometimes enshrouded him was starting to dissolve and he was finally ready to let me in.

The trees thinned out as we approached a red wooden stable. The paint was faded and chipped. Leather saddles and metal horseshoes dangled from hooks near the wide, open doors, revealing rows of vacant stalls inside. The fenced-in enclosure just beyond the barn was also deserted. The unlatched gate gently swayed in the wind as we drove past. The place didn't just feel empty, but abandoned. "Where are the horses?"

Nick took his eyes off the road and glanced over at the stable. "My father got rid of them," he said, as if he had forgotten about them. "Nobody rides anymore."

A massive stone structure appeared in the distance, like a mirage of a castle. Expansive lawns spread out on either side of the road leading up to it. But the grass was dead: all brown and overgrown, like it hadn't been tended to in months. There were definitely no automatic sprinklers here. It made me think of Nick's comment in the desert about the "real California," and how different it was from the vibrant lawns in Vista Valley that were so green they looked like Astroturf.

The road turned to gravel and ended in a circular driveway in front of the house. The looming manse was four stories tall and as wide as my school, with at least fifty small square windows evenly spaced across. The stones looked genuinely old (unlike the cheap imitation style, popular in new developments in Vista Valley), as if each one had been individually extracted from a castle in England.

"Here we are," Nick said. "Home, sweet home."

I couldn't quite read his voice, whether he was happy or nervous to have me here.

We got out and started heading toward the entrance. Viny weeds sprouted from the empty flower boxes hanging from each window, spreading across the stone facade like tentacles. They were the kind of weeds my mom spent hours trying to eradicate from her garden. She'd probably have a heart attack if she saw these. A fountain sat in the center of the driveway, its water undisturbed except for a lazy fly suspended above, seemingly drunk off the stagnant water.

My phone started buzzing with an incoming text. Shit. It was from Annie.

Where are you?????

It was fifth period—my free period—and I was supposed to be in the gym helping her. I messed up. Again.

Please don't hate me, I quickly wrote back. *Not at school. Will explain.*

"If you need to go back, I'll take you," Nick said, assessing my shift in mood.

My heart raced thinking about the repercussions, both if I stayed and if I left. It made me think about my father at my age and the story he told me. If he could disappear for all those months without telling a soul, surely I could do it for an afternoon. I slipped my phone back in my bag. "No, I'm right where I want to be."

"Good, then let's go in," he said, opening the front door. It wasn't locked, and for a second I thought maybe the entire house had been abandoned, too.

"Wow," I gasped as we stepped into the giant foyer. It had enough art on display to fill an entire museum. They looked like the kind of paintings you'd find in a museum, too: portraits of serious aristocratic-looking people painted in dark, muted colors. As I took it all in, I found myself wishing we were back at the church, or driving down the dark freeway under a moonlit sky, or even back on Skid Row. Any place where I could pretend we were equals.

"Are you all right?" Nick gave me a look of deep understanding through his messy hair and I just about wilted.

"Are your parents home?" I whispered. With the high ceilings, I was afraid our voices might echo through the entire house.

"No." There was that crooked smirk again. "I have no idea where they are."

While I tried to decipher what that meant, if they were just running errands or would be gone for days, Nick started up the stairs.

I followed him up the wide, red-carpeted staircase, while his ancestors, or whoever they were, stared down at us from their gilded frames. We stopped off on the second floor, which opened onto a long hallway. The dark hardwood floors were covered with intricately woven Persian rugs. Wall sconces dimly lit the way.

Nick walked briskly down the hall. He clearly had no intention of giving me the grand tour. I tried to keep up while also sneaking glances into some of the open doorways we passed. I couldn't imagine what use anyone could have for so many guest rooms and fireplaces, or for multiple libraries lined with leather-bound books. Everything seemed so old, including the furniture, like it was from another era. But aside from the gallery of dead people lining the walls, there was nothing personal in the house, no sign that a family lived here—that *anyone* did. It was as if the whole place had been frozen in time.

When we reached the end of the hall, Nick opened the last door and waved me in. Unlike the rest of the house, the room was small and simple. The bed was made, as if it hadn't been slept in for a long time. The bookshelves were mostly empty, and the only thing on the desk was a black globe.

"Is this your room?" I asked.

He nodded. "If you can call it that. I don't really spend much time in here."

In a way it reminded me of my room, stripped bare of the person I used to be, of the person I used to be *with*. But who or what was Nick trying to forget? "I don't either. Spend a lot of time in my room, I mean. Especially not at night. That's when I'm most awake."

"Yeah," Nick said. "Me too."

"Maybe that's what happens when you cheat death," I said. "Your reward is a life of endless waking hours."

"Or your curse," Nick said with a slight chuckle, only it didn't really seem like he was joking. I wanted to press further, to find out what he meant, but I was afraid that would just send him to that far-off place again. I didn't want to be left in this big house all alone. Even if it was figuratively speaking.

I walked over to the desk and examined the globe. I spotted England and tried to imagine how long it would take to get there. It seemed so much further away with a massive ocean staring back at me. I gave the globe a push. As I watched it twirl around on its stand, I tried to forget about next year, that Nick would be gone and that my future was a big question mark. Besides, the world didn't seem quite as big spinning around like that, with all the oceans and countries blending together.

Suddenly, I saw a silver-framed photograph peeking out from behind the globe. It was of two young boys, dressed alike in matching shorts and collared polo shirts that had a crest sewn onto the breast pocket. Their hair was cut in the same short, close-cropped style, like it was part of their uniform. They were each holding some kind of bat. And they were beaming. The boy on the left was taller by at least a head. He seemed older, too, from the way he confidently leaned his elbow on the smaller boy's shoulder. Like he was in charge, maybe the captain of whatever sport they were playing. My eyes settled on the shorter boy, the one with darker hair. A faint birthmark the size of a postage stamp shaded his chin.

"That's you," I said, touching the boy's face through the glass frame. I was certain of it. He had the same intense eyes, the same bump across the ridge of his nose. But he looked like a different person. And it wasn't just that the photo was taken a long time ago, that the cut of his hair had changed or that he had filled out since then. I recognized the difference, because Nick had changed in the same way I had. In a profound way that had nothing to do with time passing.

"It's from a long time ago." Nick appeared beside me and took the picture in his hands. His face darkened as he examined it, like he had stepped into a shadow. "My first year at Eton."

"What are those sticks for?"

"They're bats. For a sport called cricket. Ever heard of it?" I shook my head. His face was lighter, like he was reliving a pleasant memory. "It's basically an arcane English version of baseball."

My mind flashed to Easter Sunday in the parking lot. It dawned on me that Nick must have been pretending to play cricket from the roof of his car that day, not baseball. "Do you still play?"

"Not for a long time." His voice sounded nostalgic, like when he'd told me about his dad selling the horses. It was starting to feel like everything in Nick's life had been left in the past.

He was still gripping the frame in his hands. The sunlight

streaming in through the window bounced off the cracked face of his watch. "What happened at nine forty-five?" I asked, gesturing to the gold band. Just then the frame slipped from his hand. The glass shattered all over the floor. It was the first time I'd seen him falter.

"I'm sorry." I didn't mean because of the frame. Now that I'd seen his house, the fact that his watch was also frozen in time was clearly deliberate. A choice. Or maybe even a punishment. Either way, it was clear he didn't want to talk about that, either—and that I shouldn't have brought it up.

"Don't be, it was my fault," Nick said, crouching down to collect the pieces. I could tell he also wasn't talking about the frame.

"Ouch." Without looking, I picked up a jagged piece, and the sharp edge sliced my finger.

"Let me have a look." Nick came rushing over. He took my hand in his and inspected my finger. "Crikey, you're bleeding."

"It really doesn't hurt," I said. In fact, it felt really good now that he was touching me. It reminded me of the first time we met at the meeting, when I burned my hand, of how gentle he could be sometimes, how present. And real. "But can you please say *crikey* again anyway?" I teased. "It makes me feel like I'm in the presence of a true English gentleman."

"And you only just realized that now?" He pulled on the end of his T-shirt and wrapped it around my finger. "There, that should stop the bleeding."

"But it'll stain," I said as little dots of blood seeped through the white fabric.

"It's just a shirt." He released his grip and took another look at my finger. "See? It already worked. No more blood."

"Thanks," I said, wishing that he had a reason to still hold on to me. "You're a gentleman and a scholar."

"Indeed I am. At least around you," he said. "How about we go out and get some air?"

"What about the broken glass?" Most of it was still scattered across the floor.

"It's okay, I'll deal with it later. There's no way I'm letting you near it again," he said with a twinkle in his eye.

It was in moments like this that I felt most comfortable with him. Both comfortable and protected.

On our way out, I saw something at the top of the bookshelf I hadn't noticed until now. A white golf ball sitting in a glass box, preserved like a shrine. There was something engraved on the front of the box, but it was too far away to make out the letters. Most golf balls were identical, but I couldn't help but feel that it was just like the one I had kept from that day at the club, that it was part of the growing mystery that Nick wanted to hide.

CHAPTER 22

THE BLAZING SUN hit us as soon as we stepped out onto the back patio. Fallen leaves crunched beneath our feet. It seemed like they might spontaneously ignite into flames from the friction. Rusty, wrought-iron furniture with bird-stained cushions haphazardly littered the red bricks. It was obvious no one had been out here in months.

"What is that?" I said when we came to the edge of the patio. An elaborate labyrinth at least six winding rows deep spread out on the grounds just beyond. It was composed of thick hedges, which, save for a few scattered green patches, were mostly brown and dried out.

"It's a knockoff of the famous maze at Hampton Court Palace in London, former home of King Henry the Eighth. You know, the old bastard who beheaded all his wives."

I shook my head, once again slightly embarrassed by my ignorance. "I've never seen anything like it."

"The real one's in better shape."

I stared back down at the tangled labyrinth, wondering how

it had devolved into that state. It was so overgrown it seemed more like a trap than a maze. "Has anyone ever gotten lost inside?"

"Why don't you see for yourself?"

I couldn't tell if it was an invitation or a dare, but I followed him anyway, down the three steps onto a stone path, which was barely visible beneath the sea of uncut grass sprouting up on either side of it. The long, dried blades tickled my ankles and calves, some reaching as high as my knees. It felt like we had been transported to some cornfield in the middle of nowhere. Running my fingers along the tops of the blades, it was still hard to believe that I was here with Nick while my life was going on without me, somewhere else. But it wasn't really my life anymore. It was just a shadow of who I used to be.

"That's the entrance," Nick said. Two wide columns of tangled branches rose from the ground.

"They're so much taller up close." The shape of the hedges that seemed so distinct from just a few hundred feet away were lost from this vantage point. We were now headed into what looked like a wild, overgrown tunnel.

"Don't worry," he said, sensing my fear. "I'll be right here with you."

That's exactly what I was afraid of. We had been alone in secluded places many times by now. But this time felt different, like we were heading down a path of no return, a path I didn't know my heart could handle.

But it was too late to turn back. And I didn't want to.

Brittle, fallen twigs lined what seemed like a once pristine path. Nick's footsteps cracked in rhythm with mine, as if we were walking across a cemetery littered with bones. When we reached the end of the first row, I stopped to look back toward the entrance. It was no longer visible, having disappeared behind the path's curve.

"Do you want to keep going?" Nick asked.

I could see the house through a pocket of gnarled, naked branches. It was like looking through a lens, revealing the layer of quiet death that had fallen over this place. It was even worse than being frozen in time, because it was like time was moving forward without it.

"Yes," I said. "I do."

The deeper into the maze we went, the more the rest of the world and everything else fell away. Even overgrown, there was still something majestic about the labyrinth, as if buried secrets existed within its twisted walls. We got to a curve in the path where the hedges grew so close together, the branches met and crisscrossed, launching us into a pocket of total darkness.

"This reminds me of the darkroom," I said.

We were standing so close I could hear the air whistle as Nick inhaled. A gentle buzzing emerged just above the sound of his breath. A second, higher pitched tone joined in, and the two danced around each other, gradually merging into a synchronized duet. Was it the melody taking a new turn?

"Can you hear that?" Nick asked.

My body froze. It was just like the whirring buzz in my head that sometimes overtook me. *He could hear it too?* "Hear what?"

"The cicadas."

I nodded and let out the deep breath I'd been holding in. The sound was real, like the crunching twigs or the flapping parrots. It didn't just exist in my head. All these phantom noises gained clarity and context because of Nick and the worlds he opened up to me. "It's beautiful."

"The males do all the buzzing. It's like their mating call to attract the right female. They have perfect pitch, you know."

Cupping my hands around my eyes, I pressed my face against the thick, decaying wall. The buzzing suddenly got louder, growing in intensity as if the cicadas sensed my presence and were coming closer. With one hand I reached back and got my camera out of my bag, grateful that I remembered to change out the finished roll.

"They hardly ever reveal themselves," Nick said, leaning against the hedge. "You're not going to see anything in there."

"I already do." A white and orange flower poked through the tangle of branches, proof that life still existed here. Its colorful pattern was so intricate, the petals looked like insect wings. "Take a look," I said, stepping aside so he could see. "Do you know what kind of flower that is?"

Nick crouched down to get a better look. "It's some kind of orchid."

It was so different from the orchids my mother grew. "How can it survive out here when everything else is . . ."

"Dead?" Nick said, finishing my thought. "Because it's a really low maintenance plant. All it needs is the occasional rain to keep it going. And they only bloom once a year. We're just lucky to catch it at the right time."

If that was true, then what was my mother doing in the greenhouse all the time? Maybe she had her secrets too.

The camera dangled from the strap around my neck as we meandered through the rest of the maze. I took pictures of different things along the way and turned the camera on Nick when he wasn't looking. We reached various dead ends, forcing us to retrace our steps, until eventually we got to the exit on the other side. It opened out onto a big meadow. The property seemed endless.

"We made it," I said, almost wistful that the experience was over.

"And we didn't get lost." Nick peered across the meadow and tugged on my sleeve. "Come on. There's something else I want to show you."

He was already moving toward a brick wall on the other side of the field. When we got there, he unlatched the arched door in the middle and led me into what seemed like a secret garden. Inside the walls, everything was brown and overgrown, just like the rest of the property, but in the middle sat a large, round pond. Nick ran down a small hill, to a dock that floated on the edge of the water. He hopped on and motioned for me to join him.

When I stepped onto the dock, he unlatched a metal hook at the base of the wooden slats. As we drifted out into the pond, I searched for our reflections on the swampy surface. But the water was so cloudy, I could only make out the vague silhouette of our shadows. We were standing so close that they blended into one.

"I used to spend a lot of time out here when I was a kid."

The image of a young Nick was still fresh in my mind. I searched for traces of his dimpled cheek or the birthmark on his chin, which was now buried beneath his thick, dark stubble.

I started and nearly fell over as I heard something splash in the water behind us. When I looked back, a large swan was sailing toward us, a ripple of florescent green algae cascading in the water behind its white feathers. I dangled my arm in the water as it got closer, waiting to caress its smooth head.

"Careful," Nick said. "Swans can be terribly vicious creatures."

I looked up, surprised by the tone of warning in his voice. "Come on, you can't be serious."

"Scout's honor," Nick said, waving his hand in salute. "You especially don't want to go near this sad soul."

I pulled my hand back and let the swan swim past. He seemed so elegant and graceful, hardly something to be afraid of. "Why? He seems so calm."

"Looks can be deceiving. He's actually been in deep mourning ever since his mate died. He just swims around the pond like this for hours looking for her."

"Can't you get him a new partner?"

"He's too smart for that," Nick said, shaking his head. "They're monogamous for life, swans."

"How long has it been? Since she died?"

"Ten years."

"That's so sad," I said, picturing the swan swimming here like this while life went on around him.

"It's not just sad. It's tragic."

Nick shifted his gaze away from the swan and fixed it on me. Lifting the camera from my neck, he gently set it down on the dock. My knees buckled as he reached out and took hold of my hand. He opened his mouth as if he was about to say something. My heart started pounding so hard I was sure he could hear it.

"What?" I whispered, feeling shy and exposed under the intensity of his gaze.

But instead of answering he came even closer. *This is it*, I thought as he squeezed my palm. *It's happening. He's going to kiss me.* I closed my eyes and could practically feel myself levitating above my own body when suddenly, without warning, Nick jumped into the pond, pulling me in with him. Still gripping my hand, we sank down, squinting at each other through the silty layers of emerald water. When our feet hit the soft, cushioned bottom, we sprang back up amid a cloud of powdery residue, like we were free-falling through space. I wondered if I had somehow dreamt this moment before, because there was something so familiar about the sensation of being carried along, weightless, just like the oxygen bubbles all around us. Spears of amber light sprouted out from Nick's body and his skin glowed luminescent, as if he were standing on top of the sun. He looked so peaceful, like he was lit from within.

The only way for this to pass is to let go of your love . . . I see into your mind . . . Your voice is like an angel I can hear without sound.

The lyrics swam around inside my head, echoing through the underwater silence. His voice was as clear and hopeful as I'd ever heard it.

Nick stared into my eyes. Then, he mouthed two words: *I'm sorry.*

I didn't need sound to understand what he was saying. But what was he apologizing for? For yanking me in? I was about to respond, to ask him why, but before my lips could form the word we were bursting through the boggy surface and I was gasping for air instead.

CHAPTER 23

"RACE YOU BACK."

Before I could object, Nick had already taken off up the hill and disappeared through the arched doorway. The handle was still wet from where he touched it as I followed him through. I ran across the meadow, struggling to catch up, pond water still pooled in my squeaking shoes, swishing between my toes. The warm air smelled sweet as it blew over my damp skin, fanning my drenched dress behind me like a wet sail.

"No fair!" I called out as Nick made a sudden left by the maze toward the forest on the other side. "You know the short cuts!"

He slowed his pace to a light backward jog so he was now facing me. He looked so sexy with his soaking wet T-shirt and jeans clinging to his lean, muscled body. "Then I suggest you don't fall behind."

When we got to the end of the meadow, he began darting in and out of the trees. Each time he disappeared for longer, deeper into the forest.

The branches blocked out most of the remaining sun. When I looked up, I spotted the moon rising through a space between the trees. It was still faint and tissue-thin, like it hadn't yet decided how much of itself to reveal.

Nick was a steady distance ahead but kept looking back over his shoulder to make sure I was still within sight.

Without slowing down, I reached the camera up into the air, high above my head, and began snapping. I hoped the pictures would turn out blurry, that they'd be able to capture how I felt at that exact moment: Free. Happy. Alive.

The forest began to thin out and soon we were back to running on the dried out, overgrown grass, the imposing stone house now visible ahead. I had almost forgotten it was there, that the property belonged to people, not just the creatures that ran rampant on it. I pumped my legs harder and finally caught up to Nick. We ran the last stretch together, our arms and legs swinging in unison, until Nick elbowed me out of the way to go barreling first through the side door.

"I win," he declared just as I came crashing in after him. We were in some kind of mud room, a space for rubber boots and gardening tools and various things dragged in from the outside.

"If I knew cheating was allowed, I would have tripped you a lot sooner," I said between gasping breaths of air.

"Would you have, now?" The lopsided grin was back. It bordered on a real smile, but not one big enough to make his missing dimple reappear. "Then don't let me stop you."

He took off up the back staircase, the floorboards creaking under his weight. I gave chase, taking the steps two at a time.

My laughter bounced with my fast movement, echoing up the stairwell like a case of the hiccups. I couldn't remember the last time I had laughed like this, so hard I could feel it in my ribs. It reminded me of all the painful bruises I used to have there, and how they had since healed. It gave me hope that maybe everything healed eventually.

There was a sudden crashing noise, followed by what sounded like a small avalanche. Nick's shuffling feet came to a standstill. I was just about to call up to see if he was okay when I heard the high-pitched tone of a woman's voice. I froze in my tracks. Even though I had stopped, my heart raced like it expected me to keep moving. Was it his mother? I strained to make out what she was saying when Nick started talking. His voice was hoarse, like he hadn't spoken in a while.

Hugging the wall, I inched forward one step at a time until I reached the landing. An empty cardboard box and various items lay scattered at my feet. They formed a trail all the way up to the top, where Nick was standing in front of an elegant-looking older woman in a long, flowing black skirt, her white hair swooped up in a bun.

I glanced at Nick. There was no hint of the grin or the playfulness from just a minute earlier. I was about to sneak back down the stairs and wait for him at the bottom when the woman spotted me.

"I didn't realize you had a guest," she said, assessing me and my soaking wet clothes from head to toe. She also had an English accent, only hers was even stronger than Nick's, like she was related to the Queen.

I stiffened and felt my cheeks burn, suddenly ashamed for being caught here alone with him. We might as well have been naked. Nick's eyes were fixed on the mix of things strewn across the landing—books, an old set of scratched, wooden ping pong rackets, a burgundy wool cardigan and a stack of letters, loosely held together with a string. From that angle, I could only make out the first three letters of the name on the envelope: *Sam . . .*

"This is Olive," Nick said, his voice now distant. "And this is Lady Beatrice Agnes Wilkins." He gestured toward the woman. "My aunt."

"I'm delighted to meet you, Olive. Nick knows I hate that silly title, so please call me Aunt Bea." She descended the stairs as she spoke, stopping on the landing next to me. After gently shaking my hand, she began collecting the fallen items from the box. "Please do forgive me for this horrible mess!"

"Here, let me help you," I said, my body relaxing. This was not how I wanted to make my first impression with any member of Nick's family, but at least she was being kind. Up close, she wasn't as intimidating as her accent made her seem.

"No." Nick's voice was so loud and firm it startled me, and I could practically see the door closing between us.

Aunt Bea looked pointedly at Nick, then turned back to me and said, "Thank you, dear, but what you need is to get out of those clothes before you catch cold."

"I'm okay, they're almost dry." Gripping the banister, I slowly backed down a step. "It's getting late. I should probably be going, anyway."

"Come on," Nick said, his voice softer now. "Aunt Bea's right. At least let me give you something to change into."

I looked toward the door—it was already getting dark and I didn't know my way home—then back up at Nick. He swiped the hair out of his face so I could see his eyes clearly.

"Okay," I finally said, releasing my hold from the railing. Gingerly stepping over the fallen debris, I started back up the stairs.

There was a light tap on the door. "Are you decent?"

"Just about," I said, slipping the shirt over my head. I was in the library, one of the rooms we had passed on the second floor hallway earlier. I felt my face flush before he even walked through the door. Even though I was covered head to toe in a pair of light blue drawstring pajamas and a white T-shirt, wearing Nick's clothes somehow made me feel naked. They smelled just like him, as if he was already right next to me. It was completely different from Derek's scent, muskier and more natural. "Okay, I'm ready."

Nick came in carrying a sterling silver tray containing a teapot, creamer, and sugar bowl in a matching pattern. He had also changed out of his wet clothes and was now wearing a pair of navy and white Adidas track pants and a faded red T-shirt. He wasn't any less clothed than usual, but he seemed stripped down, almost as if he'd taken off a mask I wasn't even aware he'd been wearing. "Cup of tea?"

"That sounds great," I said, rubbing my arms. They were still cold.

He set the tray down on the coffee table. "Milk and sugar?"

"Just plain."

"That's not really a proper cup of tea, you know. But I'll let it slide." He prepared two mugs and sat down on the Persian rug facing the empty fireplace.

I sat down next to him. The cup felt warm between my hands, but I still had a chill running through me, even more so now.

He reached back toward the couch and yanked off a few cushions for us to lean on. The volumes of leather-bound books surrounding us felt cozy. "It's a good look on you, men's PJ's."

"Maybe I'll start a new trend." I was getting better at detecting his sarcasm, even with his accent. "I'm sure it will spread like wildfire in Vista Valley."

"Hey, you never know. Then again, you'd look good in anything."

A flurry of goose bumps broke out across my skin. I hugged my knees into my chest.

"Still cold? Here, let me start a fire." He was already pulling logs out of a secret compartment in the wall.

"You don't have to do that. It's like a million degrees out."

"Who cares if it's two million degrees, not that you're prone to exaggeration," he said, strategically stacking the wood in the fireplace in a crisscross pattern. "You're covered in gooseflesh."

"Goose*flesh*?" I said, giggling. "Is that what you just said?" Once I started laughing I couldn't stop. I had to put my cup down so it wouldn't spill.

"All right, missy, what do you call all those bumps on your arms?"

"Exactly, that's what they are, *bumps*! Goose *BUMPS*!"

He laughed. "See, that's the problem growing up in two countries. I can never remember which term to use where."

"Okay, let's find another one." I was still giggling. "Oh I know, what do you call the bathroom again in England?"

"The loo." He was crouching down, lighting some crumpled newspaper.

"The looooooo?" I said, doing my best attempt at an English accent.

"It sounds a hell of a lot more dignified than *toilet*, don't you think?" He got the fire going and sat back down on the carpet next to me. "I guess I'll just have to accept my fate as a perpetual outsider." He was joking, but something snagged in his voice.

"Why did you go to school in England when your family lives here? It seems so far away."

"It is. But when every male predecessor in the Wilkins clan has gone to Eton before you, you aren't given much choice in the matter." The first log caught fire, sending a crackling flame up the chimney chute. "History decided for me."

One question only opened the door for the next. There were so many more things I wanted to ask him. "Does your aunt live here?"

"No." Nick took a sip of his drink and stared into the fire. "She's just visiting."

"Where are your parents?"

"Back in England."

I sensed him opening up so I decided to go further. "For how long?"

He shrugged. "They don't like spending much time here."

Maybe that explained why the place was in such disarray. "Do you?"

He looked up at me, like he was startled by the question. Had I gone too far? He put his mug down and leaned back into the pillow. "I don't have a choice."

It's not what I expected him to say. Of all the people I'd ever met, Nick was the only one who truly seemed to control his destiny. It's one of the things I liked most about him. But if he didn't have a choice, maybe none of us did. Maybe we were all trapped. Just like my dad was all those years ago. Like he still seemed to be.

The fire was really going now. We sat, silently staring at the rising flames when the same buzzing sound from the maze returned.

"Is that another cicada?" I asked.

Nick stretched his neck out as if he were opening up his ears. "It is."

I gazed toward the nearest window as we listened to the pleasant noise. It oscillated between a hum and a full-on melody. I spotted the moon glowing brighter now against the dark sky. "It sounds like it's coming from inside."

"They throw off sound so it's impossible to pin them down. They're deceptive that way."

He got up to fan the flames with a leather pump that looked like a bagpipe. The gentle breeze caused my dress and jean jacket to sway on the iron grate in front of the fireplace where I'd hung them to dry.

I hoped they never would.

"They also cast off their skin, you know." He was back on the pillows next to me. "It's called molting. Sometimes you can spot the skins lying around. They look like dead bugs, but if you look closer you can see they're just empty shells. Kind of like external skeletons."

"Did you major in birds and insects or something at boarding school?"

"Hardly," Nick laughed. "I'm just a master of useless knowledge. Didn't make me too popular growing up." He touched his nose. "I have this lovely bump to prove it."

"It's not useless knowledge," I protested, "I like it." The last log caught fire. I could feel the heat rolling toward us. "Maybe we're like the cicadas."

Nick jerked his head up. "What do you mean?"

"I don't know," I said, uncertain where my thought was leading me. "Like when we die, we shed our skin too and, I don't know, move on to become something else." I paused, nervous that I was losing him, that I was beginning to sound like the crazy people in the meetings.

"Go on." His voice was soft and expectant, as if I had the answer.

"It's just that, do you ever wonder what if things happened differently? Like, what if we actually died and there was nothing near about it? What if we weren't supposed to come back?"

I'd avoided thinking of my accident and the events leading up to it for so long that I'd barely thought about what would have happened if it had all really ended that night.

He was quiet for a second. "All the time."

"Then sometimes I think we must have survived for a reason. But what are we supposed to do with that?"

"Nothing." He was so matter-of-fact, so certain.

"Don't you ever think we were given a second chance?"

"No." He said it with such finality, with no room for error or discussion.

"Why not?"

"Because I don't deserve one."

Memories from that night pressed up against the melody swimming around my head. Running out Derek's front door. Into his car. Driving off into the rain. The rest was still a blur. But no matter how many wrong turns I may have taken, they led me here. To Nick. That had to mean something.

"I think you're wrong." I watched the flames dance up the chimney, blackening the red brick chute. "I think we all do."

I reached into my bag for my music. I selected the first title on what was now a lengthy playlist. I put one bud in Nick's ear, the other in mine, then lay back down and pressed play.

The room was completely dark when I opened my eyes. It took a second to get my bearings—and to notice Nick's arm draped over my shoulder. It felt so natural, like he was an extension of me. We were still leaning against the couch, my legs still crossed in the same position, the earbud cord still suspended between us like a shared artery, even though the music had stopped. The fire had long burned down and the logs were now reduced to a pile of glowing embers. How long had we been asleep like this?

When I wake I see your face
Even through the fog that leaves no trace
I will hear you long after you're gone
Mingled with the earth your heart beats on

Another rash of goose bumps erupted across my whole body as the new lyrics spun around my head. The words accompanied a new playful twist in the melody, like they were dancing around each other in a flirtatious game. It made me think of running after Nick in the woods, how it was his face I saw when I heard the song, his heartbeat that I carried inside my own.

The voice was so loud it almost felt like it would wake Nick, but when I glanced over, he was still asleep, his chest heaving gently up and down with each breath. He looked so peaceful, his face so relaxed, like a sleeping baby. Even though we both had all our clothes on, it felt like a lot more had happened than just falling asleep. It was as if a tight-knit cocoon had been woven around us. But the cocoon didn't just insulate us from the rest of the world; it also formed a new one, a world that belonged only to me and him.

Just then, Nick's eyes sprung open and locked on mine. He didn't seem the least bit surprised by my presence, and I didn't feel a rush of embarrassment or the urge to look away, like I used to with Derek. We just stared at each other and it felt like my heart might explode. I never dreamt it was even possible to feel this connected to another person.

"Hey," he finally said, his voice just above a whisper. "Are you still cold?"

He rubbed his hand up and down my arm, which only

made my skin erupt more, but this time it wasn't because of the temperature.

"No," I said, my voice cracking after having been silent for so long.

"Are you nervous?" he asked, his face inching closer.

My heart started to pound wildly in my chest. With the moonlight pouring in through the windows, the shadows from the swaying trees dancing across the rug, it almost felt like we were waking into the same dream. Because how could happiness like this possibly be real?

I heard a gentle tap. Was that the sound of his heart? But then I heard it again, followed by Aunt Bea's distinctive, high-pitched voice. "Nick?"

She slowly opened the door and turned on the lights. Nick and I both squinted, our eyes unaccustomed to the brightness.

"Sorry to bother you, dear," she said gently, standing by the door, like she genuinely didn't want to disturb us. "But Sam's here." Nick instantly pulled his arm back so that we were no longer touching. Was it the Sam from the letters on the stairs? "She's downstairs and would like to see you."

My heart sank. Sam was a *she*. Without a word or even a look in my direction, Nick got up and followed Aunt Bea out the door. Just like that, he was gone. The dream was over. My goose bumps disappeared, but still I felt cold all over.

I waited until I could no longer hear footsteps then ran to the door, where I spotted the tops of their heads disappearing down the stairs. Confident that my bare feet wouldn't make any noise, I tiptoed halfway down the hall and stopped at the head of the staircase. I still couldn't see anything so I crept down further until I reached the landing. I crouched and peered through the banister slats, affording me a mostly unobstructed view of the foyer below where Nick and Aunt Bea were just arriving.

And then, out from behind a column that had hidden her from sight, came Samantha. She was tall, with locks of thick, luscious red hair that cascaded down the back of her form-fitting green wrap dress. She carried herself like she was older, definitely not a teen, her body curved in a shape similar to her long, wavy hair. It was as if she had materialized out of thin air. I was too far away to make out what they were saying, but when she leaned in to hug Nick, there was no translation necessary.

My eyes burned from the ocean of tears threatening to pour out, but I bit down on the inside of my cheek to try to stop them. The signs had been there all along, the clues that Nick's heart really belonged to someone else, that he also had a Derek. The only difference now was that I knew her name. And that she was beautiful.

When I got up to leave, my knee knocked into the banister. Samantha glanced up and I quickly retreated back into a shadow just as Nick was turning around. Had they seen me? I darted up the stairs and back to the library before I could find out. I went over to the grate to check my dress. It was still slightly damp, but I put it on anyway. After what I'd just witnessed, I suddenly felt all wrong wearing Nick's clothes.

I began pacing the room as I felt panic rising. I tried to breathe, to count to ten, but that only made it worse, because it made me think about Nick. I had to get out of here. I thought about calling Annie, but I didn't know what I would tell her. I didn't even know the address. I had no choice but to wait for Nick to return.

I only had to wait a few moments longer.

"It's late," Nick said, appearing by the door, his shoulders slumped, a dark expression across his face. "I should take you home now."

There was no sign of Samantha on our way out. I took some comfort knowing that her visit had been brief. Not much could have happened beyond that hug. But my relief was short-lived when I noticed a car in the driveway, a pearl-white BMW convertible with a studded pink border around its license plate. It wasn't there when we arrived and it definitely wasn't the kind of car a distinguished woman like Aunt Bea would drive. My stomach sank as my mind scrambled to find a way around the fact that the car belonged to Samantha. Which only meant one thing: that she was still there.

CHAPTER 24

WHEN I GOT to the darkroom, I locked the door behind me. Nobody used it aside from Annie. Even the janitor didn't have a key. But still, it felt safer in here with the door sealed, like I was shielded from the rest of the world. It was the last period of the day and I had independent study. I should have been free to go except for the fact that I had detention after school.

My mom had been waiting up for me when I got back from Nick's a few nights before. I saw her peering out from behind the curtains when he dropped me off. She was all in a tizzy over the call from Principal Kingston about playing hooky, never mind the fact that I had been unreachable for the last eight hours. She gave me a lecture on how we have to take responsibility for our actions, and that actions have consequences. That was why she grounded me in addition to the week of detention I was given at school. It felt like she was reading straight from a parenting handbook, under the section entitled "How to Handle Your Truant Child." She seemed almost relieved that there was a standard operating procedure for situations like this. But these consequences didn't matter. Nothing mattered compared to the possibility that I might never see Nick again, that it was over before it ever really had a chance to begin.

I clutched the finished roll of film in my hand and stood in the middle of the room. Various proofs and contact sheets, contenders for the yearbook, were tacked up all over. All the people I had known for years—classmates, playmates, and neighbors—surrounded me. If what was on these walls was my past, then I was hoping that this roll held some clue to my future. Or at least to Nick. Only now that I was here, I wasn't so sure I wanted to know what was hidden inside this plastic container. I wasn't so sure if it was better left imagined, permitted to exist only in my head. Like the song, or what would have happened last night if Samantha had never interrupted. But then I was haunted by another, scarier thought: what if this was all I had left?

I rolled up my sleeves and got started.

Even though Annie could do all this blindfolded, she still kept a set of detailed step-by-step instructions tacked to the wall. Following the directions, I pulled out the metal canisters, chemicals, beakers, and timer, all the tools I would need at my fingertips. I got the paper ready and reviewed the steps one more time before switching over to the red light.

Once it was safe, I pried the lid off the film container. It made a popping sound, like a cork coming off a bottle of champagne. I gently began to unravel the roll before loading it onto the reel. The metal spool felt icy between my fingers, the film slick. When I was done I dropped the reel into the light-tight can, poured in the contents of the first beaker, sealed it with the rubber top, gave it a shake, and hit the button on the timer. Once it buzzed a few minutes later, I got to work draining out the chemical, pouring the next one in, and resetting the timer. I repeated the process one last time for the final tray, and pretty soon I had successfully developed the negatives.

The next thing I was supposed to do was create a contact sheet so that I could pick the best ones to print. But I already knew which one I wanted to see most, the first picture on the roll. Slipping the negative into the enlarger, I set the size of the print. My hands trembled as I dipped the eight-by-ten sheet into the first tray. Within seconds, shades of blue, purple, and silver emerged, pooling over the milky paper. As I continued the process, each tray brought more clarity to the image. Two abstract blotches gradually transformed into Nick's eyes, another into the vague outline of a tree. I was finally beginning to understand why Annie liked doing this so much, developing her photos instead of going digital. There was something magical about the process, about uncovering the mysteries trapped beneath the white surface as they began to take shape.

Just as I was dipping the paper into the final tray, the door suddenly opened. A blast of light from the hallway filled the room.

"Quick, shut the door!" I said as Annie came stumbling in, laden with bags.

"Oh-my-god-you-gave-me-a-heart-attack-I-had-no-idea-you-were-even-in-here-wait-are-you-printing-something?" she said all in one breath, closing the door behind her.

When I looked back down at the photo, the image was all of

a sudden inverted. It was dark where it should have been light, and vice versa, like an X-ray. I thought my eyes were playing tricks on me as they readjusted to the red light, until Annie came up behind me and saw it too.

"Oh shit. I'm so sorry, Ol," she said, peering into the tray over my shoulder. "The light from the door solarized the print. I ruined it."

But when I looked back at the photo and watched the rest of the image emerge—Nick lying under the burnt tree in the middle of the desert—I couldn't help but think the opposite. That the effect made it seem as if he were illuminated from within, like his heart was glowing. It reminded me of the way I felt when I took the picture: electric. "You didn't," I said, using the metal tongs to transfer the dripping wet paper to the clothesline to dry. "I like it better this way."

"How do you even know how to use all this?" she asked, waving at the chemicals and equipment spread out across the counter.

"I found the camera in the cabinet a few weeks ago and just kind of started," I said. "I hope you don't mind that I took it."

"Mind? I'm blown away."

She came to the clothesline and took a closer look at the print. "You're a natural, solarized or not."

I stood and examined the photo with her. There was something about Nick's expression that still came through with the image inverted, maybe more so because of it. Even with his eyes closed, it looked like he was somewhere else, halfway between the dream world and the real one, uncertain which to cling to, if there was even a choice. My heart ached when I realized the fleeting thing I'd uncovered in this frozen moment: his vulnerability.

The song started over from the beginning. This time, the deep, smoky voice came at me with such force it felt like I was standing in a wind tunnel. There was an even deeper sense of longing and sadness in it than I'd heard before. It pierced right through me.

"Ol?" Annie reached over and stroked the back of my hair. "What's wrong? Why do you seem so sad?"

I closed my eyes as she continued smoothing out my hair, grateful that she was still here for me even after I'd been so flaky. "I'm scared this picture might be all I have left of him."

"But everything's been going so well," she said, confused. "What changed?"

I told her about ditching school the other day and about my night at Nick's house. I described the maze and the wild, overgrown grounds. Then running into Aunt Bea on the stairs and falling asleep, like really asleep, for the first time in weeks. And then I told her about Samantha.

"Why didn't you tell me any of this before?" she said, when I was through.

"I was too embarrassed."

"Derek really did a number on you."

"This doesn't have anything to do with Derek." A flare of anger swelled in me, the kind that was usually only triggered by my mother.

"That's because you still can't see it. That there's more than just one way to interpret things."

"What do you mean?"

"You said Samantha hugged Nick. Did he hug her back?"

I'd been so focused on Samantha, so distracted by her beauty and her body language, that I hadn't paid attention to Nick. But now that I thought about it, I could see him in my mind's eye: through the slats of the banister, with his arms slack by his side, his shoulders already slumped the way they'd been when he returned to the library. "No," I said, my voice lifting. "I guess he didn't."

"Exactly," Annie said, slapping her thigh for emphasis. "And you said he was in a bad mood after he saw her, right?" It wasn't exactly how I had put it, but I nodded anyway. She was on a roll and was starting to sound convincing. "If he actually had feelings for her, he'd barely be able to contain his excitement."

I thought about Derek parading down the halls with Betsy, a big smile plastered across his face, and how Nick didn't act anything like that. I'd never thought I had a choice over the way I felt, or that looking at things from another angle could tell a different story. "Okay, maybe you have a point."

"All I'm trying to say is that it's okay to trust someone again."

That was the thing. I thought I did trust Nick. Or was starting to. Now I didn't know what to think anymore. I still hadn't told Annie about the other side of Nick. The side that housed his pain. I couldn't go there without brushing up against my own. "But she was still there when I left," I reminded Annie.

"Look, who knows? Maybe Samantha is his ex and *she's* the one who's not over *him*. She was probably threatened when she saw you and gave him a hard time. But it's so clear he really cares about you, Ol. Don't let insecurity get in the way. It doesn't lead to a good place."

I was all too aware of the places it led, of the things that it could make me do. The problem was, how could I be sure when it was safe? I pulled my phone out of my bag just to make sure I hadn't missed any calls or texts in the last forty-five minutes. It was the longest I'd gone all day without checking. "I haven't heard from him in three days," I said, as the rest of my doubts started to creep back in.

"Then contact him. Who says you have to be a passive participant in your own life? Be bold, Olive Bell. Make your own choices."

I thought about all the times I'd waited by the phone for Derek to call, all those hours I'd wasted worrying when everything always turned out okay. Or almost always, up until the end. But then I also remembered what I'd told Nick, that I believed we were given a second chance for a reason. "Okay," I finally agreed.

And then just like that, my phone started chirping on the counter. "Oh my god. It's him."

"You gave him his own ring tone?"

I nodded, still blown away by his timing. It felt like a reward from the universe for getting better at taking control. "Wow," Annie teased. "This is even more serious than I realized."

I let out a nervous laugh and handed her the phone. "I can't look." Annie read the message with a puzzled look on her face, while my insides felt like they were turning inside out. "What's it say?"

"*H-I-G-Q-T*. I have no idea what that means."

"How's it going, cutie," I explained, a smile spreading across my face. That's when Annie started typing. "Wait, what are you doing?"

"Responding."

I looked over her shoulder just as the sent chime sounded. She had written *SETE*, aka, smiling ear to ear. "Annie!" I exclaimed, uncertain whether to be excited or mortified by what she'd done.

My phone chirped again. *You around 2night?*

Yes. Annie wrote back before I could stop her.

Your turn to pick.

"See?" Annie said, showing me his response. "You have nothing to worry about. So, what should I say now?"

I glanced back at the print hanging from the clothesline and that's when the idea crystallized, when I realized where I wanted to take him. "Give me that," I said, reaching for my phone.

CHAPTER 25

WHEN I GOT out of detention, I went back to the darkroom to finish developing the rest of the roll. Now that I was done, the halls were quiet, with no trace of the voices and footsteps that had filled them an hour earlier. I ran down the corridor, the sound of my squeaky sneakers reverberating off the metal lockers.

"Hello, HELLO!" I called out, half-expecting to hear the words echo back at me. "I'm here!" I yelled, louder this time, Annie's command to be bold running through my mind. "OLIVE BELL!!!"

As I ran up the back stairs, something dislodged inside me. It felt like my whole body—my soul—was suddenly breathing in sync, inhaling and exhaling through every pore. It didn't even bother me when I ran past the Pioneer, or make me wonder what Derek was doing. All I could think about was Nick. That he was still in my life. And that I would see him in a matter of hours.

I ran the whole way home. On foot I was able to see things

I normally missed driving by at forty miles an hour. Like how the roses and tulips were wilted from the day's sun. The automatic sprinklers would undoubtedly go off before they flopped over completely. Every lawn was perfectly mowed and such a vibrant green, each one could pass for a hole on the golf course. Nothing grew wild or free. There wasn't a weed, brown patch, or dried leaf in sight.

It wasn't until I got to the middle of our block and saw both my parents' cars in the driveway that I realized something was wrong. When I got to the front door I looked up at the sky. The almost full moon had risen early and was now just cresting over our roof. It was so bright I could see the craters across its surface. It seemed close enough for me to grab on, for it to whisk me away, high above my house, my street, the neighborhood, even the whole world.

But instead I put my key in the lock, turned it twice to the right until it clicked, and went inside.

As soon as I walked in, I noticed something perched on the credenza in the entry hall, where we kept our mail: a white envelope with the Georgetown logo printed in its corner. I had forgotten all about the fact that I would soon learn if I got in. It was too late to snatch it and hide it in my bag. It had clearly been placed there for my benefit.

I was just about to escape to my room when my mother came hustling in through the kitchen, her gardening apron rattling as she approached. She was always so harried, like the world lay on her shoulders, like it just might fall apart if she weren't there to prop it up.

"We need to talk," she said, picking up the letter. "We're in the kitchen."

I followed her in, where my father was leaning against the doorjamb, holding a half-empty glass of scotch. Things must be worse than I thought if she summoned him home early.

"What's going on?" I asked, waiting for the hammer to drop.

The sound of the shifting, melting ice cubes in my father's glass filled the room. "Here." My mother handed me the letter, which is when I saw that it had already been opened, that she already knew my fate.

I slipped the neatly folded paper out of the envelope and glanced at the first line. "I got in," I said flatly, "pending my final transcript." I guess Principal Kingston's threat hadn't been idle. He actually called and let them know I was failing.

"This is *very* good news," my mother said, taking the letter back, like she was surprised. Was it because of my reaction or the fact that I actually got in? "Now as long as you get your grades back up, everything will be right back on track."

On track for what? To live out what I was quickly realizing was Derek's dream? Or my mother's dream of getting a college degree? I tried to catch my father's eye. He of all people should have understood how I felt. But he kept his gaze focused on some invisible point at the bottom of his drink, like he was staring through the looking glass. It was then that it suddenly hit me why he had abandoned his road trip nineteen years ago. I did the math in my head, calculating the months backward from my birthday. It wasn't for my mother. It was because he found out she was pregnant with me, which is why she never finished college. I was the reason he couldn't keep going, the reason he had to abandon his dream.

The television started blaring from the den, where Noah was probably watching one of his shows. I wished I were in there with him, huddled under a fort of pillows, instead of here, contemplating a future I wanted to escape. I thought about the photo in the darkroom and then the low, fat moon. I couldn't help but feel like I was watching a drama unfold on TV, like this was all happening to someone else. Some other girl named Olive Bell who lived on Lily Lane.

"I should get started on my homework," I finally said, knowing they couldn't object to that.

I dropped my bag off in my room, changed into my pajamas, and went to the den to join Noah.

"Hey bud." I curled up under the blanket on the couch next to him. "Watcha watching?"

"Hailey's Picnic," he said, his eyes glued to the blaring commercial advertising face soap.

"It's *Hailey's Clinic*, silly," I said, ruffling his scruffy dark hair. The red button was alight on the cable box. It had been recording the show, week after week, long after I had stopped watching it. My heart ached thinking about Noah keeping my old habits alive without me.

"You can skip the ads," I said, showing him the fast-forward button on the remote. "You just press here."

"I know," he said matter-of-factly. "I like the commercials."

I laughed and sank deeper into the couch, letting the words and images of the beautiful, frolicking women on the screen wash over me. They looked so happy and carefree, like nothing could ever get them down. I glanced over and watched Noah bopping his head to the ad's catchy jingle. I wished I could take him in my arms and never let go, that I could protect him so he wouldn't have to go through what I had, so he wouldn't have to die in order to find a new lease on life.

"Are you really leaving?" Noah asked, still nodding along to the tune.

"What do you mean?"

"Mom says you're going away next year to college. Is that true?"

"Don't think about that now," I said, stroking his hair. "It's a long way off. But I'll tell you what. I'll make you a copy of my playlist before I go. So you can think of me when you listen to it. That way it'll be like I'm always here. Deal?"

He nodded and rested his head against my shoulder. We sat silently staring at the screen, until Noah eventually fell asleep. His small hands, smeared with green marker, gripped the edge of my shirt while his chest heaved slowly up and down, just like Nick's had the other night. I gathered him in my arms, the blanket still tangled around his body, and carried him to his bed. The gentle rhythm of his breathing against my body was soothing, steady and constant, like a heartbeat. It was the first time I had hugged anyone in a long time, and it felt nice.

The house was quiet. My father had gone back to the office or to the hotel to meet his mistress or wherever he went at night. There was no sign of my mother in the kitchen or in the greenhouse, which meant it was safe to assume she was asleep.

I hurried back to my room to change. I was about to put on a pair of jeans and a sweater when the black dress I had bought with Annie, the one with the plunging neckline, caught my eye. I thought about what she had said that day, how you don't buy a dress like this for an occasion, you create the occasion for the dress.

I had found my occasion. I slipped it on.

"Where you going, Ollie?"

Noah was standing in front of the hall bathroom, dressed in his Spiderman pajamas.

"Hey bud, what are you doing up?"

"You're awake, too." His cheeks were puffy from sleep.

"That's because I have to finish some homework." It was simpler than explaining what I was really about to do.

He squinted his eyes. "Why are you dressed up?"

"I'm just playing around in my closet." I had gotten used to lying to my parents, but I hated lying to Noah, especially since I knew he'd believe anything I said. "You should go back to bed."

I waited until he retreated back down the hall and disappeared into his room before sneaking down the stairs and out the front door.

CHAPTER 26

THE SCHOOL LOOKED different at night. With all the lights out, the concrete building practically disappeared against the dark sky. But it wasn't creepy or intimidating. If anything it was the other way around. Once all the students and teachers were gone, it was just a place like any other. Because it was the people who mattered. Not some pile of bricks or stones.

"So, what are we doing here?" Nick asked.

"You'll see."

I led him down the path around the school until we got to Mr. Owen's classroom. It was on the basement level, but the windows were accessible from the main path. There was always at least one left open to help dilute the funk of Mr. Owen's notorious body odor. He must have had some kind of condition to go on reeking like that year after year.

"Are we breaking in?" Nick asked, sidling up next to me. He was so close our arms touched, igniting a round of goose bumps.

The irony of breaking into the same place I always felt desperate to escape was not lost on me as I crouched down on my knees, slid my fingers through the narrow opening, and lifted. The window wouldn't budge, layers of paint jobs sealing it in place.

"Here, let me have a go." He kneeled beside me and wedged his hands beneath the splintered wood. Just the accidental swipe of his wrist against mine sent a tremor through my body. "On the count of three, okay?" I nodded. "One, two, three."

We leaned all our weight into the frame and hoisted. I was trying so hard I could feel veins and vessels straining under the effort. There was a slight budge, followed by another almost imperceptible shift. A few seconds later, the window came flying open.

With the resistance gone, we fell back onto the grass in a fit of laughter. We stayed like that for a minute, spread out like angels under the moon. Even though it had a couple more days to go, it looked full from that angle, like it might burst. I felt the same way.

The window was much higher than the classroom floor, so I slid through slowly until my feet hit the ground. Nick jumped down right behind me without hesitation, landing on top of a desk. The rancid stench was as strong as ever, like the walls were sweating out Mr. Owen's smell. I covered my nose and ran out into the hall.

"Wait up!" Nick called after me, jogging out into the dark corridor.

"Catch me." I darted around the corner. The sound of Nick's footsteps echoed behind me down the hall.

When I got to the darkroom, I leaned against the door and waited for Nick to find me, like a game of hide-and-seek.

"This the end of the road?" he asked, appearing a few seconds later.

My stomach fluttered. *Or the beginning*, I thought as I unlocked the door.

"Wait," Nick said as I reached for the light switch. He shut the door behind him, launching us into total blackness. "Stay like this for a second," he whispered, like he was sharing a secret. "I like the dark."

We stood inches apart. He was so close I could detect hints of licorice and fresh mint on his breath, feel the static between our clothes. When he finally hit the switch, illuminating the room, I almost forgot why we were here.

"You took these?" he asked. The finished prints dangled like flags from the clothesline where I had left them to dry.

I nodded as he examined each photo as if he were in a real gallery. He stopped when he got to the one of him lying under the tree. The one that was solarized.

"I may have taken a couple of you," I said, trying to read his expression, if he saw the same thing when he looked at his face as I did.

He grinned knowingly and continued down the line. "What happened to this one?" The background was blown out, as if it were a close-up of the sun. A swirling mass of black and white emerged where our heads should have been. Two abstract blobs melting into each other in the middle. No light had gotten in the room when I developed it, so I knew it hadn't been solarized like the other print.

"I don't know," I shrugged. "It just came out that way."

"It looks unfinished, like it needs more time to develop."

But I got the sense that he wasn't talking about the photo, that he was really talking about us. He draped his arm over my shoulder, just like the other night, and pulled me in closer. He felt so solid, so secure, like I really could melt into him. He reached his hand up into my hair, tickling the base of my skull. When his fingers found their way across the bumpy patch of my scar, he didn't flinch or pull away. And neither did I. It was the final part of myself I was ready to reveal.

"I'm so glad I met you," I whispered in his ear. "After my accident, I was so lost."

"Olive," he whispered back. "Don't. It's okay."

"I want to." The skin beneath his fingers tingled, like a current coming to life. Dr. Farmand had been wrong. My nerve endings weren't dead or permanently damaged. They just needed the right touch to bring the feeling back. "You make me feel safe. Safer than I've ever felt."

I reached up and caressed his cheek. It was much softer than I expected, even with his facial hair that was now approaching a full-on beard.

Nick released his hold on my neck and stepped back. He was gone, no longer with me, the electric current dead. "Olive . . ."

"You don't have to say anything."

"I don't think I can see you anymore." His voice was firm, leaving no room for interpretation.

"What?" I shook my head, trying to process what he just said. "But I don't understand . . ."

"Look, I never meant for you to take any of this seriously."

He suddenly seemed rigid, like a different person from the one captured in the eight-by-ten dangling in front of us.

"Then what *did* you mean?" My head started running through all the possibilities of what had gone wrong.

He bowed his head. "There are things you don't know."

"Like what? That you have a girlfriend?" I was shaking so much, my voice vibrated inside my head. I couldn't believe this was happening. Again.

"I never died. I didn't have a near-death experience. I was faking it."

I felt like I'd just been kicked, like the wind had been knocked out of me. It was the last thing I expected him to say, a factual omission I never imagined. I searched his face for some hint that this was all a bad joke. But it was unflinching, a mask with no remorse. A spark of anger flared up inside me as his words began to sink in.

"Then why were you at those meetings?" He kept staring at the floor. His silence only made me angrier. At him, at Annie. At the whole word. "Was this all just a big game for you? Trolling the meetings for vulnerable girls so you could take them back to your rotting mansion to seduce them? Because what kind of freak fakes a near-death experience?"

Nick whipped his head up. There was no sign of the softness or the hope or any of the other things I convinced myself that I saw when I looked at him. "I figured it was a good place to meet crazy chicks. And you know what? I was right."

The room started spinning, slowly at first, picking up speed until everything blurred together—the dangling prints, the trays, the chemicals, and Nick disappearing at the center of it all. My legs started moving mechanically, like they belonged to someone else. They carried me out the door and back down the unlit hall. It felt like I was drowning underwater, fighting to get to the surface, the world distorted and unstable around me.

I made it to the front entrance and crashed through, setting off the alarm. I sucked in the crisp air, each breath cutting into my lungs like a knife as the siren bellowed out around me. The pain ran so deep, the only way to stave it off was to keep moving, to keep putting one foot in front of the other.

The moon followed me no matter which way I went, like it was mocking me. I ran until my legs cramped and couldn't carry me any further, until I exhausted my body beyond the point of pain, until I couldn't feel anything and collapsed on the path leading up to our front door.

CHAPTER 27

"HERE YOU ARE."

I jerked my head around and squinted at the narrow-shouldered silhouette looming over me. It was Derek. I was huddled in a corner cubicle at the back of the library and must have fallen asleep.

"I've been looking for you," he said.

"Well, you found me." I sat up, pushing my hair off my face. I was sure I looked a mess, but I didn't care.

He pulled a chair over from the next cubicle. "Were you sick?"

I hadn't been to school in almost a week, not since the night I'd come here with Nick. It was the last time I'd heard from him, too. Unlike with Derek, I wasn't filled with some delusional hope that Nick would come back, that we could gloss over his lie. I was certain it was over and that I'd never see him again. My father had come home that night to find me out on the front steps. He carried me to my room and woke my mother, who got me undressed and into bed. She didn't ask me where I'd been, why I was so dressed up, or how I'd ended up on the doorstep in the middle of the night. Probably because she'd been too consumed with the fact that my father had just come home at two in the morning. I wondered if she'd smelled another woman's perfume on his jacket or spotted a lipstick stain on his collar. She didn't press me the next morning either, or object when I said I felt too sick to go to school. It was like I suddenly had this power over her that made her walk on eggshells around me. Or maybe it was that I was finally catching up on homework, and that was all that mattered. I'd been holed up in my room, tackling months of missed assignments. It was ironic how after the accident, doing homework reminded me too much of Derek. Now, it helped me forget Nick. One week later, I didn't feel sad or depressed or even angry anymore. I didn't feel anything at all.

"Are you stalking me or something?"

"Why, do you want me to be stalking you?" Derek laughed like I was flirting with him. I wasn't. I was just talking to him like a regular person, not someone I needed to impress. He tipped his chair back, balancing it on its two hind legs.

"Careful," I said, instinctively reaching over to stop him.

"Still looking out for me." He tipped it forward and leaned his arms on the table. "You always have."

Now he was the one who was flirting. A rush of heat rose to my cheeks. Why was I blushing? "I have a lot of work to do," I said, turning my head so he couldn't see my face.

"It's Senior Spring. Everyone knows grades don't matter anymore."

"I've missed a lot this year," I said, smoothing my hand over my notebook. I stopped short of telling him about my conditional acceptance to Georgetown. It no longer concerned him.

"What are you reading?"

I was still trying to get through *Mrs. Dalloway*. For some reason it was the one assignment I couldn't face. "It's for a term paper."

"If you'd taken econ with me like I suggested, I'd have given you all my notes and you wouldn't be stuck here."

"That doesn't exactly help me now."

"Yeah, but the Cliff's Notes will." Maybe he had a point. I was already caught up on all my other homework. All I cared about right now was passing so that I could at least be done with this place.

He picked up the book and started flipping through the pages. "Hey, was this your mom's?"

"Yeah, how'd you know?"

"Her handwriting. It's still the same." He pointed to one of the notes she'd written in the margins. It was funny how he and I could look at the same thing yet see something entirely different.

He edged his chair closer so his knee brushed up against mine, but I was still too numb to feel anything. "What are you doing for prom?"

I had forgotten that prom was only two weeks away. It used to be the day I looked forward to most, the very pinnacle of my high school fairytale, only now I had no intention of going. "Why?"

"Are you going with that guy?"

I pulled my leg away so we were no longer touching. I'd forgotten he'd seen me with Nick that one time. They were from two different worlds and I wanted to keep it that way, especially now that Nick's world no longer existed. "No."

His face brightened. "Well, I thought . . ." He stopped midsentence. Derek never hesitated or was at a loss for words. "I just thought if you weren't going with him, that maybe we could go together."

"What about Betsy?"

"It's over." He cleared his throat the way he did on the stand during a debate when he was about to make his closing argument. "She doesn't get me. Not like you do, Wollie. It's not too late to go back to the way things were. And we have Georgetown next year."

I heard him, but nothing sank in. Not the fact that it was over with Betsy, that he wanted me back, that he assumed I'd gotten into Georgetown, or that we'd spend the next four years there together, just like we planned in another lifetime.

My mind flooded with memories of Nick, still frames from the past few months: waltzing out into the middle of traffic, his banged-up car, the dead garden, his empty home. And the last time I saw him. Pieced together, they didn't tell the story I had imagined, about two lost souls bound together by one shared experience, one shared pain. In this version—reality—I was all alone.

"Okay," I finally said. "I'll go with you."

A hopeful smile blossomed on his face. "It's like you always said: we're meant to be."

I felt the slight twinge of my heart opening up just enough to let Derek back in. He had a point: here we were, a few months later, right where we left off. We could step back on the same path, like nothing had changed except for the date on the calendar. I knew better now than to try to fight it. All I had to do was accept that he finally wanted me back, that he was giving me the second chance I dreamed of, that this had been my fate all along. I wasn't going to let my anger over Nick take that away. Besides, Derek had already apologized. Now it was time for me to forgive him.

He walked me to my next class. Even though he said it was over with Betsy, I was relieved we didn't run into her in the halls. I knew how it felt, and no matter how mean she had been to me, I still didn't want to rub it in her face. I waited until Derek was gone before slipping back out into the hall. I made a beeline for the darkroom. There was still one thing holding me back and I needed to fix it.

"Whoa, slow down," Annie said as we collided at the door.

I ignored her and went straight for the clothesline. It was empty. "Where are they?"

"Where are what?" Annie said, setting her bag down as the second bell rang.

"My prints."

"I put them over there," she said, pointing to a neat stack on the counter.

I could see Nick's face staring back at me from the top of the pile. I ran over, picked it up, and began tearing it apart.

"Ol, don't . . ." Annie said, coming toward me.

She tried to pull the other prints away, but I boxed her out and quickly made my way through the rest of the pile, ripping each photo to pieces. When I got to the blurry one Nick had taken of us, I finally realized why it had come out like that. Because it was a picture of nothing, a picture that was trying to capture something that didn't exist.

"Not the negatives!" Annie gasped as I snapped the crisp film cleanly in half. I kept going until the pieces became too small to break apart. When I was done, I slumped to the floor.

"Will you please tell me what the hell is going on?" She dropped down to the ground next to me.

"Don't you have class?" I said, swiping my legs over the scattered remains, like they were used confetti.

"I don't care." She reached for my hand. "I'm worried about you."

"Don't be," I said, pulling it away. "I'm fine."

"No, you're not." Annie knew something had happened with Nick, but I refused to tell her the details. I would only share that it was over and I never wanted to hear his name again.

"Derek asked me to prom."

"Ha!" Annie scoffed. "I can't believe the nerve of that—"

"I said yes." I picked at the tiny, sharp shards of film that were stuck to my palm. They looked like amber splinters. "We're probably getting back together."

"Ol, no matter what happened with Nick . . ."

"This has nothing to do with Nick. You don't know what it's like to have your life fall apart. This is my chance to get it back."

"Derek isn't good enough for you. You're making a big mistake."

"Well, good thing it's none of your business."

"Oh I get it, it's only my business when you need a ride or a scapegoat."

"I wish you'd stop telling me what to do, pressuring me to be somebody I'm not. I should never have listened to you to be bold."

"So this is all *my* fault? I'd like to know when you'll start taking responsibility for your own life, including the crash, because we both know it didn't happen because you were late."

"What do you even know about relationships anyway?" I flared. She had no right to question my judgment, to challenge me about that night. Once I started, I couldn't stop. The simmering rage I didn't realize had been building up inside flowed out of me like lava. "Skyping with someone a million miles away doesn't count. Not that you'd have the guts to call Jessica your girlfriend even if she lived next door. You pretend you're different, but you're just as fake as everyone else."

I took a deep breath and felt a knot unravel in my chest. But as I saw the look of devastation spread across Annie's face, another one began to form. I wondered if Nick felt the same way after he told me the truth, after he detonated the connection between us.

"I figured you'd change after everything you've been through." Annie's voice was low and deep. She sounded like a different person, a stranger. She kneeled down and started picking up the broken pieces. "Now I know there's no cure for selfishness because you're worse than you were before, if that's even possible."

The knot in my ribcage tightened and began to throb. I got down on my knees to help her, when Annie briskly stood up to leave.

"Leave your key on the counter when you're done." She gathered her things and paused at the door. "There's no reason for you to be in here anymore."

CHAPTER 28

"HOLD STILL AND keep your eyes closed." My mother was inches from my face, clamping the curler down on my eyelashes. I had always sworn I would never allow her to use it on me, but like most things, I'd learned it was easier not to resist.

Now that I was getting my grades up and hadn't pulled any more rebellious stunts, there had been a sort of détente between us. And of course, it didn't hurt that things were back on track with Derek.

"Don't get too carried away, Mom. I'm just going to the gym." If it were up to me, I'd be going in jeans instead of the Laura Ashley floral gown my mom had come home with when she noticed I still had "nothing to wear." I had taken the black dress and all the new clothes I'd gotten with Annie and buried them at the back of my closet. They reminded me too much of Nick, and of Annie, and of the person I was pretending to be.

"It's *not* the gym tonight. It's Atlantis!" That was this year's theme. The prom committee had apparently ordered ice sculptures in the shape of sea animals and all sorts of other ridiculous decorations to try to cover up the fact that it was still the stinky gym where basketball was played. I could think of a million better uses for that money, and a part of me even felt guilty for lending my support to the stupid tradition by showing up. "I'll never forget dancing with your father at our prom. I still have my corsage, you know."

"Well, it was different back then." I wondered if my father was already dreaming of his escape when he danced with her that night. If he was just going through the motions, like I was. But I was doing this for Derek, because the tradition suddenly seemed to be very important to him. He was the one who'd arranged everything for tonight, like ordering the limo and the corsages, figuring out what time we needed to be there and which after-parties we'd hit. He'd handled all the details I used to imagine I'd be in charge of. It was like there'd been this role reversal between us, like he was doing all he could to make up for lost time.

"You just wait and see," she said. "You're going to look so beautiful. Derek won't know what hit him when I'm through with you."

Derek would be ringing the bell soon, waiting at the door in his rented tux while the stretch limo idled outside. I tried to tell him that a cab would be good enough, but he insisted, saying he only wanted the best for me. My mother would be beaming, poised with her camera, and my father ready to pop a bottle of champagne while they waited for my grand entrance. I could see the whole night unfold before it even started, like a scene in one of the teen soaps I used to watch.

"Open your eyes." My mother took a few steps back to assess my face before coming at me with the blush brush. "And that about does it. Take a look!"

I went over to the full-length mirror on the back of my parents' bathroom door and stared at my reflection. With the help of about a hundred bobby pins, she was able to pull my hair back into a bun. It almost looked like I had never cut it. But even so, I hardly recognized myself in that dress, with my red lips, pink cheeks, and glittery eyes. It wasn't just the clothes and makeup that seemed foreign. It was deeper than that, like I had left my body and another eighteen-year-old girl had taken over, telling me when to sit or stand, when to speak or smile.

"Oh no, it's starting to drizzle," my mother gasped, peering out the window as the sky darkened. "Tonight of all nights."

"It doesn't matter," I said, trying to appease her, like it was *her* prom that was about to be ruined. "We're going to be inside anyway."

"But the pictures!" She threw her hands up in the air in defeat. "I wanted to get some of you two in the garden."

Now that Derek was back in our lives, she delighted in throwing around that term, *you two*. It had only been two weeks, but in just a couple of days, we had slipped back into our old routines: sitting together at lunch (where my place had been reinstated), hanging out after school, watching movies on Friday night. We still didn't hold hands in the hallways, but now it was because of my terms. I still wasn't ready to kiss him, even in private.

Neither of us mentioned the accident. It was like I had stepped into an alternate universe, where we never broke up and I didn't crash his car, where Nick didn't exist, and where my heart never got broken. Everything looked exactly the way it had always been. It reminded me of a movie my father showed me once, *The Truman Show*, where Truman's whole world turns out to be fake, where everyone's in on the secret except for Truman himself. But in my case, it was the other way around. I was the only one in on the joke, the only one who could see that everything in my world was superficial, and that just beneath the surface, it was a whole different story.

The rain started coming down harder now. The louder it got, the more it calmed me, its pitter-patter replacing the rhythm of my own heart.

"He's early!" My mother squealed as the doorbell rang. "You stay here, I'll get it."

She giggled and ran downstairs. I stood in the middle of the room, staring at the reflection of the strange girl in the mirror, the girl everyone expected me to be.

The front door creaked open. Over the sound of the rain, I detected a slight strain in my mother's voice, even though I couldn't make out what she was saying. The door closed again, and I heard her footsteps shuffling back upstairs.

She came back in, her brow furrowed.

"What's wrong?" I asked through the mirror's reflection.

"It's not Derek. It's that boy from the club. From that day—"

"What?" I whipped my head around.

"He insisted on speaking with you. He has an English accent. I thought you said he was from school."

My heart started to quiver, sending quick, sharp jabs into my chest. She searched my face for guidance but I couldn't move or speak. "I'm going to send him away."

"No, wait," I spat, finding my words. "I'll do it."

Without thinking, I moved past her into the hall, practically tripping over my dress. I gathered it up off the floor and ran the rest of the way. I hesitated when I got to the door. Did I really want to do this? Leaning into the black wood, I pressed my right eye against the peephole and peered through.

It was really him.

Suddenly lightheaded, I reached for the doorknob to steady myself and opened the door. Nick was standing under the awning, sopping wet like he'd been out in the rain for hours. It was as if everything was happening in slow motion, as if I wasn't in control of my own limbs.

"Olive." His voice caught, like he could barely utter my name.

The rain blew in, drops spraying across my dress. Despite the breeze, my cheeks burned and my skin pricked with heat. "What are you doing here?"

"I had to see you."

His shirt and jeans were soaked through. The way his wet hair stuck to his forehead exposed his face completely, revealing a scar above his left eyebrow. It looked pink and tender, as if it had never fully healed.

"What else is there to say?"

"There's something . . ." His voice cracked as three beads

of water rolled down his cheek. Were they raindrops or tears? "Can we talk?

If I said yes, I knew I wouldn't be inviting just Nick in, but all the painful feelings I'd pushed down and cemented over. But as I looked into his gray eyes, I knew it was already too late.

"Come inside," I said, opening the door wider.

CHAPTER 29

MY MOTHER HOVERED nervously in the front hall. "You better finish getting ready," she said, even though we both knew I was done. Perfectly primped and packaged.

"This won't take long." I led Nick upstairs to my room. It was the only place where we'd have any privacy.

I had been so completely convinced that I would never see him again, but here he was, walking into my room, just as I was about to go to prom with Derek.

"You can sit here," I said, gesturing toward the armchair.

"I prefer to stand, if that's okay," he said, shuffling on his feet. It was the first time he ever seemed nervous, out of his element.

"I don't have much time," I said, glancing at the clock on my bedside table. Derek would be here any minute. "It's prom."

He probably thought the whole idea of prom was ridiculous compared to all the balls and fancy parties he was used to, but I didn't care. I didn't care what he thought of my room, or the goofy family pictures lining the hall, the size of our house, or even my mother. I had nothing left to hide.

A single raindrop clung to a clump of wet bangs and dangled precariously above his nose. It looked like it was suspended in midair. "I'm sorry," he croaked.

He had the same look on his face that he'd had the day he apologized in the pond, underwater. Only this time, I could hear him clearly. This time, I knew what was wrapped up in that expression. It wasn't love. It was guilt.

"I'm so sorry," he repeated, bowing his head. "About what I said to you in the darkroom. It wasn't fair. I wasn't at the meetings looking for unstable girls. That's not how I think of you. Far from it."

Had he come all this way just to say that? It was a little too late. And it still didn't change the most important thing of all. "You lied to me."

"I know. It's the second-worst thing I've ever done."

My back stiffened. "Is that supposed to make me feel better?"

"I came to tell you about my accident. I did have one. That part was true." He walked over to the window and tugged on the braided rope that dangled next to the curtains.

"It doesn't matter anymore." I clenched my hands into balled fists. I couldn't tell what I was feeling, fear or anger or both. "I don't want to know."

"Please, Olive. If you never want to see me again, I promise I'll leave you alone forever. Just hear me out."

He was wearing the white T-shirt he had on that day at his house. Even though all his shirts were identical, I knew it was the same one because it still held the faint trace of my blood.

"Fine." I sat on the edge of my bed. My legs felt too weak to stand. "You have five minutes."

He cleared his throat and began. "I came back to Los Angeles last June, right after graduation. It was the first time the whole family was home together in almost two years. Me, my parents, and . . ." The color drained from his face. "And Theo. My older brother."

His brother? His voice wavered and my mind flashed to the frame on his desk. "The boy in the picture," I said. "That was Theo."

He nodded and looked down at the floor, unable to meet my gaze. "I was supposed to go travel with friends for the summer, but I came back so I could spend the summer with him. We hardly ever saw each other anymore, not since he graduated Eton and joined the golf tour. It was his passion and it took him all over the world. But he'd just accepted a job as the pro at a country club and was going to be home for the first time in ages."

I knew exactly which club he meant. Our eyes met as the pieces slowly started to take shape. It reminded me of the way images gradually formed out of nowhere in the photo developing trays. "You can stop," I said, my voice softer now.

But he didn't.

"My father had just bought a Learjet, his latest toy that sat unused in the hangar, so I decided to get my pilot's license. But by the third lesson, I became impatient. Screw the license, I thought. Why did I need a piece of paper to fly my own plane? I was convinced I already knew how."

My stomach tightened into knots as I listened, afraid of where he was going, unsure I wanted to know. I focused on the silk fringe of the curtain brushing up against his fingers as he continued.

"Then, on the morning of June twenty-ninth, I invited Theo out for a flight before work. It was overcast with the type of fog that normally burns off quickly, a typical June gloom morning. But when we got to the airport, the fog was even worse. Theo suggested we wait for a clearer day so we'd have better views. He said we had the whole summer ahead of us. But I insisted. We were already there and it'd be a waste to turn back. 'We'll fly above the clouds,' I told him. 'Just a quick spin.' I was so desperate to impress him. I wanted him to be proud of me in the way that my father never was, the way he was only proud of Theo."

Nick pulled down on the string, drawing open the curtains. It was already so dark from the rain, his reflection bounced off the wet glass. "When we were headed down the runway, I looked up at the wall of fog and hesitated for a second, thinking that maybe we should turn back. But I was too proud to admit I'd made a mistake, that Theo was right."

Nick stopped and turned around, shifting his weight from one foot to the other, his eyes fixed on some point on the carpet.

"Takeoff was smooth, and the plane soared up into the clouds. Within a few minutes we were cruising at fifteen thousand feet. It was so quiet and magical up there, like the whole world was on pause. I looked over at Theo and I remember thinking that I'd never felt so at peace before. That *this* was what life was all about. That very moment. That's when everything changed. The wind suddenly picked up, catapulting us back down into the clouds. I tried to regain control of the plane, but it was like an invisible force had taken over and was dragging us down. No matter what I did, no matter how hard I tried to pull the nose back up, nothing worked. Wisps of cloud and rain started whipping past us so fast it felt like the windows were going to crack. The next thing I knew the ground was coming at me at an unstoppable speed. Then there was the piercing crash of metal and glass and . . . and . . ."

When he tried to speak, small gasps came out instead of words.

"Nick," I said, my own voice scratchy.

"The last thing I heard was Theo calling my name," he said, his voice now a hollow whisper. "The doctors said it was a miracle I survived. But going through every day for the rest of my life knowing that I killed my brother, that's not a miracle. It's torture."

I wanted to go over and reach out, to touch him, but something was still holding me back. "Is that why you went to the meetings?"

He nodded. "I spent the first few months after he died basically catatonic. It became so unbearable that I became obsessed with trying to find answers, something that could make sense of the mess I'd made. That's when I found out about the Near-Death Society through a random Google search about the afterlife. I had this crazy delusion that someone who'd been to the other side could reassure me that Theo was in a better place. But the more I went, the more I was convinced there is no other side. It's all hell."

I swallowed hard, trying to take it all in. "Why didn't you tell me any of this before?"

"After he died, I couldn't function or even have a normal conversation. Day and night, all I could think about was Theo. But when I met you, something shifted and I felt an old part of myself start to come out. I was racked with guilt about it because I didn't think I deserved another minute of happiness again. I knew that even telling you would be a form of relief, so I couldn't bring myself to do it."

My limbs pricked and felt heavy, like they were waking from a long sleep, stirring feelings that had been put to rest. Even though Nick didn't technically die, he'd felt more dead on the inside than I ever had. "Is that why your parents are gone?"

He nodded, fiddling with the strap on his watch. That's when I realized why it was frozen on the number nine, why he never took it off. It was the time of Theo's death.

"They couldn't stand being here anymore. Everything reminded them of Theo—the stables, the pond, the maze where we grew up playing hide-and-seek. And especially me. They couldn't stand the sight of me anymore. Theo was always my father's favorite, his 'young grasshopper.' He never said it, but he didn't have to. My dad did everything with Theo—ride horses, golf, hunt. All the things he never did with me."

My heart felt like it was breaking all over again. But not because of my pain, because of Nick's. I stepped closer so that I was standing next to him now.

"Aunt Bea came to pack up Theo's things. That box of stuff she was carrying that day on the stairs, that was for Samantha."

He was talking faster now, like he wanted to make sure he got it all out. "That's something else I couldn't explain. Samantha was never my girlfriend and never would be because she was Theo's. He was going to propose at the end of the summer. She was there that night to pick up the box Aunt Bea put together for her. It was the first time I'd seen or spoken to Samantha in months. Since his funeral."

The final pieces were starting to emerge and connect. Only I was still standing too close to see the completed puzzle. "What changed?" I kept my eyes trained on the ground, on the space between his feet. His red Converse looked black from all the mud and rain. "Why now?"

"It was much more painful without you in my life. Even though the pain is what I deserved, you didn't. So when I realized that depriving myself was also hurting you, I couldn't bear it, and I had to try to make things right."

There was a knock at the door and my mother poked her head in.

"Derek's here." Her voice was pointed and firm. Our time was up. She opened the door wider, shedding light from the hall into my darkened room.

I kept my gaze fixed on the same point on the carpet between Nick's feet, completely paralyzed. Pressure started to build up behind my eyes, like a storm brewing in my head.

"Thank you for listening," Nick said. "That's all I wanted. I'll see myself out."

After he left, the vague outline of his stance remained indented in the rug where he'd been standing. His confession swirled around me, the words impenetrable as if they were spoken in a foreign language I didn't speak.

"Is everything all right?" My mother came up and tucked a loose hair behind my ear. "You know you don't have to go tonight. You can always stay home with us."

"I can't," I said, smoothing out the wrinkles on my dress. This was my second chance, and it had nothing to do with Nick. "Derek's waiting for me."

When I got to the foyer, Nick was just making his way out. Derek looked on, his fist balled around the pink carnations that made up my corsage. In his rented black tux with the matching carnation boutonniere, he looked much younger than Nick, like he was playing the part of a grown-up for the night.

Nick paused before he closed the door, letting in a gust of rain. With his hand still gripping the doorknob, he turned back to face me.

"There's one last thing you should know. When we were on the dock that day, right before I pulled you into the pond, you were right. I was going to say something. I was going to tell you how beautiful you are."

Something fluttered beneath my scar, like a small goldfish was trapped behind it, wriggling madly to be free. It felt like my whole head was spinning out of control.

"You're the most beautiful person I've ever met. I just thought you should know that," he said, before shutting the door behind him.

CHAPTER 30

"WHAT THE HELL was he doing here?" Derek demanded once we were in the limo. It was decorated like a disco inside, with multi-colored flashing bulbs lining the sides and ceiling.

I had managed to avoid the topic while my mother took pictures and my father handed out the champagne, like we were headed to our wedding, not our Atlantis-themed prom.

"I didn't know he was coming." I felt a headache creeping in with every blink of the lights. I cracked open the window to let in some air. "I haven't spoken to him in weeks."

"What was all that bullshit about you being beautiful?" His nostrils flared as he spoke, like an angry bull's. "Did you sleep with that guy?"

"No!" The words stung, like it was hardly believable that someone would find me beautiful without getting something in exchange. Derek had never complimented me before. Not even tonight, when it was basically an obligation. "I'm here," I said, more to convince myself than him. "I chose you."

"I don't want you to even talk to that guy," he barked.

"You don't see me hanging around with Betsy anymore, do you?"

In all the time I'd fantasized about being Derek's girlfriend again, I'd forgotten about this, how he sometimes spoke to me like I was his bratty little sister. I sank deeper into my seat, digging my hands into the sticky leather cushion, while Derek poured himself a glass of vodka from the mirrored mini bar.

"No thanks," I said as he started to pour a second one.

"Great," he scoffed. "You're not going to be any fun tonight, are you?"

He downed his drink and my half-filled glass before refilling them both immediately. He was already well on his way to being drunk. I had only seen him wasted once before, when the debate team went to drown their sorrows after losing a match and I had to pick him up. He didn't even thank me for getting dressed at midnight and driving all the way to get him. He just made fun of the minivan and my pink slippers with the pig face on the toes, like the team's failure had been my fault. Why were all these bad memories suddenly coming back to me now?

"Can you close that thing?" he yelled to the driver.

The tinted glass divider lowered, shutting us in. He slid in closer across the seat, squeezing me in against the door. He groped around the layers of material of my dress until his hand found my thigh buried underneath. He gripped hard. I used to like it when he touched me that way, with a firm, rough hand, like he never wanted to let go. But now it made me feel like I was suffocating, like he thought I *belonged* to him.

I opened the window more, letting in a stream of big, fat

raindrops. I couldn't help but think of Nick, dripping wet. Where had he gone? Were these same drops falling on him right now? The way they felt, landing on my cheeks in splats, made my stomach coil into knots. It wasn't just Nick. I had felt this way before—the rain settling into a mist over my face, the pain in my gut, the uncertainty—like a memory from another life. That's when I remembered the last time it had rained this way: the night of the accident.

"I booked a room at the Sheraton for later," Derek announced as we pulled into the school driveway behind a line of other rented limos. "And look what I brought for the occasion." He flashed open his jacket. A small, square, florescent green packet peeked out from the inside pocket. It was a condom, just like the ones we had bought together at the Vista Valley Mart all those months ago. "I figured we can, you know, pick up where we left off."

My stomach heaved and swelled like there was a tidal wave trapped inside me. "Okay," I said weakly.

The driver came around to my side first and opened the door, holding out a black umbrella. I slid out from under Derek's hold but could still feel the spot where he had been gripping my leg, like it had been permanently marked by his fingertips.

I paused on the walkway. The rain was pelting down in sheets, blowing onto my hair and dress. A giggling group of dressed-up couples spilled out of their limo and splashed past me, racing for dry cover. Derek ran with them, making a beeline for the front entrance. He didn't turn around or even notice I hadn't moved until he reached the doors.

"What are you doing?" he called out as the wind battered a bouquet of balloons behind him. A silver one broke free from the bunch. I followed its path in the sky as it flew higher and higher above Derek, above the building, up into the source of the storm, until I couldn't see it anymore. Suddenly I wasn't standing outside the school, but in front of his house that night, the rain coming down on me just like this. "Olive, come on! You'll get soaked."

As his voice reached me, I shook off the feeling, reminding myself where I was. I ran up the walkway to meet him.

The whole building felt like it was shaking from the thumping bass. We headed in the direction of the sound, the rows of lockers on either side of us plastered with the same nautical-themed streamers and balloons covering the front entrance.

"We're going here first," Derek said as we approached the Pioneer. It had been so long since I'd staked out the door, waiting for Derek to emerge, pretending I just happened to be walking by whenever he finally did. "We stashed a keg in here this morning."

The pre-party was already packed. Hip-hop streamed from the iPod docking station, drowning out the Katy Perry song blaring from the gym. It was hot and humid inside, the windows completely fogged over from the rain. I looked around, taking in my surroundings. All these years, I'd built the Pioneer up in my head to be this amazing, secret hideout. But it was just like every other classroom in the building, with the same drop-panel ceilings, the same fluorescent lights, and the same dry-erase board up at the front. Other than the fact that you needed a key to get in, there was nothing special about it.

"Bro!" Jed, one of Derek's teammates, greeted him with a high five. Even though Derek had his arm around me, Jed acted like I wasn't there. "Now we can really get this party started. This one's for you!"

Jed downed his beer in celebration and then immediately started pounding the one in his other hand. A small crowd cheered him on. A group of girls nearby excitedly admired one another's outfits. A couple was sloppily making out in the middle of the room. And here I was, with Derek, a part of it again. This had been exactly what I wanted. Only now that it was happening, why did I feel like I was suffocating?

Derek dropped his arm from my shoulder. "If you're just going to mope all night, tell me now."

"No," I said, dredging up the biggest smile I could muster. I was sure I looked just like my mother. "I'm happy to be here."

"I'm going to get some beer."

He pushed his way through the thickening crowd toward the keg, greeting his teammates with "bro-hugs" along the way, like they were football players. I moved off to the side and watched him. All this time I'd been so convinced that getting back together would reinstate my identity, but I never stopped to question what that identity even was. Because the more I thought about it, Jed's behavior was no different from how it used to be before the accident. He never talked to me or asked me questions about my life. None of Derek's friends ever had. I was just the girl on the side, the one who watched from the stands during debates and sat quietly during lunch, listening to them laugh at their inside jokes. It suddenly dawned on me why Derek had wanted me to dress up as a cheerleader for Halloween. It wasn't so he could live out some private fantasy. It was so I could look like what I already was: his personal cheerleader. In the end, it was probably why he chose me over Betsy. He didn't have to worry about sharing me with an entire team. I only cheered for him.

My eyes aimlessly scanned the crowd until they rested on a head of long, blond hair. I knew who it belonged to before she even turned around. Betsy Brill. What was she doing here?

She intercepted Derek as he made his way back, juggling two yellow plastic cups overflowing with beer. Leaning in, she whispered something in his ear. My body froze as her dress slipped off her shoulder, revealing her bra underneath. It wasn't just any bra. It was red, with a delicate, white lace trim. Tiny pink heart-shaped polka dots covered the bust. Even though the hearts weren't visible from where I was standing, I knew they were there because it wasn't the first time I'd seen them.

My lungs suddenly felt like they were shrinking, fighting for small gasps of air. Everything grew hazy, the room off-kilter, like I was the one who'd been drinking. I looked down at my dress, still streaked with rain. It felt like I was standing outside looking in through the steamy windows.

And that's when the truth came barreling toward me, forcing me to confront everything I didn't want to think about or remember. One by one, each detail came into sharp focus, like I was reliving the whole experience all over again. It felt so real and vivid, like I'd been transported back in time to that night, and I was no longer standing in the Pioneer, but in Derek's bedroom. Naked.

I'd begged him to let me keep some of my clothes on, but he said he wanted to see all of me when it happened. He told me to trust him. And I did. I always did. The bed squeaked as he lay down on top of me. Using his hand, he guided his way in. I stifled a scream and bit down on the inside of my cheek. Pulling down on the ends of my hair, Derek thrust his body into mine over and over until he rolled off with a grunt. And just like that it was over. I was no longer a virgin.

When I'd reached down to retrieve my shirt from the floor, it snagged on something hidden under the bed. A red bra with heart-shaped polka dots and a white lace trim around the edges.

The song suddenly blasted in my head. The lyrics jumped on top of each other, out of order, like a traffic pileup. There was an added urgency to his voice, but I couldn't tell if it was meant as a sign or a warning. The melody crescendoed until it seemed like it had nowhere left to go, like it was dangling on the precipice of a deep canyon. One more step and it would drop, free-falling into the abyss. The sound and scope were so big it felt like the melody could no longer fit in my head, a prisoner banging his fist against the contours of my skull.

I'd become so convinced the song was trying to tell me something, but I was beginning to realize that maybe I was going about it all wrong, that it was up to me to decipher its meaning, to decide what to do next.

A nudge on my arm brought me back, the blinding fluorescent lights reminding me where I was. "There's only beer," Derek said, handing me a cup.

I reflexively stepped away, his breath already sour and stale from drinking. Betsy's eyes met mine from across the room. A sly grin spread across her face as she readjusted her dress, hiding the lacy strap. And that's when I knew: she had wanted me to see it.

"It was hers," I muttered under my breath. "It was Betsy's."

I had long suspected the bra belonged to her, but I was beginning to discover the true power of denial. Uncovering the truth stirred something so deep within it was like excavating a corpse, that part of me I wanted to keep hidden even from myself.

Because the alternative was too shameful.

"Relax," he said, crumpling his empty cup. "She's here with someone else."

The haze around me began to clear. It wasn't just about Betsy. It was the things Derek did and said, the way he looked at me. The way he made me feel when I was with him: more alone than I felt when I was by myself. None of it reflected the person I wanted to be. The person I was starting to become, until we got back together.

"I need to get out of here."

"Wait." Derek reached out to stop me but caught hold of the corsage on my wrist instead. Pink and white petals fell to the ground.

"Hey, watch it!" Jed called out as I bumped his elbow on my way out, jostling his cup. Beer sloshed all over his shirt, some splattering on my dress, but I didn't stop. I made it to the door ahead of Derek and sprinted back down the hall, my legs pumping so fast that the rest of my body could barely keep up. I stopped by a bank of lockers and leaned against them, gasping for air. Derek came bounding around the corner, practically tripping over me.

"What the hell has gotten into you?" he said, wiping his moist brow with the back of his sleeve. "If this is about Betsy, I told you it's over."

I stood to face him. My mind was no longer fuzzy. It reminded me of what happened when the aperture on the camera was wide open: lots of light came through. And that's what it felt like now. The aperture on my life was opening, and for the first time, I could see Derek for who he really was.

My voice came out strong and clear.

"It's about everything," I said. "That night, you made me feel like I was the one who'd done something wrong, that I was the reason you cheated. That I even deserved it." As it started to come out, I realized that I'd been directing my feelings of betrayal and mistrust at the wrong person. "You disappeared when I needed you most. What's worse is you didn't defend me. You let everyone believe I'd done it on purpose."

"Well, didn't you?" he said, his face all blotchy and red. "Nobody forced you to take my car. You were completely out of control."

I started to back away as I thought about the rest of that night. How he said I'd made him wait too long, that love wasn't always enough. I had felt like I was choking and that the only way to breathe again was to run away, to get as far away from him as possible. It was exactly how I felt again right now. But instead of leaving and letting him have the last word, I turned around one last time.

"You know, I actually feel sorry for you. You're the kind of coward who will never be able to think for himself. You'll always have to hide behind lies and other people's ideas to feel like a real person. But, believe me, the truth will always find you." I gathered my dress in my hand. "And since I didn't have the guts to do it the first time around, let me be perfectly clear. I'm breaking up with you."

I ran down the hall, away from the thumping bass, the balloons, and Derek. This time, I knew he wasn't going to follow. And I didn't want him to.

I had almost reached the door when I ran right into Annie coming out of the girls' bathroom, knocking her camera bag off her shoulder. I scrambled to catch it but it was too late. It fell to the ground with a dull thud.

"Oh shit," I said, kneeling down to get it. "I hope I didn't break it."

We had passed each other in the halls many times since our fight in the darkroom, but this was the first time we'd actually spoken. It was also the first time I realized just how much I'd missed her.

"It's fine." She slung the bag back over her shoulder. "There's a reason there's so much padding," she said, tapping the thick outer case.

"I'm really sorry, Annie."

"I know." She played with the zipper on the camera bag.

"I didn't mean those things. I was totally out of line. I was just angry and confused."

Annie dropped the rest of her bags and we both sat down on the floor. "But you were right. There I was telling you how to live your life when I wasn't even being honest about my own. I was too afraid to accept who I really am."

I pulled my knees into my chest and leaned against the lockers. The metal felt cold against my exposed back. "Sometimes that's the hardest part."

"Well, because of you I finally did it. Jessica is now officially my girlfriend and she's moving back to L.A. in the fall. I even came out to my parents, not that they were surprised."

We both laughed. "That's amazing, Annie! I'm seriously so proud of you."

She nodded toward the gym. "Aren't you supposed to be in there being crowned prom king and queen?"

I squeezed my eyes, trying to blink back a tear. "It's over. For good this time."

Annie nudged her shoulder into mine. That was all it took. The dam broke and months of pent-up tears came pouring out of me. Every time I tried to say something, another swell took over. It was the kind of full-body, chest-heaving crying where you have no choice but to surrender.

"I feel so humiliated," I finally said between sobs.

"You have no reason to be." She reached for my hand. "I was way too hard on you."

"But there's something you don't know." I swept my tongue across the inside of my cheek where I had bitten it so many times over the last few months. It was finally starting to heal. I sat up straighter, swallowed hard, and told Annie everything about that night. About finding Betsy's bra in Derek's room and his reaction. And finally, about losing my virginity to him right before. She held my hand and listened. My throat burned when I was done. "You must think I'm an even bigger idiot for taking him back after all that."

"I don't," she said, squeezing my hand. "Now I understand why."

Then I told her about Nick showing up sopping wet at my door, how even after everything he confided about Theo, I still chose Derek. "But when I saw him talking to Betsy tonight," I explained, "something snapped. It wasn't jealousy. I just felt like I was going to suffocate if I stayed a minute longer. So here I am now. A total mess." I wiped my face into my dress. "I guess it's what I deserve for not learning from my mistakes."

"But you have learned. You stood up for yourself and you didn't stick around when it didn't feel right. Don't you see, Ol? You have changed." She let out a laugh. "I just wish I could have seen the look on Derek's face when you ditched his sorry ass in his rented tux."

I smiled. "You've got to admit it's a little extreme that I had to die to learn what a jerk he was."

"I don't know," Annie said. "I think you were starting to change a long time ago. I mean, you were the one who walked out that night, right? If you didn't have the accident, you probably would have realized it a lot sooner. But then, you would never have met Nick."

"I turned him away when he needed me most," I said as reality sank in.

With a glint in her eye she released my hand. "Get up. You're coming with me."

I followed her into the bathroom, where she slipped out of her purple silk dress.

"What the hell are you doing?" I asked, laughing.

"You're right. You're a mess and you can't go see Nick in whatever that is." She dismissively pointed at my dress. "So hurry up and take it off before I freeze to death," she said, standing half-naked in the middle of the sticky linoleum floor. "We're switching."

CHAPTER 31

I WAS BACK on the front walkway, only now I was wearing Annie's dress. Even though she was about three sizes smaller than me, it somehow fit, the folds of the purple silk draping around my body like it was made for me. With my hair down and the layers of caked makeup washed off my face, I felt much better. I felt like myself again.

With the rain still pelting down, I hurried toward the driveway where our driver said he'd be waiting for us. I scanned the row of identical black stretch limos when a pair of headlights flashed twice.

The driver stepped out and came up the path with his umbrella. This time I didn't refuse. I was grateful for the dry cover as he escorted me back to the car.

I got in and settled into the same spot in the back. A pink petal from my corsage was stuck to the leather cushion.

"Over already?" the driver asked, sliding down the divider.

"Something like that." I picked up the petal and caressed it between my fingers.

"Are we waiting for anyone else?"

I slid forward on the seat, anxious to get going. "No."

"Then where to?" he asked, peering at me through the rearview mirror.

"I don't know the address," I said, opening the window a crack. "But if you take me to Bel Air I can show you how to get there."

He nodded, made a U-turn, and started heading toward the freeway. The limousine drove up the slick on-ramp, spilling us out onto the 101. All five lanes were practically empty.

"It sprinkles a little and everyone acts like a hurricane's coming," the driver chuckled, his Southern accent emerging. "I'm from New Orleans, where practically every house comes with a row boat. But look at it here. A ghost town. Just means we'll get there faster."

Even though it was coming down harder now, I lowered the window. I liked the way the wind felt, whipping my hair back so my face could absorb the raindrops. "It can't be fast enough."

"In a hurry, huh?" he said, nodding knowingly. "What's his name?"

Startled, I glanced toward the front and met his eyes in the mirror. "Is it that obvious?"

"In my line of work, you learn a thing or two about the heart."

"His name is Nick." Just saying it gave me butterflies.

He glanced back at me again and studied my face. "You made the right call leaving the dance."

I released the petal out the window and watched it get carried away in the wind. "I know I did."

The city lights glittered in the distance. I looked up at the hills to my right, trying to get my bearings. "It's the exit after this one."

Even though I couldn't name the streets, the route was embedded in my memory. I was more certain of every turn the closer we got.

"Make a right at the light up ahead, next to the gas station." I remembered because it was the last sign of civilization before Nick's. The rest of the way was entirely secluded. "When you get to the top of the hill, veer left and take the road as far as it'll go."

"Got it, doll."

I leaned back and closed my eyes. Taking a deep breath, it finally hit me. Annie was right. I had changed. For the first time, I was making my own decision. I was trusting myself.

"Is this where you want to be?"

The car idled at the end of the road and my heart soared. The tall, black, wrought iron gates were wide open, as if Nick was expecting me.

"It is," I said, reaching my arm out the window. The rain had stopped and an unexpectedly warm breeze blew in. "I'm going to walk the rest of the way."

He put the car in park. "Should I wait?"

I gazed up at the full moon, a perfect circle. "No."

He chuckled. "I didn't think so."

I watched the car's red lights retreat down the street until they disappeared, then started down the path. The wall of trees that stretched out on either side of the private road seemed taller and more densely packed up close and on foot. Not even moonlight penetrated the thick foliage. The wind picked up, shaking free pools of rainwater that had collected on the leaves. I lifted my face up toward the sky and opened my mouth, letting the cool, swollen drops land on my outstretched tongue.

I began to run toward the house, kicking up sticks and pebbles along the way. A branch whipped past, scratching my cheek, but I didn't care. The burn even felt good, a reminder that I *could* feel again. And I realized why: my heart was no longer broken.

The trees began to thin out when I passed the empty stables. Off in the distance, I spotted Nick's car parked in the same spot by the water fountain. I ran even faster now, past the meadow of overgrown weeds and grass. Gravel crunched underneath my feet as I raced up the driveway. Not even the sharp pebbles biting through the thin soles of my soaked shoes could stop me.

The house was dark and silent. When I reached the front door, I took a deep breath and rang the bell.

No answer.

I rang again.

Silence.

I banged the brass knocker against the weather-beaten red door. I slammed it again and again, so hard I thought the old wood might crack.

Where was he?

Finally, the lanterns on either side of the door lit up, bathing me in their soft glow. I looked down at my mud-splattered dress. I couldn't help but smile. Now I was the one showing up on Nick's doorstep like a wet puppy.

But my smile began to fade when Aunt Bea appeared at the door in her robe.

"Olive," she said, taking in my disheveled appearance. "Get yourself inside before you catch cold."

"I'm sorry to bother you so late," I stammered. "I came to see . . ." My heart began to sink before I could get the words out. The answer was written on her face.

"I'm afraid he's already gone, dear. Back to England," she said, perceiving my devastation. "His flight left half an hour ago."

"He's gone," I repeated, the words detonating inside me like bombs. Was he on his way to the airport when he came to see me? Was he planning to leave all along? The alternative was too painful to contemplate. "His car . . ." I muttered, pointing to the beat-up Jag, parked at an angle as if he was coming right back, but nothing else came out except a steady stream of tears.

Aunt Bea ushered me inside to a cozy room off the foyer. The last few embers of a fire crackled in the fireplace, their low flames casting distorted, wavering shadows against the dimly lit walls. She went to the kitchen and came back a few minutes later with a cup of tea. It was just like the tea Nick had brought me that day. I sipped it slowly, but not even the hot liquid or the warmth of the fire could stop me from shivering. It reminded me of the time when I was nine and had gotten lost out in the rain on my bike. A stranger found me crying on the side of the street and took me in until my father arrived ten minutes later with a cup of hot chocolate.

"You can stay the night," Aunt Bea said, handing me a blanket. "There's plenty of room."

I smiled weakly and politely declined, realizing there was one person I wanted to call.

My father arrived less than an hour later. He didn't ask about my tear-stained face, where Derek was, or how I had ended up so many miles away.

"You can explain when you're ready," he said as we pulled away from the property. Through the side mirror, I watched the black gates disappear behind us.

As we merged onto the freeway, I suddenly had an image of my dad at my age, driving down a road like this one. "How far did you get?" I asked.

"I'm not sure I follow," he said, confused.

"I mean when you drove across the country."

"Oh, then." He sighed like he hadn't thought about it in a long time. "Not very far. Just to Kansas."

Kansas always made me think of *The Wizard of Oz*, especially the part at the end when Dorothy wakes up in her own bed, surrounded by the people who love her, and that's when she realizes that after everything she's been through, there's no place like home. I was beginning to understand what she meant. I wondered what Nick called home, if he felt he still had one or if Theo's death had destroyed that, too.

"Do you still think about it? Do you ever wish you never came back?"

"No, never," he said emphatically. "It was stupid to have taken off like that. When I found out your mom was pregnant,

I was scared about life changing so fast and I didn't know what to do or how to stop it. But you can't stop it. That's just life. It'll go on with or without you. And I realized I didn't want to miss it. The adventure didn't mean anything without your mom." He glanced over at me. "Or without you."

I looked out the window. The wind stretched the remaining raindrops into long, diagonal streaks across the tinted glass.

"I know about the hotel," I suddenly blurted. "I know that's where you've been going at night. That you're not really working late."

I couldn't believe I said it, just like that with no build-up or warning. But it felt right, like another weight was lifting.

"It's not what you think."

"I'm not judging you." And I wasn't. "I just thought you should know that I know."

My dad paused for a moment. He turned on the right turn signal and eased the car over one lane. The windshield wipers squeaked back and forth.

"That night, when we got the call . . ." His voice trailed off and he tightened his grip on the leather wheel. "I thought I lost you. Your mother and I both did. Even though you survived and even though the doctors assured us you were going to be okay, I still had nightmares. I'd wake up at all hours of the night screaming, convinced you were gone. That's why I started going to the hotel. So I could sleep without worrying that my nightmares would disturb everyone. Especially you and Noah." His eyes glistened, pooled with tears. "But they're over now."

"Does Mom know about any of this?"

"Of course," he said, laughing. "It was her idea."

I looked down at Annie's ruined dress and at my red toe peeking through the hole on the tip of my shoe and started to laugh with him. "So what's Mom going to think about all this?" I asked, gesturing to my appearance.

"The same thing I do," he said, glancing over at me. In that instant, I imagined him laughing just like this nineteen years ago, speeding down another highway. "That you're growing up."

When we got home, I quickly got undressed and went straight to bed.

When I woke up, it was still dark out. It took me a second to notice that I was no longer in my bed. I was floating. When I looked down, I could see someone lying motionless on a small patch of grass beneath a tree, off to the side of the road, surrounded by twisted red metal and broken glass.

That's when I realized who I was looking down at: me.

The distant sound of sirens filtered in. As they got closer, spinning red lights reflected off the wet asphalt below. Even though my eyes were closed, I could see the moon radiating through the leaves. Gravel and dirt filled my mouth but when I inhaled, my breath flowed freely. Big, fat raindrops splatted down on my face. One after the other they fell, steady and constant like a leaky faucet. When I reached up to wipe my cheeks, they were dry.

An ambulance arrived. A team of paramedics spilled out and got to work.

No pulse . . . we're losing her . . . she's gone . . . keep at it . . . don't give up . . .

Their muffled voices overlapped, reaching me in a whisper. When I looked down, the ground was barely visible, my body now a small speck, swallowed up by the darkness. But I was still drifting away like a balloon, higher and higher into the sky until I came face-to-face with the light. It was so blinding it canceled out everything else, all sight and sound and existence, like the inverse of a black hole. The light was warm and loving and drew me in closer until it enveloped me tight like a cocoon, like I could stay that way forever: weightless, illuminated, free.

A voice wafted in, an irresistibly wistful voice that whispered two words in my ear.

Let go.

When I opened my eyes again, I was back in my own bed, Annie's purple dress in a ball on the floor where I left it. I went over to the window and opened the curtains. The sun was shining. It was a new day. This time I really was awake. Gazing down at the sprinklers coming to life, spraying a light mist across my mother's lush lawn, the hazy details of my dream slowly started coming back to me. As I thought about the girl on the ground beneath the tree, and the one floating above her, I realized it hadn't been a dream, but a memory. A very real and vivid memory of what happened when I died. And it had been just the way everyone in the meetings described it.

Magical.

CHAPTER 32

CLASSES WERE OVER and I'd made it through my last high school exam. There were no more excuses. It was finally time to face my English essay. This paper was the last thing standing between me and graduation. Between me and the rest of my life.

I'd found a bunch of plot summaries online and even bought the Cliff's Notes like Derek had suggested. It would have been easy to cobble something together that was good enough, that would guarantee a passing grade. But as I sat there under the willow tree with the moonlight filtering through the leaves, something in me knew that I had to try my best. If I had learned anything over the last few months, it was that giving up was no longer an option.

There wasn't a day that went by when I didn't think about Nick. I knew I'd probably never see him again, and that was hard to accept. But as the days passed, I wondered if I'd already experienced all the moments with him that I was meant to. Maybe I should feel grateful to have met him at all.

I hadn't heard the song in my head since prom. I had thought it would never go away, that there was more I was supposed to remember. Or maybe I just didn't need to hear the rest because it had already done its job. Even though I could no longer hear it, I knew it would be a part of me forever.

I leaned against the thick trunk and opened the book to the first page. I needed to go back to the very beginning. I needed to start over.

"Mrs. Dalloway said she would buy the flowers herself."

Unlike all those other times when I couldn't get past page 10, I didn't move or stop reading until I reached the end. The further I read, the more I found myself relating to Clarissa Dalloway. She wasn't just a bored housewife with a perfect life. She was so much more. She was a woman with regrets and dashed hopes, insecurities and flaws. But above all, she was a woman who felt trapped, backed into a corner with no way out.

"Are we not all prisoners?" Mrs. Dalloway asks herself toward the end of the book. "She often went into her garden and got from her flowers a peace which men and women never gave her."

I realized then that maybe my mother felt that way, too. That we both did. That maybe she and I weren't so different after all.

I opened my notebook and wrote out the assignment at the top of a clean page: *Virginia Woolf created Septimus Warren Smith as a double for Clarissa Dalloway. In what ways are they similar? In what ways are they different?*

I began to write. Within minutes, I lost track of time and where I was. With all these ideas churning in my head, the essay flowed out of me, fully formed. Not only did I finally understand the question, but I also knew how to answer it. Septimus Smith, a troubled war veteran, is so haunted by disturbing memories from his past that he gives up and commits suicide. Clarissa Dalloway is also haunted, for different reasons. But she doesn't kill herself. She realizes she has a choice.

She chooses life. Just like I did.

I tore the finished pages from my notebook when I was done. Hopefully Miss Porter would accept a handwritten essay. Somehow it felt more honest this way.

The sun was just rising and a golden light coated the lawn. My stomach growled. I got up and headed for the house. The damp grass squished between my toes, tickling the soles of my bare feet. The garden had changed over the last couple of months. The vines along the fence had grown, now spreading out like octopus limbs. They no longer divided our property from the Grays' house—they isolated us. The swollen rose bushes had thickened since the spring. The early summer heat invited back the mosquitoes, their buzz filling the air. The sweet, fragrant scent of the blooming roses, lilies, and gardenias blended together into a single intoxicating aroma.

It smelled like home.

I heard a noise as I passed the greenhouse. The door had been left open a crack. My mother was adamant about keeping it shut so that the neighborhood skunks and squirrels couldn't get in. I went over to make sure no rodents had destroyed her plants, when I saw my mother sitting cross-legged in the middle of the floor. Her eyes were closed, her hands resting face-up on her knees.

I paused by the door. Something about her was different. As she inhaled and exhaled each even breath, I realized what it was. Her forehead was smooth, free of the lines I had come to associate with it.

"Olive?" Her eyes popped open.

"I didn't know you were in here," I said, backing away.

"It's okay, stay." She got up and stretched her limbs.

"What were you doing?" I stepped further inside.

"Oh, nothing." She tightened the apron string around her waist and hauled a giant bag of earth onto the counter.

"It didn't look like nothing," I said, dropping my bag. "I mean, it looked like you were doing nothing on purpose."

She smiled. "I like how quiet it is here. Sometimes I feel like it's the only place I can think."

I reached my hand into the open bag and grabbed a handful of dirt. It felt cool as it sifted through my fingers.

"I've been spending a lot of time out here, too," I said.

She pulled a small shovel from her apron pocket and began scooping out clumps of earth from the bag into an empty pot. "I know."

I snapped my head up. "You do?"

"Of course," she said. "Under the willow tree."

"Why didn't you say anything?"

"Because I understood it's what you needed." She set the shovel aside and started kneading the soil like dough.

Guilt rippled through me. "I'm sorry I ruined your plants." We still hadn't talked about it, or any of the horrible things I had said to her that day.

"You didn't," she said. "Come here."

I followed her to the other side of the greenhouse. The sun poured through the east-facing wall onto a row of short, flower-less plants. Their tangled, bone-colored roots poked out from the fresh dirt, sprouting vibrant green leaves. "See?"

"They're the same ones?" A hint of a fuchsia petal was starting to sprout on one of the plants, replacing the ones I had trampled.

She nodded. "Orchids look delicate but they're a lot sturdier than you'd think. That's why they've been around since the dinosaur age. They just need a little TLC."

It reminded me of the lone orchid that thrived in the dead maze at Nick's, reminded me that life went on even when you thought it couldn't.

"I don't want to go to Georgetown next year." I still wasn't certain if my acceptance would stand, but staring at the tiny bud on the verge of blossoming, the idea took root. "I want to find a college that's a better fit for me." I thought about the spin-ning globe on Nick's desk. "And I want to take a year off to see the world." It wasn't so I could go find Nick, or anyone else. It was so I could continue finding myself.

"I think you should." She released the dirt and took my hands in hers. They were soft and warm. "I've seen how you've changed. How you're continuing to change and grow. I don't want to hold you back."

The warmth of her hands spread through my body. "What about Dad? Do you think he'll go for it?"

"I know he will. All we both want is for you to be happy."

She smiled and her whole face lit up, practically morphing her into another person. For the first time, it wasn't my mother I saw facing me, but a woman with her own path, her own series of moments. Maybe she always looked this way and I was the one who wasn't paying attention.

She reached for another pot off the shelf to continue planting. When she wasn't looking, I snuck my camera out of my bag and started shooting.

"I look awful!" she protested, smoothing out her hair with her muddy hand. The sun picked up a stray green leaf that had gotten stuck in it.

"You actually look really beautiful, Mom."

"Oh please," she said, shooing the air. "Wait, you got it! Is it the one you wanted?"

She was referring to my brand new 35 mm Nikon camera purchased under Annie's expert guidance. It was an early graduation present from my parents, even though my final transcript hadn't come in yet.

"Yes, and it's perfect."

"Why don't we go inside," she said, putting her arm around me. "I made some coffee."

When we came in the kitchen, my father and Noah were dipping into the icing of a cake that rested on the counter.

"Hey, that was supposed to be for dessert tonight," my mother chided. But I could tell she wasn't really angry, because she was smiling.

"Not our fault you forgot to hide it," my dad said, a smear of chocolate running across his chin. "Right, buddy?"

"Right!" Noah agreed, swiping his finger across the top again.

My mother took down four plates and grabbed a handful of forks before sitting down at the table. "I guess we're having cake for breakfast."

"Yes!" Noah pumped his fist and reached up to high five my dad.

I was suddenly filled with a deep sense of love and gratitude for my family. It felt like I was floating again, full of peace and calm and hope all wrapped into one. The floating feeling wasn't just reserved for dying, or for those few suspended moments in the in-between. It was happening in my real life, too. It reminded me of how I felt on the day Noah was born. Complete. Like a family.

"I'll be right back," I said, already moving toward the hall.

I ran to my room, my head spinning with all the possibilities that lay ahead. No one was holding me back and my life was now firmly in my own hands. It was all up to me. But there was one thing I needed to do before this new chapter could begin.

Pulling a fresh piece of paper from the printer tray, I chose my favorite purple pen from the jar on my desk and began to write a letter.

It was to Nick.

Just like with the essay, the words poured out of me. I may not have been able to say these things to his face, but it didn't mean I couldn't express them in some other way. I wanted to thank him for seeing the real me before I even knew she existed. For believing in me and giving me the courage to get to where I was now. For waking me from a deep sleep that began long before I crashed Derek's car. And finally, I wanted to tell him about the song. Maybe Theo had a song, too. I hesitated before writing one last thing. I told him that I had seen him at the club that day standing on the roof of his car, that I had run after one of the golf balls and kept it, because I had seen something in him that I wanted to hold on to. Only now it was time that I gave it back so he could find the peace that he deserved.

My heart twitched as I signed my name, a reminder of my old pain and how far I'd come. I neatly folded the paper into three, put it in an envelope, and got dressed. On my way out, I grabbed the golf ball and slipped it in my pocket.

"We saved you a piece!" my dad said when I came back to the kitchen. He held out a plate with the saddest looking excuse for a slice of cake.

"Ahem. *I* saved it, or at least I tried to," my mom said, playfully taking the plate from him as Noah tried to swipe his finger across the icing.

"I think you missed a bite," I said, pointing to the trail of crumbs that traveled down my father's tie.

"You know what I think this family needs?" my dad announced, popping the fallen pieces into his mouth. "An adventure. School's out so I think this calls for a day off. Where should we go?"

"Disneyland!" Noah yelled.

"Marian?" my dad asked, clearing it with her.

"I think it's a great idea," she said, beaming. "Olive, how does that sound?"

"Perfect. There's just a quick errand I have to run first."

"Oh, I'll take you," my mom volunteered. "Let me just change."

"Actually," I said, "this is something I need to do myself. Can I borrow the car?" I tucked my hair behind my ear. It had grown so much these past few weeks that it stayed in place on its own.

My parents exchanged a glance.

"Why don't you take the Buick," my father said, reaching into his pocket for the keys. "We'll be here waiting for you when you get back."

I turned the radio up and sang along the whole way to Nick's house. I had no idea where he was, so Aunt Bea was my only hope that this letter would eventually find him.

It was still early when I arrived. As the house emerged in the distance, I braced myself for a surge of sadness to overcome me. But with the morning sunlight casting a warm, pink glow across the weathered stones, it reminded me of Nick's smile, of his voice, of everything he had given me. And I felt at peace.

I decided against knocking and instead left the letter on the welcome mat by the front door, using the weight of the golf ball to keep it in place. I took in the house one last time before getting in the car and starting back home.

Before I knew it I was back on Vista Boulevard, at the corner of Hyacinth Circle. Without thinking, I turned left and started up the street. As I drove, the scent of hyacinths blew in through the open windows, jogging another buried memory.

Various things jumped out at me as I edged up the road, like a bright yellow mailbox in the shape of a birdhouse.

And then I saw it. The street lamp at the curve in the road. Looking closely, I could still make out the dent in the pole and the faint trace of the black tire marks leading up to it.

This was where it happened.

I slowed the Buick to a crawl. I waited for my heart to skip, for my breath to catch, for something to happen. And then I was reminded of a line in *Mrs. Dalloway* that had stayed with me for days: "Life, London, this moment of June." It described my life, too. Only instead of London I was in Vista Valley. Alive and happy, full of hope.

I tried to hum the song, but the melody kept coming out wrong. It was like trying to catch a mosquito droning nearby; you could hear its buzzing, but it remained just out of reach. I liked to think it was because I didn't need it anymore, because I had already passed the song on to Nick. Hopefully, wherever he was, it was quietly humming in his ear now instead.

And he'd know it was from me.

CHAPTER 33

THE ALARM CLOCK blared, waking me from a deep sleep. It was only six thirty and work didn't start until nine, but it was all the way in Santa Monica and Annie liked getting an early start to beat rush hour traffic. Most mornings we got there early enough to take pictures on the beach. Every time I stared out at the ocean, I pictured Nick on the other side of the globe, somewhere over the horizon. Some mornings, when it was still overcast and the fog hadn't yet lifted, I imagined I could hear his voice being carried in by the roiling water.

Right after graduation, a position became available at the photo studio where Annie had a job lined up. It was run by a collective of photographers who made most of their money from head shots and family portraits. But they also did fashion shoots and magazine ads. Although Annie and I were just interns, it was exciting to see professional photo shoots in action. We even got to help out when they needed an extra hand. In just six weeks, I had already saved enough to buy a round-trip ticket to pretty much anywhere I wanted to go. I just hadn't decided where yet.

When I got outside, Noah was already sitting on the top step waiting for the bus to day camp. His Spiderman backpack and matching lunchbox, which my mother had prepared the night before, were propped next to him.

"You beat me." I joined him on the steps and mussed up his hair. "Are you going anywhere fun today?"

"Yeah," he said, his eyes alight with excitement. "The zoo."

The automatic sprinklers went off on the Millers' lawn across the street, scaring off a squirrel that had been dissecting a fallen avocado. He tried to carry it with him as he scurried off, but it was too big and clunky. He paused, dejected, before eventually abandoning it to take refuge in the nearest tree.

"Did you know that most animals' hearts beat the same number of times throughout their lives?" I asked.

Noah squinted up at me, the glare of the rising sun behind my head. "How many times?"

"A billion."

He stopped to think for a moment.

"Is that more than a million?"

"Much more," I said, trying to come up with an example that could convey such a large number. "It's as many as all the stars in the sky, or all the grains of sand on the beach."

"That sounds like forever."

I thought about my own heart. "In a way it kind of is."

Annie's bug came chugging down the street just as the old yellow bus approached from the other direction. It looked like the same one I had taken to camp a decade ago.

"Don't forget your lunch box, Noah," I said as he started running toward the curb.

I got that feeling again on the drive into work, the one where I was floating. It lasted throughout the morning, as I answered phones, greeted clients, and sat in on a couple of shoots. And it remained there through the end of the day. Once everyone had left, I rolled my chair over to the computer at the receptionist's desk and pulled up the world map I had bookmarked. It was interactive, where information and statistics about each country popped up when you scrolled over it.

The front door jingled as someone entered the studio. With the sun's glare, I couldn't see much, except that the silhouette appeared to be a man's.

"We're closed!" Annie called out. She was sitting next to me on the floor, catching up on some filing.

I shut my eyes, blindly moved the mouse over the screen, and clicked. It was a silly game I liked to play, letting fate determine which countries I'd visit on my trip. The list was getting long. This time when I opened my eyes, the pink hourglass shape of the United Kingdom filled the screen.

When I glanced back up, the silhouette was still standing there, sunbeams poking out around him like spokes on a bicycle. "We're closed," I repeated as he started moving toward me.

"I know," he said as he came closer.

When he reached the counter, I studied the figure standing before me. With the sun still blurring my vision, he looked just like an angel. As he stepped forward out of the glare, his features gained form and clarity.

There was no mistaking him. Even with his short, closely shorn hair fully exposing his face, and his beard gone, revealing the still-faint birthmark on his chin. My heart started beating so wildly it felt like it was going to combust.

"You cut your hair." My voice was hoarse, as if it was my first time speaking after a long sleep.

"I did."

"You look more like yourself."

"I feel more like myself," Nick said, breaking into a full smile, forming two deep dimples on either side of his face. Just like in the picture with Theo.

My skin tingled from the sound of his voice, like it was awakening that last part of me, the part I had put to rest. "How did you know where to find me?"

"Your mother told me."

"I knew it," Annie said, popping up from the floor like a jack-in-the-box. "I knew you'd come back!"

I had forgotten she was there and practically fell off my stool, which made us all laugh.

Nick stepped forward to shake her hand.

"You Brits, you're way too formal," Annie teased, pulling him into a hug.

Nick smiled, returning the hug. He was wearing a pair of shorts and a clean white shirt. I had never seen him look so free and light, his face so calm and open, with no trace of the darkness that used to lurk there.

"Want to get out of here?" I asked, still trying to absorb the fact that he was standing in front of me.

He nodded and waited while I gathered my things. We walked a few blocks until we reached Ocean Avenue and made our way down the public stairs to the beach below. When we got to the boardwalk, we strolled along in silence, the sand and ocean expanding out before us.

"I came to find you," I finally said, tears pooling in my eyes. "That same night, but I was too late. I wrote you a letter—"

"That's why I'm here," he said, reaching for my hand. "That's why I came back."

A group of cyclists raced past us on the boardwalk. The wind in their wake practically knocked me over. I was so light-headed, so dizzy from Nick's presence, it already felt like I might fall over at any second.

"There's something else, something I haven't told anyone before," I said, stopping in the middle of the path as the realization dawned on me. "Something I haven't even been able to admit to myself . . . about my accident."

"It's okay." He caressed his thumb over mine.

I knew what I was about to say could change the way Nick saw me. But if I had any hope of letting go of the past, I had to make sure it could no longer hold onto me.

I turned to face the ocean. The tide was on its way out.

"The thing is, I'm not so sure it *was* an accident. I mean, I saw the curve in the road that night. I knew I couldn't take it at that speed, especially not in the rain. I don't know what I was thinking, or if I was even thinking at all, but I didn't slow down. I was out of control." Derek's words from prom rang in my head, and for the first time I realized that he was right. Annie and my parents and even Dr. Green had a right to be concerned, to want to make me face the very thing I couldn't accept. "A part of me wanted to die that night." I took a deep breath. "So there you have it. The truth. Now you know who I really am."

"Olive," he said, sweeping a piece of hair off my face. "I already know who you are."

I felt his steady gaze but I still couldn't turn to face him. "You don't think I'm crazy?"

"I think everyone gets to the edge sometimes," he said, taking a step closer. "Maybe you went a little further than you intended, but you came back. You didn't stay there. One single action can't define who you are forever. You're the one who taught me that."

He reached into his pocket and pulled out the golf ball, the one I had left on his doorstep. Pivoting his shoulder, he pitched it out toward the ocean. I watched it arc up into the sky, just like I had the very first time I laid eyes on Nick. Only now, he wasn't burying his past, he was releasing it, setting it free.

As I watched the tide get lower and lower, it felt like the shame I'd buried so deep was being swept out to sea with it. Above the sound of the crashing waves and the cawing seagulls, the faint hint of a melody came into my head.

It was my song. It was back. I could hear it again.

Nick gently squeezed my hand, exactly in rhythm with the beat of each note.

I gasped. "You can hear it?"

"I can see him, too," he said. "Over there."

I followed his gaze a few hundred feet to the right, where a guy on the sand was strumming a guitar. A warm feeling exploded inside me as the lyrics kicked in. They were the same words, sung by the same velvety voice I had heard all those times before.

"That's it," I whispered, looking up into his eyes. "It's the song I told you about in the letter. He's singing my song."

Nick squeezed my hand harder, his heartbeat pulsing through his palm.

"How is this possible?"

"Because anything is."

He pulled me in until our bodies were pressed up against each other, as the melody and the voice danced around us. We were so close, our hearts beating so fast, I couldn't tell which was mine and which was his. He wrapped his arms around me and held on tight. It was the only thing keeping me from drifting away.

"You taught me that too."

Cupping my face in his hands he leaned in, his lips gently grazing against mine, soft like a petal. I felt another rush of warmth coursing through my body, like my blood was on fire, as he leaned in and kissed me again, longer this time. The way our lips locked and our bodies folded so naturally into each other made it seem like we had done this all before.

Like this was meant to happen.

The song built in intensity, overlapping chords getting higher and higher like the singing cicadas. This was the part where it used to loop around in my head and go back to the beginning. But this time it didn't. The notes kept escalating higher, like they were climbing a mountain, until they reached a climax.

It was the chorus.

On the infinite horizon

Where you and I belong

As the silver moon is rising

That's when they'll play our song

And in that instant everything suddenly became clear.

Our song

Why the song remained incomplete.

Our song

Why I could never find it.

Our song

It was because when I died, I didn't go to heaven or travel to my past or even get stuck in some kind of in-between. I got to experience a moment from my future. A moment that was my reason to hang on. But it was just a glimpse. Now that I had caught up, the rest was finally happening.

"You saved me," Nick whispered in my ear.

His voice echoed in my head.

"No," I said. "We saved each other."

I'm indebted to the following people for helping me bring this book into the world:

At ICM Partners: Kate Lee and Tina Wexler, for believing in me from the very beginning, and for being my champions every step of the way.

At Razorbill: Ben Schrank, Laura Schechter, and Caroline Donofrio, for their guidance and insight, and for helping me take this book to the next level.

All my friends who graciously offered their time to read parts of the novel and give advice, but especially Paula Yoo, Oritte Bendory, and Kathryn Himoff.

My dog Rocky, for giving the best cuddles through all the highs and lows.

My husband Alex. My love, my best friend, my wellspring of inspiration.

And finally, my daughter Eva. She was just an idea when I began writing this book. Now she is the reason I strive to be better.